A nameless  er.

Alicia's pulse qui[...] next move. The very ai[...] like a fire leaping [...]

Without uttering a word, he gathered her into his arms. He clasped her body tightly against his. She inhaled sharply at the contact, intoxicated by his warm, manly scent. She felt her blood coursing through her veins like a flooding mountain brook in springtime. His broad shoulders heaved as if he had just run a footrace. His hard-muscled thigh brushed against her hip, sending a thousand sparks dancing up her leg. The touch of his hands on her spine, firm and persuasive, invited more intimacy. Abandoning her shyness, she wound her arms around his neck, and locked herself within his embrace.

"Alicia." He murmured her name like a prayer. His warm breath fanned her face.

Her thoughts spun….

Dear Reader,

This month we've covered all the bases. You'll laugh, you'll cry, *you'll find romance.* To begin, Tori Phillips is back with her third Cavendish knight—the one who's often flanked by his three canines in the aptly titled *Three Dog Knight.* In this charming and clever tale, a shy earl and an illegitimate noblewoman forge a marriage of convenience based on trust, and later love, despite the machinations of an evil sister-in-law. It's no wonder critics have described her books as "superb," "SPLENDID!" and "delightfully mischievous."

We are also delighted to feature Ruth Langan's *Blackthorne,* her first medieval novel in nearly four years! Packed with intrigue and emotion, this is the story of a haunted widower, the lord of Blackthorne, whose child's governess teaches him how to love again. And be sure to look for *Apache Fire* by longtime author Elizabeth Lane, about a Native American army scout on the run from vigilantes, who finds shelter in the arms of a beautiful young widow.

Rounding out the month is *Lost Acres Bride* by rising talent Lynna Banning. Here, a rugged, by-the-book rancher must contend with the female spitfire who inherits a piece of his land—and gets a piece of his heart! Don't miss this fun and frolicking Western!

Whatever your tastes in reading, you'll be sure to find a romantic journey back to the past between the covers of a Harlequin Historicals® novel.

Sincerely,
Tracy Farrell, Senior Editor

Please address questions and book requests to:
Harlequin Reader Service
U.S.: 3010 Walden Ave., P.O. Box 1325, Buffalo, NY 14269
Canadian: P.O. Box 609, Fort Erie, Ont. L2A 5X3

Three Dog Knight

TORI PHILLIPS

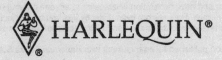

HARLEQUIN®

TORONTO • NEW YORK • LONDON
AMSTERDAM • PARIS • SYDNEY • HAMBURG
STOCKHOLM • ATHENS • TOKYO • MILAN • MADRID
PRAGUE • WARSAW • BUDAPEST • AUCKLAND

ISBN 0-373-29038-1

THREE DOG KNIGHT

This edition published by arrangement with Harlequin Books S.A.

® and TM are trademarks of the publisher. Trademarks indicated with ® are registered in the United States Patent and Trademark Office, the Canadian Trade Marks Office and in other countries.

Printed in U.S.A.

Books by Tori Phillips

Harlequin Historicals

*The Cavendish Chronicles

TORI PHILLIPS

After receiving her degree in theater arts from the University of San Diego, Tori worked at MGM Studios, acted in numerous summer stock musicals and appeared in Paramount Pictures' *The Great Gatsby*. Her plays, published by Dramatic Publishing Co., have been produced in the U.S. and Canada, and her poetry is included in several anthologies. She has directed over forty plays, including twenty-one Shakespeare productions. Currently, she is a first-person, Living History actress at the Folger Shakespearean Library in Washington, D.C. She lives with her husband in Burke, VA.

To my three nieces—
Anni Peduzzi, Sarah and Louise Welling
who all love cats

ACKNOWLEDGMENTS

I am deeply grateful to all my friends in the
Richard III Society, especially Laura Blanchard,
Carol Bessette, her husband, John (of the Loyal
Opposition) and particularly to Judie Gall, who allowed
me to purloin her excellent work, *FERNE-AGO*, a
dictionary of medieval words and terms.

Chapter One

"And dog will have his day."
—William Shakespeare
Hamlet, V, i

Wolf Hall, Northumberland, England
October 1487

"She's a long-limbed lass," observed Sir Giles Cavendish, Earl of Thornbury. "Looks like a spring colt."

The girl's guardian, Sir Edward Brampton, forced his smile, though the earl's assessment of his darling Alicia made him fearful for her future. Aloud, he replied, "Aye, and one fine day she will grow into a beauty. You have already noticed that she has inherited her father's height. She also possesses the family's legendary good looks."

Indeed, Alicia was the spitting image of her royal sire, although she did not enjoy the protection of a legitimate birth. A cold shiver raced down Sir Edward's spine at the mere thought of what would happen to his ward if Henry Tudor's agents learned of her existence.

Her first cousin, the poor half-witted Earl of Warwick, already languished in the Tower at the new king's pleasure.

The earl shifted his gaze away from the golden-haired child who amused herself with a game of cat's cradle at the far end of the hall. "Does the lass know of her parents?" he queried.

Sir Edward shook his head. "Nay, she thinks her family were yeomen farmers who died of the plague when she was a baby." He gave a rueful smile. "She believes that my lady and I are the goldsmith of York and his wife. I thought it safest to keep the truth from her until she is of age—or married." He allowed the last word to hang in the air between them.

Sir Giles sipped from his pewter tankard of ale. "Why have you chosen my family?" he asked. "Would it not be better for the girl to marry within her own class and be lost amid the bustle of York?"

Sir Edward furrowed his brow. "That is precisely the reason why I have come to you, my lord. She was born higher than any merchant of York. Though her father lifted skirts from France to the Scottish borders, he was also our late King Edward, God rest his soul." He made a hasty sign of the cross.

Sir Giles followed suit. "Amen to that." He stared at Sir Edward, while he drummed his fingers on the wide-planked tabletop. "You have told me an interesting tale, Lord Brampton. I especially like the part when King Richard called you to his tent before the battle of Bosworth, and gave his brother's waif into your care." He leaned forward in his chair. "But what proof do you have?"

Sir Edward drew in his breath. The next few minutes would decide Alicia's fate. "Did you know King Edward well?'' he asked, as he fumbled with the buckle of the worn leather pouch on his lap.

"Aye, as well as I knew my own wife of blessed memory." The old earl chuckled. "My lady often swore that I preferred Edward's company to her own. Bestrew me, but at times I did, for the woman tended to nag." He sighed, then took another swallow of ale. "Now that she has gone to her heavenly reward, I miss her. But to your point, my lord."

Sir Edward drew a blue velvet bag from the pouch. "Perchance you recognize this?" He cradled a jeweled brooch in his palm.

Sir Giles's eyes widened when he beheld the splendid oval ruby nestled in a golden setting. A large teardrop pearl dangled from it. "Aye, 'tis a gladsome sight to see it again. 'Twas His Grace's favorite bauble to deck his cap. He is wearing it in a portrait that I have hidden away."

"A fitting dowry for his last child." Sensing his goal within reach, Sir Edward lowered his voice. "King Richard gave me a bag of gold sovereigns to accompany the brooch. He did not wish Alicia to come to her husband as a pauper."

The earl glared at him. "The jewel is enough, though the coin would make my tax burden lighter. May the Tudor and his minions rot in hell! They will squeeze the country dry with their damnable taxes. I can barely make ends meet. My tenants are already destitute."

"I warrant you, 'tis equally as hard on honest goldsmiths, my lord." Sir Edward held up the brooch. The light from the hearth fire brought the ruby to life. "'Tis a match then? Your son for my fair Alicia, daughter of Edward IV?"

Sir Giles stroked his chin. "I have three boys."

"Alicia needs only one of them for a husband." Sir

Edward glanced at the young girl on the bench. The pale rays of the sun shining through the high-arched window caught the red-gold of her hair, turning it into a blazing halo about her heart-shaped face. An angel, he thought with a surge of pride. Just like all the Plantagenets. Sweet Jesu, protect her from the Tudor upstart.

The earl cleared his throat. "My eldest, John, is near twenty. He has been married once already, but she died. When he takes his next wife, she must be descended from…legitimate parentage, as John will be the Earl of Thornbury after me."

"Just so." Sir Edward drank deeply of the ale in his tankard lest he be tempted to challenge the earl's thinly veiled insult.

"William, my second son, is betrothed to one of Bedford's quiverful of daughters. That boy is a wild one. Only sixteen, and already he's gotten two of the village maids with child."

By the tone of the earl's voice, Sir Edward suspected the young rogue's father was secretly proud of his son's proven virility. He cleared his throat. "Alicia needs a strong arm and a loyal heart to protect her." She should be loved and cherished, his heart cried out in silence, as I have loved and cherished her since she was in leading strings.

Thornbury sighed, and drained his tankard. "Then there is Thomas." He chewed on his lower lip. "Just fourteen, but as big as the other two. Rides well. Best sword arm of the lot."

"He sounds promising." What was the problem? Sir Edward wondered. Was the boy poxed? With growing misgivings, he waited for the earl to continue.

Sir Giles refilled their tankards from the clay jug on the table between them. "The lad is…honest and true as the day is long. Methinks he does not know how to lie. He speaks his mind plain—that is, when he decides to speak at all.''

Sir Edward blinked. ''Your pardon, my lord?''

The earl sank back against the cushions of his chair. ''Methinks the boy was coddled by his mother too much. From childhood Thomas shunned the company of his brothers and my fosterlings. He grew even more reclusive after my wife died in childbirth. Now he spends most of the day out of doors, either at practice in the tilt yard, or hunting in the forest.''

Sir Edward found himself holding his breath. Alicia needed the protection of a strong family loyal to the Yorkist cause. If his future plans proved successful, the child would be the half sister of the rightful king. Young Richard of York lay hidden away in the countryside of Flanders, waiting until he was old enough to claim his birthright. Sir Edward measured his next words carefully.

''Your Thomas sounds like the very match for my ward.''

Sir Giles massaged the bridge of his nose. ''My Thomas may have the strength of an ox, but he has the brain of one as well. He hardly talks, and when he does, 'tis usually to one of his damnable dogs. In plain truth, my third son is a lackwit.''

''Oh.'' Sir Edward felt like a fool's inflated bladder after some unfortunate person had sat upon it.

God in heaven, how could he possibly betroth Alicia to a half-wit? What other choice did he have? By the stain of her birth, she would be an outcast at the court of Burgundy, where the Yorkist sympathizers resided. Should he send her over the border to Scotland, or into a nunnery? She would whither away in either place. Nay, Sir Edward had given his solemn vow to King Richard to marry Alicia well. That oath had been sworn the day before the king had been cruelly slain by the Tudor dog who now wore his crown.

A ripple of silvery laughter interrupted Sir Edward's dark musings. At the far end of the hall, Alicia slid to the floor to intercept an apricot-colored mastiff puppy. It scampered up to her on oversize paws; a long pink tongue hung from its wide, black muzzle. The little fellow greeted the girl with wet affection. The sound of spurs scraping the flagstones, and several male voices speaking at once heralded the arrival of the earl's sons.

One of the blond giants spied Alicia. "Good sooth, what have we here?" he greeted her. "'Tis an angel come down to earth."

Sir Giles shook his head. "My second son, William. *He* is never at loss for words."

"Good day, young mistress," added the older son, giving Alicia a small bow.

Holding the puppy in her arms, Alicia rose from the floor in a fluid motion. "God give you a good day, my lords," she replied in her clear, sweet voice.

Despite the wiggling animal, she executed a lovely curtsy. Sir Edward smiled at his ward. Only seven years old, yet she carried herself like a princess. If the fickle fates had been kinder, she would have been a true one, he thought. God forgive Edward Plantagenet's philandering ways.

William shouted across the hall. "How now, father? Is this one my new bride? By the stars, mistress, you are a lofty creature! I like my women small. They are easier to subdue."

John clapped a hand on his brother's shoulder. "You are frightening the child," he admonished mildly. To Alicia, he added, "Welcome to Wolf Hall."

"Ah," she replied with a pert smile. "Is this one of the dreadful wolves?" She held up the puppy.

"He is mine." Stepping out of the shadows, the third son took the dog from her hands.

God's teeth! The boy was a handsome brute, Sir Edward thought. Blonder than either of his brothers, with well-defined features yet unblessed by a whisker, Thomas Cavendish reminded Brampton of an avenging angel chiseled in marble. At fourteen, the third son stood as tall as the other two. His wide shoulders and loose-hung arms and legs gave promise of the powerful man he would become when fully grown. Sir Edward searched the boy's face for some sign of mental incapacity. Surprised, he saw none. Instead of retreating with his pup, Thomas stood before Alicia as if rooted to the spot.

"You see what I mean?" the earl muttered to his guest. "Says nothing." He motioned for his sons to join him. The older two obeyed. Thomas either did not see his father beckon to him, or he chose to ignore it. Instead, he allowed Alicia to pet the dog.

"John, William, this is…ah…"

"Master Roger Broom, goldsmith, my lords." Sir Edward slipped into his daily guise. He bowed with the deference of a merchant before nobility. "I am honored."

"Just so," the earl rumbled under his breath. "And the child is Alicia Broom."

"My daughter," Sir Edward added smoothly.

"A pretty wench," William remarked, appraising her over his shoulder.

Sir Edward did not like the roving gleam in William's eye. Thank all the saints Alicia was too young yet for bedding, or that young man might attempt to do her mischief. Silently he applauded Sir Giles's prudence to contract his second son as quickly as possible. He was glad that the earl had not offered William for Alicia.

The rogue would make life a merry hell for any poor woman.

John elbowed his brother in the stomach. "Forgive William's manners, master goldsmith. Methinks he forgot to put them on with his hat this morning."

The earl growled an oath under his breath.

Sir Edward flourished another bow. "Youth must be served, my lord."

"Avaunt, you two! Begone!" Sir Giles snapped his fingers several times. "We desire some conference with Thomas—in private."

William brayed a laugh. "What ho! You plan to apprentice old Tom to a goldsmith? What a jest!"

"Out!" roared Sir Giles. "Thomas! A word with you—and put that damnable dog down!"

"Or better yet, marry him to the goldsmith's daughter!" William jibed as John hauled him up the broad stairs at the near end of the hall. "When you need instruction in the arts of swiving, Tom, call me and—"

John's audible blow between William's shoulder blades put a quick end to the young man's lewd suggestion. Flinging oaths at each other, the two brothers disappeared into the gallery above.

Sir Giles poured himself a third tankard of ale. "The devil take all offspring. I fear that my family makes hawks look as tame as robins. Thomas! Come here!" To Brampton, he murmured, "Now you will see what I mean. A good boy—but he does not know the letter *B* from battledore."

Alicia stepped closer to the tall lad. "If it please you, my lord, I could hold your dog while you speak with your father." She held out her hands. "Come, let us all go together."

Thomas handed the puppy back to Alicia. "His name is Georgie."

Georgie greeted her with another long slurp of his tongue. She giggled, then tucked the pup under one arm. She slipped her free hand into Thomas's. Startled by the contact, the boy looked as if he might pull away. Alicia merely cast him a beatific smile. Without a word, they presented themselves to Sir Giles.

They look well together, Brampton thought. A sun-blessed giant and a golden princess. Then he noticed a fresh bruise on the boy's left cheekbone. *He must have tripped over his large feet.*

Sir Edward cleared his throat. "My daughter, Alicia Broom, my lords."

Once again, Alicia dropped a perfect curtsy while keeping a firm hold on the excited puppy. "I am most honored, my lord earl," she said in bright, sunlit tones. Then she added in a whisper, "Prithee, my lord, will you be serving us supper?"

Sir Edward coughed in warning. He should never have mentioned that possibility to the child. He prayed the earl would forgive her indiscretion. Being a simple merchant's daughter, she had never met anyone from the upper levels of the nobility.

Before Sir Giles could recover his surprise, Thomas turned to her. "Do you like apple tarts?"

She closed her eyes in rapture. Her little pink tongue darted between her lips. "Aye, I do so adore them!"

"And I, as well," the young man confided. "Let us visit the kitchens now. I am famished."

Alicia giggled, and held up the puppy. "And so is Georgie, methinks."

Turning back to his father, Thomas inclined his head. "Father?" he asked.

Sir Edward detected a flicker of fear in the boy's remarkable blue eyes before he looked down to the stone floor. Brampton considered the bruise again, and wondered if Sir Giles beat his sons, Thomas in particular.

The earl coughed, blew his nose, then waved away the children. "Take her to the kitchen. Give the lass all the tarts she can eat. Well, don't just stand there like a hobbledehoy. Be off, Thomas!"

For the first time since he had appeared, Thomas smiled. By all the saints! Sir Edward could scarcely believe the handsome change that came over the lad's face. The boy threw a sidelong glance at Alicia, who grinned at him in return.

"Let us away, before your papa changes his mind," she whispered.

Thomas nodded. With hasty bows, the young couple departed.

"Do you like your tarts with cream?" he asked as they went out the far door.

"With lots and lots," Alicia replied.

Thomas's deeper voice echoed back into the hall. "Me, too."

The earl stared wide-eyed after them, then drained his ale. "God's teeth! Did you hear that, my lord? Thomas has not spoken that many words in my hearing for years. What magic does your little changeling weave?"

Love and acceptance, Sir Edward wanted to tell the amazed father. Instead, he replied, "I know not, my lord. Alicia has a way with folk—with animals, too."

Sir Giles struck the tabletop with the flat of his hand. "If you say aye to Thomas, then 'tis a match. We can draw up the contract—after that supper your little minx requested. God's sooth! She has her royal father's charm."

Sir Edward exhaled, and found the experience a soothing one. "You have my word upon it, my lord.

Come Alicia's eighteenth birthday, I shall bring her to Wolf Hall to be wed to Thomas.''

Sir Giles rose and extended his hand. "We are agreed, Brampton." He regarded his guest with his piercing blue eyes. "You did say the lass gets along with animals?"

"Aye, you saw as much, my lord."

The Earl of Thornbury smiled. "Good, for she will be living with a damnable kennel."

Come, it lacks a minute of midnight; I shall bring thee to Wolf Hall or be wed to Thomas.

Sir Oliver rose and extended his hand. "We are agreed, Bannoner," he began to his friend with his piercing blue eyes. "You will say the last vows along with me?"

"Aye, you and I."

The Earl of Thornbury scowled. Yet our future will be filled with...

Chapter Two

Wolf Hall
Early August 1497

"**M**y lord, you have guests." Dane Stokes pounded on the thick oaken door of the tiny library. "My lord?"

Thomas Cavendish, the new Earl of Thornbury, hunched deeper in the chamber's only chair. He pretended to read the Latin text in his hands. Perhaps if he ignored his steward's battering long enough, Stokes would give up, and send away the unwanted visitors. A wide black mourning band slipped down Thomas's arm to his elbow. Scowling, he hitched it back up.

Blast the Fates! He had never wanted to be the earl. Had never even considered such a laughable idea. A little over a month ago, his father had been alive and healthy. William and his wife fought like cats, but that was not unusual for them. John's wedding to a young, wealthy heiress was to be celebrated at the Harvest Festival in September. Meanwhile, Thomas had spent the bright sunlit days pursuing badgers.

"Caught a fair lot of them, did we not?" he asked

the undersize brown-and-white terrier of mixed pedigree who nestled on his lap.

Lifting his head, Taverstock perked his ears and licked his lips in reply.

Stokes pounded on the door again. "Sir Thomas, 'tis some high-and-mighty lord who awaits your pleasure in the hall. Him and his ladies."

Thomas groaned softly. Not more women. He had one too many as it was. William's ferret-faced wife, Isabel, refused to accept her widowhood with good grace. He wished that the witch would pack up her chests of clothes and return to her father.

"And leave me in peace," he added aloud as he scratched the sleek head of the fawn-colored miniature greyhound, who reclined beside his chair.

Vixen looked up at her master with open affection in her deep brown eyes.

"Aye, Vixen, you are the only lady in my life," Thomas continued, massaging her velvet ears.

Impatient with his master's misdirected attention, Taverstock pushed his wet nose against the open page of Thomas's expensive copy of *The Comedies of Plautus*. Clicking a reprimand with his tongue, Thomas closed the book, and placed it on the table beside him.

Stokes knocked once more. "My Lord Cavendish, do you hear me?" he persisted. "What am I to do with them?"

Send the high-and-mighty lord to the devil and dispatch the ladies after him. Thomas sighed. "Things are not the same as they were, eh, Tavie?"

The terrier licked his lips again, then sneezed wetly.

"Please, my lord. The company has come a long way to see you."

"Who?" Thomas thundered at his persistent steward. His loud tone woke the mastiff dozing in the nearby corner. The dog lifted his gray-flecked muzzle, then yawned, displaying two rows of large, sharp teeth.

"'Tis Sir Edward Brampton and his lady wife. Sir Edward says he requests a most urgent conference with you."

"Never heard of him," Thomas told his three canine companions. "What in blazes do you suppose he wants?" In a louder voice, he asked Stokes, "What for?"

"I know not, my lord, save that the younger lady has brought all her baggage with her. Sir Edward said for me to tell you…" Stokes's voice trailed away.

"What?" Thomas bellowed.

"That he has brought your…your…" Stokes's voice quivered.

"Spikes and thorns, man! What has he brought me?"

"Your betrothed!" Stokes yelled through the wooden panels. "And Sir Edward is in a great hurry to be off and away, he said."

Thomas opened his mouth to hurl another oath at the steward, but a distant memory stopped him. A tall, thin girl-child in a plain blue woolen gown with her red-gold hair barely covered by a wide blue ribbon and a thin white veil—the goldsmith's daughter. William had teased Thomas to distraction over his unlikely betrothal. It had been the first time Thomas had ever knocked one of his older brothers unconscious. The earl had whipped Thomas raw for it, but the punishment had been worth the pain. His brothers had never dared to provoke Thomas again. As for the girl—he presumed that she had been married off to the son of another merchant. He had heard nothing of her since their only meeting years ago. Alicia—that was her name.

"'Tis some mistake, I'll warrant," Thomas told Vixen. "What would a high-and-mighty lord like this

Brampton fellow be doing with the daughter of a goldsmith? Nay, the word has gotten out that the new Earl of Thornbury is a rich young bachelor.'' He grinned at the terrier in his lap. ''Oh, and I am somewhat scattered in my wits, as well. We must not forget that part. I wonder if my Lord Brampton is the vanguard of prospective fathers-in-law? God shield me!''

''My lord?'' Stokes whined through the keyhole. ''What do you want me to do?''

''Come in!'' Thomas roared back at him.

The brass latch turned, then Stokes poked his head around the door. ''Aye, my lord?''

''The wench. What does she look like?''

A sheepish grin spread across the steward's face. He reminded Thomas of a lovesick swain on a May Day morn. The sight was enough to put a man off his feed.

Stokes sighed. ''Sweet and young, my lord. Fair and tall. The face of an angel. The voice of a lark. The figure of a willow. The—''

''Peace with your moon song, knave!'' Thomas curled his lip.

A plague upon it! The little witch had already enchanted his steward. She would have to stir up all the charms of hell to ensnare Thomas in her coils. Blasts and fogs! He did not need more woman trouble. He snapped his fingers to his three best friends.

''Up, Georgie! Let us meet this…female who claims me.''

Thomas found Lord Brampton pacing before the cold fireplace in the great hall. The heel plates of the visitor's riding boots grated against the flagstones. Brampton had thrown one side of his thick black wool riding cape over his shoulder, revealing his brown velvet garb. Thomas noted that the clothing was well made.

A lady, presumably the impatient lord's wife, sat in a nearby chair. Her travel cloak showed mud-stained signs of a rough journey. Her pale face held an anxious expression. When she lifted her cup of wine, her hand trembled.

Planting himself in front of his master, Taverstock bristled the fur on the back of his neck. He growled once or twice in challenge. Vixen leaned against Thomas's left leg. Georgie halted, lifted his nose, quivered, then with a thundering bay, he bounded down the length of the hall toward the startled guests.

The lady screamed as the great dog came closer. Her husband stepped in front of her, and drew his sword.

"Georgie!" Thomas shouted, dashing after the dog. What had gotten into the old boy? Brampton's sword looked sharp.

"Georgie?" A tall young woman stepped into the band of sunlight cast from the window. Its golden beams caught the fire in her hair. With a delighted thrill of laughter, she sank to her knees and held out her arms to the great mastiff. "After all these years, is it really little Georgie?" She buried her face in his thick furry neck.

Taverstock whined, and danced a few side steps on his short bandy legs. Vixen froze in place. Her dark expressive eyes remained fixed on her master.

At the sound of the girl's voice, Thomas skidded to a stop. He blinked. The goldsmith's daughter of his youthful fantasies had returned as a beautiful woman. Her voice was lower, but still held the same tone of merriment. Stokes had not exaggerated. Her figure was indeed that of a graceful, supple willow. Her laughter reminded him of a clear, sweet spring on a hot summer's day.

"Hold very still, Alicia," Brampton whispered as he advanced upon the pair on the floor. "I shall take—"

"Nay!" Grabbing the man's wrist, Thomas twisted it. The naked sword clattered to the floor. Taverstock barked with approval.

"What foul knavery is this?" Brampton whirled on Thomas. "You would set your cur upon my child? Is this your idea of hospitality?"

"Edward, peace!" His wife rose from her chair and came to his side. "'Tis no harm done. See? Alicia and the dog are in perfect friendship." Turning to Thomas, she smiled at him. "Forgive my husband, Lord Cavendish. Our journey has been in haste, and with some danger. I fear we are much agitated."

Thomas took a deep breath to steady his nerves. Out of the corner of his eye, he saw Georgie lie down, then roll over on his back while the girl cooed endearments to him, and rubbed his tummy. The great beast wriggled with pleasure. A sudden twinge of envy took Thomas by surprise. With reluctance, he returned his attention to the fuming man before him. Brampton looked familiar, yet Thomas could not place him.

"You wished to see me?" he asked brusquely.

Brampton patted his wife's restraining hand, then straightened his cap that had been knocked askew. "I told that whey-faced servant that I wished to speak to the earl." He glared down at Taverstock, who sniffed at his boots. "You are Thomas, as I recall?"

"I am, and I am."

Brampton rolled his eyes to the heavens. "I am glad you are Thomas," he said, drawing out his words. "Now, may I please speak with your father?"

"You cannot," Thomas snapped. Sweet Jesu! How he wished that Brampton could. He helped himself to a cup of wine from the table.

Brampton sputtered. "By heaven, sir, we have come on a matter most urgent. I have no time to talk in riddles."

"Nor have I." Thomas drained his wine. Over the rim of his cup, he watched the girl try to entice Vixen into her charmed circle. Sweat popped out on his brow. Very warm for this season, he thought with discomfort.

Brampton slammed his fist on the table, rattling the wine pitcher. "Where is the Earl of Thornbury?"

Thomas replaced his cup with deliberate care. "You are speaking to him."

Brampton's jaw sagged open. "You jest!" He appeared to deflate under his cloak.

"Nay." Thomas readjusted his sliding black band. "Gaol fever. My father, then my brothers. They caught it in June at the assizes in York." Pausing, he pressed his lips together to hold back the pain that welled up inside of him. "I remained at home."

"May God have mercy on their souls," Lady Brampton murmured, making the sign of the cross.

"Amen," Thomas muttered under his breath.

"Amen," echoed the girl in a soft voice. The heartfelt emotion in her simple word pierced Thomas to his heart. He couldn't look at her.

A stricken expression swept across Brampton's face. "All dead?"

Thomas nodded, not trusting his voice.

The older man shot his wife a quick look, then asked, "Did your father ever chance to speak to you of your marriage?"

The young earl grimaced. His father had rarely spoken to his third son except to find fault with him or one of his dogs. The old earl had never talked of gentler matters. Thomas shook his head.

"God save us!" Brampton poured himself more wine, then downed it in one gulp.

At this rate, Thomas wondered which of them would get drunk first. He held his tongue as he studied the older man. Long experience had taught him that people grew uncomfortable with silence, and would gabble anything to fill the void. By and by, he would learn Brampton's innermost thoughts.

Sir Edward drew himself to his full height. Even so, he was still half a head shorter than Thomas.

"I am sorry for your loss," his guest began in a firmer tone. "But my mission is still the same. Ten years ago, your father and I struck an agreement whereby you would marry my Alicia at the proper time." He glanced fondly at the girl seated amid the dogs. "I had planned to keep her one more year. She is barely seventeen."

Suddenly Thomas remembered the man. "You are the goldsmith—Roger Broom."

Surprise widened Brampton's dark brown eyes. "By the book! You have a better memory than I expected. Aye, 'twas a disguise. Your father knew my true identity. But no more of this, the hour hurries past us. My wife and I must race for the coast before our ship sails for the Lowlands."

Thomas grunted in reply, though his mind whirled at this news. Why disguised? Now why the flight?

"Alicia?" he asked aloud.

"By written agreement, and the dowry I paid to your father, Alicia is contracted to marry you. And the sooner, the better for her sake," Brampton added in almost a whisper.

Thomas felt as if a lance had struck a blow against his chest. He glanced at the girl. She smiled back at him. He couldn't breathe. She rose from the floor, then stepped over the sated Georgie. Hoy day! She stood nearly as tall as Brampton. She tossed her thick braid of hair over her shoulder as she advanced toward Thomas.

His heart thudded against his chest. She must hear its pounding, he thought. A drop of sweat rolled into his eye. He blinked. Her lush red lips parted. Her white teeth gleamed like little pearls. His hands grew clammy. A roaring filled his ears. He had never been this close to such perfection in his four-and-twenty years. His tongue seemed to swell two sizes larger, then it cleaved itself to the roof of his mouth.

She looked directly at him with a sparkle of her laughter in her matchless blue eyes. "Tell me, Sir Thomas," she asked in tones of purest crystal. "Does your cook still make the most wonderful apple tarts in the world?"

Air! Thomas needed to breathe, or he would expire at her feet. He opened his mouth to answer that all the tarts in Wolf Hall were hers for the asking, but only a strangled gargle came out. Without attempting any more conversation, he wheeled around, and fled out of the hall. Taverstock and Vixen followed in hot pursuit. Georgie, that lumbering traitor, remained behind to enjoy more of Alicia's caresses.

In the corridor, Thomas barely paused when he encountered his startled squire. "See to my guests," he snapped at Andrew.

The slim boy lifted his eyebrows with surprise. "Aye, my lord."

"Put *her* in the royal suite," Thomas tossed over his shoulder. Tavie scrambled in his wake.

"Aye, my lord," Andrew called after him. "I presume you are not referring to Vixen?"

The little greyhound gave him a reproachful look as she limped by.

"Go to the devil, Andrew." Thomas shouted as he rounded the corner. "And take my Lord Brampton with you," he added under his breath. He flung open the outer door. Fresh air! He drew in deep, cleansing draughts as he raced across the meadow to the safety of the sun-dappled forest.

"I am the greatest fool in all England!" He consoled himself by banging his head against an unforgiving tree trunk. Tavie and Vixen lay down among the dry leaves to watch their master make a complete idiot of himself.

Sir Edward threw his hat to the floor. "Bolts and shackles! A plague take him! I have half a mind to follow the jolthead, and bring him back to beg your forgiveness. What simpleton have I tied you to, Alicia?"

Lady Katherine laid her hand on his arm. "Peace, my husband. Methinks the young lord is consumed with grief at his sudden loss. Such a misfortune is apt to muddle one's wits."

"His wits were none too steady ten years ago," Sir Edward growled, staring at the empty doorway. "But I had hopes that he would grow more wise with time." He put an arm around Alicia. "Forgive me, my precious child. I have done you and your royal father a great disservice."

Alicia shook her head. "Nay, Papa...I mean, Edward, I think not. I recall that Sir Thomas was kind to me when I was a child. Methinks the idea of a wife on his doorstep has much to do with his current distress." She laughed softly. "Do you remember Peter Martext, the draper's son? He often visited our shop. When I asked him if he needed help to choose a gold chain, he merely stared at me. You remarked he did not know how to converse with women. Perchance that is the case with Sir Thomas.''

Alicia's lighthearted tone belied the twist of fear in her heart. Dear Lord in heaven, what if her betrothed was truly mad? Though he looked to possess the strength of his Viking ancestors, what would she do if he could not protect her?

Yet the shy boy had grown into a most handsome man. Alicia had never seen such a pair of broad shoulders on anyone. His tight black hose left very little to the imagination. His waist tapered to slim hips and buttocks. His stockings bulged with large thigh and calf muscles, indicating a man who lived in the saddle. The black velvet of his mourning doublet set off his bright blond hair and flashing sapphire eyes. Those eyes did not reflect madness, merely shock.

Lady Katherine squeezed her husband's arm. ''Aye, Ned. I believe Alicia has hit upon the core of the problem.'' She smiled up at him, a little too brightly.

Edward slapped his riding gloves against his palm. The huge mastiff rolled over, and regarded him with interest.

''What am I to do now? We must flee the king's vengeance, yet I fear to leave you here alone, child. You must be safe.''

Alicia swept her gaze around the hall. The wainscoting of oaken panels appeared more black than a natural brown color. The plastered walls above the wood, once whitewashed, had taken on a gray color from many years of sooty fires and neglect. The carved pillars, also blackened by smoke, rose into the darkness of the vaulted ceiling. A faded red banner, looking more like a rag than a battle flag, hung crookedly over the chimneypiece. No gentle housekeeping hand had touched

Wolf Hall in many a year. What the poor new earl needed was someone to let some fresh air and sunshine into his life.

"Wolf Hall looks stout enough to withstand an army," she remarked, trying to sound braver than she really felt. "The only enemy I see is dirt and mismanagement."

Sir Edward gathered her into his embrace. She was tall enough to look directly into his eyes, and to read his apprehension. "You have always been the practical one, my dove, but thick walls will not save you from the Tudor's grasp, if the heart that rules within this castle is a weak one."

Before Alicia could frame a reply, she heard someone cough discreetly behind her.

A youth, dressed in the height of fashion, but with colors of gray and black, swept them a bow. "My Lord Brampton, Lady Brampton, Mistress Broom, welcome to Wolf Hall."

Sir Edward released Alicia, then strode toward the young man. "Who the devil are you?"

The young fop swept him another bow. "Andrew Ford, my lord. I have the honor of being squire to the Earl of Thornbury."

Brampton groaned under his breath. "This farce grows worse and worse. An idiotic bear is served by a preening peacock," he noted in an aside to his wife.

Undaunted by Sir Edward's glower, Andrew Ford approached them. The slim boy looked no more than sixteen. His sleek, nut-brown hair fell to his jawline. The boy's hazel eyes hinted of mischief.

"I have come to beg your pardon for my master's hasty exit, my lord." Andrew threw him a guileless smile. "Sir Thomas is unused to company of any sort—and most particularly that of two such beautiful ladies as yourselves.'' He bowed again to Lady Katherine and Alicia.

Alicia regarded the boy with hidden amusement. *This one must dine and sup on honey, and keep the tailors of York in constant employment.*

Sir Edward assumed his most dignified demeanor. His ward had rarely seen that side of him in all her years of living under his roof. She still found it difficult to accept that he was a noble lord, while she, herself was...

Alicia pushed away the thought of her true identity. She must try to forget it completely. The sooner she cast off the name of Broom and became a Cavendish, the safer it would be for her. After that, she hoped she could bury the dangerous secret of her existence deep within the heart of Wolf Hall. She prayed that Sir Thomas would honor his father's bond and marry her.

She did not want to be locked away in a nunnery for the rest of her life. She craved the love and companionship of a husband, and children to bear and nurture. Sunshine. Flowers. And especially animals. She glanced down at Georgie, who returned her look with a hopeful one of his own. Alicia leaned over, and rubbed his tawny ears. Georgie closed his eyes with a sigh of satisfaction.

Sir Edward towered over the boy. ''When next you speak, Master Ford, pray do so with some firm purpose. Your lord has treated us in a most shabby manner, and has dishonored his bride. He is an ass.''

Though Andrew shook his head at this insult, his smile never left his face. ''Hear me, my good lord, and so find understanding in your heart. My master is a good man, strong and true. He means no disrespect, and certainly not to so fair a maiden as Mistress Broom.'' He turned his smile up a notch at Alicia.

She continued to rub Georgie's ears. Best not to give the boy too much encouragement. He looked like the sort who fell madly in love every day of the week and twice on Sundays.

Sir Edward snapped his fingers several times. "Speak to me, squire. How can I be sure that my ward will be safe if I leave her in this…" He glared at Georgie. "In this kennel. Does your master often bolt from his chambers? Can he speak in more than a growl? Does he have the wit to be married? Can he care for my precious girl?"

"Aye, my lord, the earl can do all this and more. Mistress Broom will be safe at Wolf Hall. You have my word upon it."

"Ha!" Sir Edward bared his teeth. "The word of a strutting popinjay? Tell me, Master Ford, does a razor frighten your beard yet?"

Two red spots appeared in the boy's smooth cheeks. His smile clouded, but did not disappear entirely. "My lord, I am sorry if my apparel and my manner offend you. I had the honor to spend my formative years in the household of the Duke of Buckingham, where I learned how a gentleman should conduct himself. Even though I serve Sir Thomas in the wilds of Northumberland, I take pleasure in maintaining my little refinements. When I am full grown, I hope to find a place at court. In the meantime, I do not intend to become a barbarian while residing in the countryside."

Alicia hid her smile behind her hand. She suspected that Andrew Ford made gladsome company in this old, neglected castle.

Sir Edward regarded the slender lad. "Very well, Sir Motley, I will leave Alicia—at your word. If I hear that she has been ill-used by your master or anyone else at Wolf Hall, I shall personally seek you out. When I am done with you, I will stuff you, your fine manners and your princely garb into an eel-skin, and feed you to the swine. Do we understand each other, squire?''

Andrew's Adam's apple bobbled up and down the column of his throat. He squared his thin shoulders in their thickly padded jacket. ''Aye, my Lord Brampton, perfectly. 'Twill be my honor to serve the countess as I now serve her lord.''

Alicia blinked. Of course! She would become a countess upon her marriage. How quickly the world turned upon itself! She moistened her dry lips. Only last week, she had been serving customers in the goldsmith's shop near the Micklegate. Now everything had turned topsy-turvy. The merchant's daughter ceased to exist. Yet the new Countess of Thornbury was still a figment of her imagination. Who was Alicia Broom now? A hunted enemy of the usurper who sat upon the throne of England. Her hand trembled as she stroked Georgie's coarse fur.

Lady Katherine drew closer to Sir Edward. ''My love, the sun begins to sink in the sky. We must hurry.''

Sir Edward grunted in his old familiar way. Alicia knew he was not happy with the decision he had to make. Her beloved foster parents must ride like the wind, or they would never reach their ship in time. If she thought she was in danger, how much more so was it for these two dearest people whom she had called Mama and Papa for so long?

Leaving Georgie to doze, she slipped her arms around their waists. ''You must go. I shall be in good hands. Methinks Sir Thomas only needs a little time.''

''He needs more than that,'' Brampton grumbled.

Alicia kissed his cheek. ''And you have the word of Master Ford that I will be well taken care of. And I shall write to you often, and tell—''

Sir Edward gripped her, and whispered, "Nay, you must not write at all, my sweet. A letter could be intercepted, and could lead to your half brother's death."

Dickon's handsome face, so like her own, rose up in her memory. She had not seen the little prince since he had been sent into hiding across the North Sea over a decade ago. Four years later, disguised as a Flemish boy named Perkin Warbeck, Dickon had returned to the south of England, where he challenged Henry Tudor for the throne. For six heart-stopping years, Dickon's fortunes had waxed and waned.

Two weeks ago, sweet Dickon had been captured by Henry's forces. Once again, he was imprisoned in the Tower of London, where he had been confined as a child. Her brother's only hope for his life lay in the fact that no one realized that he was the true Richard, Duke of York, and the rightful heir to the throne. Sir Edward hoped that Dickon would be released, just as another pretender named Lambert Simnel had been. Her brother played his part by claiming he had been duped by greedy men. God save him.

Alicia hung her head. "I had forgotten. Forgive me, Papa...my lord."

Sir Edward hugged her. "I am no lord to you, poppet. Though I could never take the place of your esteemed father, I pray that you will always think of Katherine and me as your loving parents."

Tears pricked behind Alicia's eyelids, though she swore to herself that she would not allow them to escape. It would make the parting more difficult. The time for tears came later. "How I love you both! I shall remember you forever."

Katherine kissed her on the forehead. "And you will always be in our thoughts and prayers, child."

"If you must contact us, do so by messenger—one

that you can trust—and send to Bruges in care of the Goldsmith's Guild there. But do not write unless 'tis a matter of life and death. Oh, my child!'' Sir Edward kissed her on the forehead. "Know that I leave my heart with you. Take good care of it until I return.''

Alicia bit her lips to keep them from quivering. "When will that be?''

Sir Edward's brow darkened. "If your brother can escape, and make his way back to his aunt's court in Burgundy, then I shall see you soon. If not...'' He sighed.

Alicia traced her thumb over the furrows in his brow, wishing she could wipe them away. "Let us not think of the alternative. I shall pray for you and for Dickon.''

"If God hears anyone's prayers, he will certainly hear yours, sweetest child.'' After giving her another hug and a kiss, Sir Edward retrieved his hat from the floor. Then he bellowed at the waiting squire. "And you, Sir Twig! I hold you accountable for her in every respect.''

Andrew swept him another jaunty bow. "You have placed your trust wisely, my lord.''

"In whom, I wonder?'' Brampton mused under his breath.

"In my good master, Sir Thomas Cavendish, my lord,'' the youth replied. "And in myself, as his obedient servant.''

With a muttered oath, Sir Edward took his wife's arm and propelled them both toward the castle's entranceway. Pausing under the arch, he glanced back to Alicia. She smiled and waved at him, while her heart broke within her breast.

"Jesu, you were such a tiny thing when first I held you in my arms. Who knew what an angel you would become?''

"Papa..." Alicia could not utter another word.

Then they were gone.

She bit her knuckles to keep from bursting into tears on the spot. She must not show weakness now, especially in front of her betrothed's squire.

Andrew offered her his arm. "The first night is the worst," he confided.

Alicia blinked back the moisture from her eyes. "Your pardon?"

"The absence of your parents." Andrew tucked her hand within the crook of his arm. "'Tis worst the first night, then becomes easier. I know."

She sniffed. "How did you come by this sage knowledge? Were you homesick at the Duke of Buckingham's?"

Andrew grinned. In a faint way he reminded her of Dickon. "Nay, 'twas when I came here to be Sir Thomas's squire. Cried my eyes out that first night."

"Oh?" Alicia wondered if she would cry all night. She had a sinking feeling that she would.

"Aye. When one of the serving men complained to Sir Thomas that my blubbering had kept him awake, my master bade me sleep on the trundle bed in his own chamber."

She couldn't help but be interested in the boy's story. "And did you keep Sir Thomas awake?"

Andrew laughed. "Nay. 'Twas *he* who banished sleep by telling me the most amusing stories until my eyelids fell of their own accord. When I awoke the next morning, I found that Vixen had joined me, and had warmed me all through the night."

Alicia gasped with shock. "Fie on Sir Thomas for that! How dare he debauch so innocent a boy in his care! And just who is this vixen, pray tell?"

Andrew laughed even harder. "Vixen is a small greyhound, Mistress Alicia. You saw her earlier with my master. Methinks you will like her.''

Ah, but will Vixen like me? Alicia wondered. And what about the dog's handsome master?

Chapter Three

"What?" Lady Isabel Cavendish hurled a chamber pot at the trembling maid. "You lie, you slut!" A cushion from the nearby stool followed after the smashed clay receptacle.

Meg ducked as the heavy pillow sailed past her. "Nay, 'tis gospel true, my lady."

Isabel snatched up one of her satin slippers from the disordered pile of her footwear on the floor. "Thomas betrothed? 'Tis as much to say that we shall catch larks when the sky falls. How now, Meg? I am in no mood for jesting."

The maid backed closer to the door. "I do not wag my tongue, my lady. I saw the woman with my own eyes. She has come, bag and baggage. Master Andrew has put her in the royal bedchamber, and there she stays. I came straightway to tell'ee, my lady."

Isabel lowered the slipper. "And Thomas? What has he said?"

"Naught." Meg hid a giggle in her apron. "In truth, he sputtered and goggled like a pike on a hook, then he bolted from the hall."

Isabel curled her lips. This unwanted guest was as

much a surprise to her brother-in-law as she was to Isabel. No doubt the great Earl of Thornbury now cowered somewhere in the home park with those filthy hounds of his. Isabel presumed that he wouldn't return until after sunset. All the better. This bold wench could be well on her way back home by the time Thomas gave her a second thought. A tiny smile crept around the corners of Isabel's mouth.

"Bring her to me," she ordered. "I shall deal with this unpleasantness myself."

Meg bobbed a curtsy. "Very good, my lady." She turned to go.

"And, Meg?"

The maid paused. "Aye, my lady?"

"Tell no one of my conference with the woman. Do you mark me?" Isabel narrowed her eyes. Meg was such a taddle-toad. "One word, and 'twill go very badly for you, I promise."

The maid swallowed. "Aye, my lady." She bobbed again, then dashed away.

Isabel picked her way around the heaps of discarded clothing that littered the floor of her chamber. She stopped before the large sheet of costly Venetian looking glass that William had imported especially for her, and wrinkled her nose at her reflection. She hated to wear black. It made her look plague-racked. Who in this godforsaken castle cared what Isabel wore? She could roam the corridors stark naked for all the interest she stirred in Thomas.

She skimmed her hands across her breasts and down to her narrow waist. William had always complimented her figure. He appreciated a beauty when he saw one. Not like his father, the old earl. All that man had ever said to Isabel was, "When are you going to do your duty, mistress? When am I going to hold my grandson?''

God knows she had tried hard enough to get pregnant. William had mounted her almost nightly—twice a day when they were first married. Isabel sighed at the memory. Though she had often complained at the time, she missed her dead husband now. Thomas couldn't possibly hold a candle to William, yet she had little choice. She must marry Thomas, or be sent back to her father's crowded household where she would have to fight her enormous number of sisters for every scrap of food on the table. Farewell to fine gowns, bright jewels and looking glasses with which to admire herself. Isabel shook out the folds of her black damask skirt. How could she possibly attract Thomas if she looked like a pinched crow?

Behind her, someone cleared her throat. Isabel whirled around. A tall creature, dressed in a plain green woolen gown, dropped a curtsy. Despite her height and apparent low estate, the stranger's posture remained perfect, even when she rose. Isabel drew in her breath. This woman was a giantess. No doubt her feet were as large as shovels—nothing like Isabel's own dainty ones. She relaxed a little. Nothing to fear from this long drink of water. Cavendish men liked their women petite.

"I am Lady Isabel Cavendish," she announced as she seated herself upon the only chair in the room. She spread out her skirts around her. "My husband was Sir William, second son of the Earl of Thornbury." Isabel paused, then corrected herself. "The *late* earl, that is."

"May God have mercy upon his soul, and upon the soul of your dear, departed husband," the chit replied in a low tone.

Isabel fumbled in her reticule, then drew out a fluttering snippet of white lawn and lace. She dabbed her dry eyes with a corner of the handkerchief. "Poor William!" she murmured. "It pains me to think of him." Which was the truth. She had finished shedding her tears over his inconvenient departure a fortnight ago. Now she had other amusements to console her grief.

"You have my deepest sympathies, my Lady Cavendish." The stranger appraised Isabel's tender little scene.

Isabel wished she had learned to cry at will like several of her sisters could. It was an extremely effective method to get what one wanted out of a man. She prayed the woman before her did not notice the absence of tears. Best to get down to business.

"Who are you, and what do you want at Wolf Hall?" Isabel waved the handkerchief in the air before her as if the visitor was accompanied by a foul odor. "You may speak freely to me, as I am Sir Thomas's chatelaine."

A faint blush hovered in the woman's cheeks. The color unfortunately made her look a little pretty.

"Mistress Alicia Broom, my lady. My...my father is...was the goldsmith by the Micklegate in the city of York."

Isabel wanted to laugh out loud. The daughter of a merchant claimed to be Thomas's betrothed? No wonder the man bolted for the woods. Naturally he left the distasteful task of getting rid of the strumpet to Isabel.

She pretended to yawn, barely covering her open mouth with her hand. Let the goldsmith's gawky daughter catch sight of the colorful gems decking Isabel's tiny fingers.

"I fear you have made a long journey to no purpose, mistress. As you can see, I am in mourning, and am not in the mood for buying new baubles. Come back to see me during Advent. Mayhap I shall give you some custom in honor of the Christmas season.''

The pink in the girl's cheeks turned to a deep crimson, though she did not change the soft tone of her voice. ''I fear you have been misled, my lady. I have not come to sell my father's wares, but to take my rightful place at Wolf Hall.'' She drew herself up even taller. ''I am pledged to be Sir Thomas Cavendish's bride.''

Isabel could not contain her laughter. The mere idea of this plain stick as the Countess of Thornbury was too ludicrous. ''I thank you, mistress, for providing me with a spot of mirth to gladden this sad time.''

''I do not jest, my lady,'' the merchant's daughter replied, with a hint of steel creeping into her voice. ''The contract was signed, and the dowry paid ten years ago between my father and the late earl. I can understand your wonderment, but—''

''But nothing!'' Isabel snarled. How dare this brazen creature invade Isabel's domain, and claim it for her own? ''Either you have been sadly misinformed, or else you deliberately pretend to a place that is not yours either by birth or by right. You are most fortunate that I have a mild disposition, or else I would bring you before the bailiff on a charge of deception, fraud, counterfeit and…and…'' Surely there was something else with which Isabel could threaten Mistress Broom. Treason, perhaps? That word always inspired terror.

A blue fire leapt into the other's eyes. ''The law is on my side, my lady. I have a copy of the betrothal contract to prove my claim.''

How dare she challenge me! Isabel stood, though she barely came up to the woman's shoulder. ''What does my Lord Cavendish have to say to all this nonsense?''

Mistress Broom bit her lip, though she did not lower her eyes as Isabel had expected. This jade was a proud one, and needed a good beating to bring her down a peg or two.

Isabel tossed her dark curls. "Methinks he said nothing. Typical! Thomas hates discord of any sort. He leaves all such matters to me. Very well, goldsmith's daughter, mark what I say to you. I am betrothed to marry Thomas once the period of our mourning is over."

Mistress Broom's eyes widened at this piece of perfidy. Isabel became even bolder. "Aye, already a courier has been sent to the Archbishop of York to procure a dispensation for the marriage between my brother-in-law and myself. Our wedding will be celebrated before the Advent season. Therefore, I suggest you remove yourself immediately before my darling Thomas returns, lest his anger grow hotter than mine."

The goldsmith's brat lifted her chin. "I will speak with my Lord Cavendish first," she replied, snapping off her words. "If *he* tells me to go, I will. But if he bids me to stay, then I will take the place that was promised to me. I vow this, as God is my witness. Good day, Lady Cavendish."

Without asking permission to go, Mistress Broom turned on her heel and left the room. The wench did not even bother to curtsy before her better. Isabel crossed to the table that held a jug of wine and several cups. She helped herself to a long, but unsatisfying drink.

The devil take the baggage! She is just the sort who would appeal to Thomas. And then, pray tell, what will happen to me?

Thomas squinted into the red-orange rays of the setting sun. Andrew's dark silhouette blotted out the beauty of the sky's palette. "Well?" he barked at his squire.

"Mistress Broom is lodged in the royal chamber as you instructed me, my lord." The boy flopped down on the log next to his lord. Vixen pushed her needle nose under his arm, then laid her sleek head on his lap. She closed her eyes with contentment when Andrew began to stroke her flank.

Thomas drew in a deep breath. "What do you think of her?" he asked, not looking directly at the youth. Andrew was too clever for his own good, and could read his master's face as easily as Thomas could read Greek poetry.

The squire chuckled. "She is bonny and fair, and a perfect match for you—aye, especially in bed. Hip to hip, knee to knee—"

Thomas cuffed him. The boy toppled backward off the log. Vixen bestowed a reproachful look on Thomas for interrupting Andrew's massage.

"You will speak with a civil tongue in your head when you speak of Mistress Alicia," Thomas growled. "Remember, she is under my protection."

He thought of her lovely eyes looking into his very soul, and of her slim body, draped in green. His manroot tightened between his legs. By the book, what witchery had Alicia wrought upon him in so short a time?

Andrew stretched out on the leafy ground where he lay. Lacing his fingers together, he pillowed his head in his hands. Vixen curled up next to him. "Aye, my lord. Tell my Lady Isabel of your chivalrous inclinations. Methinks she has already poured some of her venom into the shell pink ear of Mistress Alicia."

Thomas groaned. If Isabel had not claimed she was ill with grief, he would have packed her off on a post-horse to her father's home right after the funerals were over. The woman made his skin crawl. What's more, she hated his dogs, and the feeling was returned tenfold by the three canines.

"So Madam Spider has already stretched out her web? What happened?"

Andrew sucked air through his teeth. "I do not know. Lady Isabel trapped Alicia in her lair for a private conference. By the time I could get close enough to overhear their conversation, 'twas finished." He sat up. "When Mistress Broom left my lady's chambers, I saw that she fought back tears. Nearly ran me over in her flight. And yet..." Pausing, he smiled with the look of a contented cat.

"What?" Thomas snapped. He had no desire for this young jackanapes to fall in love with his betrothed. By the rood, Alicia was his.

Andrew blinked. "She stopped, and apologized very prettily to me as if I were the lord mayor of York. Alicia may be a merchant's daughter, but she has the manners of a noble lady."

"Humph." Thomas chewed on his lower lip. "Just remember, maltworm, *Mistress* Alicia will be the Countess of Thornbury." That title sounded very odd on his tongue.

"Not if Isabel has her way," the squire replied softly.

"How now?" Thomas bellowed.

"Methought I heard Lady Isabel say that she would wed *you* before Advent. And she called you her darling Thomas." Andrew made a face as if the words tasted bitter. "By my troth, my lord, I would not mingle my blood with hers in a basin, much less in bed. I often wondered how your brother could stand her."

"They were a matched pair," Thomas muttered, scooping up Tavie with one hand.

"Aye." Andrew dismissed the couple with a graceful

gesture. "'Tis said they matched very well in amorous pursuits." He ducked when Thomas tried to cuff him again. "Peace, my lord. I speak only the truth. If you are to marry Mistress Alicia, then 'tis time you thought of bedsport for yourself. I have had some experience in this area, sir. 'Tis a very pleasant occupation."

Thomas scratched Tavie's belly, and pretended to ignore Andrew's last remark. Only his squire knew of Thomas's chosen celibacy. At least, Andrew had the wit to keep his observations private. Everyone else at Wolf Hall, from the steward to the scullery maid, imagined Thomas was a stallion like his lusty brothers. In actual fact, the female of the species scared the living hell out of him.

Andrew jumped up from the ground, then brushed the clinging bits of leaves and pine needles from his expensive clothes. "'Tis suppertime, my lord."

Recognizing one of his favorite words, Tavie yipped several times. Then he licked his master's hand before springing to the ground. Thomas regarded his smallest dog with open fondness. "Now you have done it, Andrew. Taverstock will give me no peace until he can dance attendance under the table."

He stood up from the rough bark log that had been his afternoon's retreat, and rubbed his backside. "I suppose the ladies are expecting me to sup with them?"

Andrew's eyes danced with merriment. "Aye, my lord. Methinks they have already drawn up their lines of battle. Their weapons will be winsome looks and sharpened wit. 'Twill be a rare treat to watch."

Thomas groaned. "Perchance I will take supper in my chamber."

"Coward!" the boy whispered, dancing out of his lord's reach.

Thomas studied the purple twilight as it crept across

the sky. The evening star winked back at him. "Aye, you speak the truth. I have never run from a fight, Andrew, and I am not about to start now. Lead me on to these warring females, but, by the book, do not leave me alone with them!"

Alicia stood at the high-arched window of her chamber. Drawing in a deep breath of the cool evening air, she savored the unfamiliar scents of wet earth, fields of new-mown hay and the sharp tang of woodsmoke that curled up from the blacksmith's forge. Everything seemed so fresh and clean in the country after a lifetime spent within the walls of York. Alicia stared at the farthest tip of the horizon, and prayed that Sir Edward and Lady Katherine had arrived in good time at their rendezvous on the North Sea coast. A thick lump rose in her throat. She might never again hear Katherine's sweet singing while she went about her chores. Never again feel Edward's whiskery good-night kisses on her cheeks. A tear burned her eyelids.

Do not be a goose, Alicia. What is past is past. Look to the future. You are mistress of your own fate now. Tears are not going to win Thomas. You must be strong. Everything depends upon it.

The huge mastiff at her feet looked up at her with an expectant expression.

Bending over, Alicia scratched his tawny back. "What is it, Georgie? Is your master coming?"

Georgie rose and padded over to the closed chamber door.

Alicia studied his behavior. "Is someone out there?" she asked in a low voice.

The dog gave himself a shake, as if to banish the last vestiges of his afternoon nap. He continued to stare at the door.

Has that awful Lady Isabel set one of her minions to spy upon me? Alicia tiptoed across the wide, smooth floor. Without making a sound, Alicia put her hand to the latch. With a sudden twist, she yanked open the door. A young girl with a tousled mane of flaxen hair fell across the threshold. Georgie greeted her with slobbering kisses.

"How now?" Putting her hands to her hips, Alicia regarded her surprise visitor. "And who might you be?"

The girl laughed in answer as she hugged the huge dog. "I wager that Georgie told you I was here," she said, pulling herself into a sitting position.

Her pretty gown of dove gray silk and linen showed signs of an active day spent out-of-doors. Smudges of dried mud decorated the hems of her skirts, and deep grass stains showed where the child had propped herself up on her elbows. *'Twill be the devil to get those marks out of the cloth. What was her governess thinking to let her frolic in so fine a dress?*

"Aye, Georgie is a wise animal," Alicia replied. She crossed her arms over her chest, and waited for an introduction.

The girl hugged the great dog again. "I thought as much. Isabel says that he is useless because he is so old. Pooh! She is the one who is useless, unless 'tis for her own pleasure." The golden child folded her hands in her lap, then looked up at Alicia. "They said you were tall."

Alicia bit back a grin. Seeing that the girl intended to remain on the floor, she decided to join her. Judging from the richness of the child's attire and her resemblance to Thomas, she presumed that her mysterious guest was a member of the family, and not a kitchen maid. Perhaps Alicia could win an ally for herself. She sank down onto the floor in front of the girl and dog.

"Not too tall now, methinks," she remarked with a smile.

The child giggled. "Nay, just right. Too bad we have

nothing to eat. We could have a feast right here, all by ourselves. I do so love feasts and merrymaking.'' Wrinkling her nose, her expression grew solemn. '''Tis been a sad house since my papa died.''

Alicia had the urge to gather the child into her arms, but restrained herself, lest she act too forward. She did not even know the winsome girl's name.

''May God have mercy on his soul,'' she murmured. ''And may his sweet angels keep watch over you.''

''Amen,'' the girl breathed. Then she ran her hand down Georgie's broad back.

Alicia stroked the animal's other side. Georgie closed his eyes with a look of pure bliss. No one spoke for several minutes.

''I heard what Isabel said to you,'' the girl announced.

Alicia paused in midstroke. ''And what did you hear?''

''Do not believe a thing Isabel says. She has a viper's tongue.''

Alicia widened her eyes. '''Tis not polite to speak that way about a member of your family.''

The child snorted in a very unladylike fashion. ''Thank the good Lord she is not a blood relation.'' She lowered her voice. ''And she is *not* going to marry Tom at all. He cannot stand her.''

Alicia moistened her lips. ''How do you know? Did my Lord Cavendish tell you this piece of news—or did it float through a keyhole?''

The lass giggled again. ''Both. That is why *you* must marry my brother without delay.''

Alicia pretended to be surprised. ''Oh? I am merely the daughter of a goldsmith. How can I marry a great lord?''

The other shrugged her shoulders. ''My papa betrothed Thomas to a goldsmith's daughter years ago. I was weaned on that tale. William often teased poor Tom about it.'' She regarded Alicia with a pair of bright blue eyes. ''Methinks my papa made a wise choice for him.''

Alicia laughed. ''How do you know? Why, you do not even know my name.''

''Mistress Alicia Broom.'' The girl shot her a triumphant look.

''My, my, your ears must be overflowing with gossip. I fear you have me at a disadvantage, for I do not know who you are.''

The child swept her flyaway hair out of her eyes, then straightened her posture. ''I am Lady Mary Elizabeth Cavendish, so please you.''

Alicia smiled as she inclined her head to Lady Mary. ''It pleases me right well to make your acquaintance.''

Mary clapped her hands. ''Good! I want us to be friends. Do you like to play games?''

Alicia blinked at the lightning shift in the conversation. ''Aye, though it has been a while since I had the opportunity. What sort of games do you have in mind?''

Mary sighed with anticipated pleasure. ''Every kind under the sun. Shuttlecock and battledore, hoodman's bluff, hoops, cards. I *love* games.'' She made a face. ''Isabel does not. She is such a mud hen! You must pay her no mind. She only wants Tom to marry her because she wants to be the Countess of Thornbury. She does not love him at all. In fact, she thinks my brother is half-witted.''

''That is a very shameful thing to say, Lady Mary,'' Alicia remarked in an offhand manner, though her heart raced under her tight bodice.

The girl did not look the least bit dismayed, but continued to stroke Georgie. ''Aye, but I did not say it. Isabel did. I heard her.''

''Through a keyhole, perchance?''

Mary grinned at her. ''Aye! How else am I to learn what happens under our roof? No one tells me anything. Was your governess a witch?''

Alicia bit her cheeks to keep from laughing out loud. "I fear that the daughters of goldsmiths do not have governesses, though my...my father taught me to read and write."

The child sighed. "Lucky you! Mine is Mistress Vive—her real name is Genevieve, but 'tis a mickle mouthful to say if one is in a hurry. She is utterly a perdition!" Mary flopped over backward with a dramatic groan.

"I am sure that she tries her best."

The sprite made a rude noise with her lips. "Not so! All she wants to do is nap or eat sweetmeats the live-long day. Every time I look at her, she clicks her tongue at me and tells me that my husband will have to horse-whip me to make me behave." She snorted. "I am not past twelve years. What do I want with a husband?" Rolling over onto her stomach, she gave Alicia a very shrewd look. "But *you* will do very well as Tom's wife. You already like his dogs, and that is half the battle."

"Tell me something about your brother," Alicia prompted. She had seen Thomas for only a moment, and she still wasn't sure if she had pleased or shocked him. Andrew's assurances had done little to calm her apprehensions.

Mary grinned. "He is the sweetest and gentlest of men. John was nice enough to me, but he was always away on Papa's business about the estates. William was...a great roaring boy. In plain truth, a bully. I hated him then, but I do miss him now. I never truly wanted him dead."

"I am sure that you did not," Alicia soothed.

Mary's eyebrow rose up. "Oh, I confess, I sometimes thought about it, especially when William got me into trouble with Papa or Mistress Vive, but now..." She gave herself a little shake. "Tom often reads stories to me from one of his books. He plays chess very well, though sometimes I can beat him. He lets me have extra sweetmeats after dinner, and he has a lovely singing voice, though no one hears it but me and the dogs.''

"Why is that?'' Alicia breathed.

"He does not like to call attention to himself. William treated Tom shamefully every chance he got. I do not blame Tom for staying out in the woods until all hours, or for finding his dogs better company. Pray, do not be fooled by my brother, Mistress Alicia. 'Tis all a ruse. He is sparse of words by choice. 'Tis true, he is very shy among company. But make him lose his temper, and bang!'' She clapped her hands, which startled Georgie out of his reverie. "Thomas spews forth such speeches that would make the Archbishop of York faint with surprise.''

Alicia tucked this piece of intelligence away in her memory. "Most interesting.''

A gong sounded in the chamber below them. Its tones reverberated from the stone walls of Wolf Hall.

Mary and Georgie both jumped to their feet. "Supper!'' the lass chirped over her shoulder as she and the mastiff hurried out the doorway. "Remember what I said.''

"Aye, 'tis graven upon my mind.'' Rising from the floor, Alicia brushed off stray tawny dog hairs. Lady Mary Cavendish had said quite a lot, she mused as she tightened her braid. She prayed she could remember it all.

Chapter Four

Thomas heard Isabel's nasal whine before he saw her. She seemed to be particularly prickly tonight.

"Must be my new guest who has set her mind a-whirl," he muttered to Vixen, who hugged his side as usual. Thomas allowed his fingertips to run along the top of the greyhound's narrow head. "Not that my Lady Tart-Tongue has much of a mind to disorder. God shield me."

Vixen licked his fingers in answer. Thomas cast a quick look at her thickening middle. Unfortunately, Vixen was a little too generous with her favors.

"Where is my cushion?" Isabel screeched as Thomas entered the hall. "Why isn't it at my place? Cream-faced loon!" She delivered a sharp blow to poor Stokes's nearest ear.

"Hold!" Thomas roared. How dare the little shrew raise her hand to his steward.

Isabel's sharp fox face smoothed into an expression of pleasure. She swept him a curtsy. He wondered what piece of mischief she brewed now.

"Thomas!" she cooed. "'Tis a joy to see you look-

ing so fit and fine this evening. I have ordered everything in readiness for your supper. All is prepared—''

His tongue curled with disgust. "Peace, woman!"

In the nine years she had lived at Wolf Hall, Isabel
had never lifted a finger or voice to order anything from
the kitchen, unless it was a plate of pastries or sweetmeats for her own private enjoyment.

"Tom! Tom!" Mary called from the wide staircase
as she half ran, half tumbled down the steps.

Her big brother smiled as he caught her. "What is
amiss now? Mistress Vive?" He didn't know whom he
pitied more, his little minx of a sister or her tiresome
governess.

"Nay!" Mary laughed as she wriggled out of his
grasp. She dropped a fleeting kiss between Vixen's ears.
"You will never guess in two months of Sundays! Alicia knows all sorts of wonderful new games, and she is
going to teach me one this very evening after supper."

Barely hearing the rest of Mary's excited prattle,
Thomas looked up the stairway. Alicia stepped out of
the shadow cast by a pillar. He caught his breath. Great
Jove! The maid looked even more beautiful than he recalled from their brief afternoon's meeting. Lifting her
skirts a little above her ankles, she descended the stairs
in a single fluid motion, like honey rolling down a knife
blade. Georgie followed behind her. Her skin glowed in
the torchlight, and her hair seemed to have a golden
sheen of its own. Thomas realized that he was holding
his breath.

When Alicia reached the bottom of the staircase, she
dropped a graceful curtsy to him. She shouldn't do that
to me, he thought.

"Oh, *there* you are!" Isabel's voice jarred the moment. "The kitchen is through that far door. Tell the

cook that I said you may have some bread—and whatever else might be lying about.''

Thomas brushed past his sister-in-law. Anger ignited in his soul. He pressed his lips tighter, lest a harsh word escape them. He offered his arm to the vision of beauty who shimmered before him. He could not think of a thing to say to Alicia that would be appropriate for such a goddess's ears.

''Thomas!'' screeched Isabel. ''That woman is not fit for the head table. She's only a common merchant's daughter.''

Grinding his teeth, he ignored the wasp in her expensive widow's weeds.

''Good evening, Sir Thomas,'' Alicia murmured as he seated her on his right. ''I trust you had a good walk this afternoon?''

Thomas looked into her eyes to see if she mocked him. Instead he felt himself drowning in their sparkling blue depths. Her smile warmed him to his toes.

''Middling.'' Without looking directly at her, he pushed their shared trencher a little closer to her.

''Thomas! You have not heard a word I have said!'' Isabel plunked herself down on the seat at his left hand.

''Nay, sweet sister-in-law, and he will not hear you until you get the wet cat out of your craw,'' Mary retorted across the table.

Isabel seemed to swell in size. Her hands shook. ''Children should be silent when in company!''

Mary stuck out her tongue in reply. Several of the castle inhabitants at the lower table tittered at the exchange. Thomas groaned inwardly at this very poor introduction to his family.

Alicia chuckled softly. ''I like your little sister very

much, my lord. She explained a number of things to me this afternoon.''

He exhaled with relief. When he glanced at her, he saw that her smile had increased in its warmth. "Good,'' he muttered.

The devil take me! I should tell her how glad I am that Isabel did not drive her away before my return. How can I possibly apologize for my churlish behavior toward her guardian?

Andrew proffered the first course of the cold supper. "Eels in aspic, my lord?''

Avoiding his squire's knowing smirk, Thomas regarded the black-and-gray jellied mess on the platter in front of him. His appetite withered at the sight. Why couldn't Isabel do a better job of the household management—especially in the kitchens?

"Serve the lady first,'' he instructed the boy.

Without hesitation, Andrew turned to Alicia. "Eels, mistress? The serving wench assures me that they are fresh—somewhat. I would not swear by the creatures at all, myself, but 'tis better than starving.''

The cheek of the stripling! How dare he flirt with my bride-to-be? Before Thomas could open his mouth or Alicia could help herself, Isabel lunged across the table and speared the choicest morsel with her silver eating knife.

"Methinks you are sand-blind, Andrew,'' she reproached him with a sweetness that dripped poison, "or you have a great deal of wax in your ears. Thomas instructed you to serve the *lady* first.''

Andrew bestowed her a smile of angelic innocence. "Aye, and so I did, Lady Isabel.''

"Check and double check!'' chortled Mary. "Yahoo!''

Infected by Mary's good spirits, Taverstock barked under the table. Georgie added a note or two in a deep bass. Vixen chose to remain silent, though she made her presence known to Thomas by pressing against his leg. He cut off a small piece of his eel for her. He slipped the morsel under the table—and encountered Alicia's fingers also holding a tidbit of the slippery fish. He sucked in his breath.

Her gorgeous eyes widened at the contact, though she did not move until Vixen had licked both their fingers clean of the last trace of gray aspic.

Thomas allowed a small grin to ruffle his lips. His skin burned where she had touched him.

Alicia returned his smile with one of her own that seemed to light up the furthermost corner of the gloomy hall. "Your hound must eat well, my lord, if she is to deliver healthy puppies," she said, her gaze never wavering from his. "I pray your pardon if I have given offense by feeding her while at table."

His heart swelled within his doublet. It hammered against his chest. "No offense," he muttered. "On behalf of Vixen, I give you her thanks."

"Rot!" spat out Isabel. "But what can you expect from an unlettered, common wench?"

"She can read and write," Mary chirruped while she helped herself to a piece of cold roasted chicken. "Can you, Isabel?"

Thomas grinned behind his hand. He knew that the Earl of Bedford had not bothered to school any of his eleven daughters. Isabel's father did not consider women's brains capable of understanding numbers and the alphabet. That Alicia could read came as a pleasant surprise.

"'Tis true?" he asked her. "You know your letters?"

"Aye, my lord," she replied, returning his gaze. "Both Latin and English, and I can cipher accounts as well."

"She...stretches the truth, methinks," Isabel sputtered. "She will say or do anything to catch your interest, Thomas. No doubt she lifts her skirts for an empty compliment."

The color drained from Alicia's cheeks. Looking down at the trencher, she swallowed. Conversation at the lower table ceased altogether. Even Mary was shocked into silence. Thomas clenched his fist until his arm throbbed.

"You will keep that vicious tongue of yours within your mouth, madam, or I will be compelled to relieve you of it altogether," he thundered at his sister-in-law.

"I only meant—" Isabel began, but Thomas cut her off.

"You drip poison from every pore, and have broken this evening's good company," he continued, his words spewing forth without control. "You will not fling mud at those who partake of my hospitality, and who are under my protection. Since you have forgotten your place in my household, methinks 'tis time for you to return to your father's castle."

He paused as he gulped for air. He looked at the shocked faces around him. Stones and bones, damn his unruly temper! The fair beauty at his side must think she has landed in a nightmare. To keep himself from venting any more spleen, Thomas grabbed a chicken wing and stuffed most of it into his mouth.

"More wine?" Andrew asked cheerfully.

* * *

Isabel's ears rang with Thomas's last words. Across the table, Mary grinned at her elder's discomfort. Plague take the little chit! What the brat needed was a good whipping. Isabel gripped her wine goblet as if she held Alicia's long neck between her fingers.

Go back to Bedford Chase? Back to the chaos where she would be but one more face around the table? Share her bed with a quarrelsome sister—or two? Isabel gritted her teeth. Never! She choked down the bile that rose in her throat. There must be a way to remain at Wolf Hall, and to turn Thomas's heart from ice to fire for her. The food in her mouth tasted of ashes, while her thoughts tumbled from one idea to the next. She did not taste the poached pears at the end of the meal. Her preoccupation with her troubles shattered when Thomas suddenly rose.

"Mistress," he muttered to the thin woman on his right. "Would you like to see the garden?"

The creature laughed, then replied, "'Twould be a great pleasure, my lord. They do say that the soul of a home is reflected in its garden."

What drivel! Isabel curled her lips. She must win her way back into Thomas's good graces this very night, before his threat of banishment hardened into iron resolve.

She forced a light laugh. "You have hit upon the mark, Thomas! 'Tis a fine evening for a twilight stroll amid the…" Rot it all! What was in bloom at the moment? She hated anything that got her hands dirty, especially mucking in a garden. "Roses!" There *had* to be roses.

Thomas cast her the briefest of looks. "Start packing," he snapped. Blue fire flashed in his eyes.

Isabel shivered within her mourning dress. William

had often warned her about his younger brother's temper, but she had rarely seen it in full blast. Now she realized that she should have been more careful. Damn William! Why did he have to die and leave her in such a wretched situation? Wolf Hall was her domain by right.

Before she could utter another word, Thomas and the woman swept from the hall. The pack of hounds followed behind him, as usual. Mary sniggered.

"Do you need help, Isabel?" she asked with ill-contained glee. "Methinks 'twill take you all night to fill your trunks with your finery."

Leaning over the table, Isabel glared at the horrid child. "If you do not leave the hall this minute, I will pluck out your hairs one by one until you are bald!"

It gave her satisfaction to see the brat pale. Without another word, Mary rose, then dashed up the stairs. At the landing, she paused.

"Since I expect you to be long gone before I wake up tomorrow, sister-in-law, I wish you a pleasant journey. May your way be plagued with ruts and rain!" she yelled. As a final insult, the little wretch stuck out her tongue. The servants clearing the tables did not bother to conceal their grins.

"May your bed be filled with lice!" Isabel retorted after Mary's fleeing figure.

She wished she could scratch out that little cat's eyes. Thomas spoiled his sister entirely too much. No wonder the child had such atrocious manners. She patted her gray veil in place. Mary would change her tune once Isabel became the Countess of Thornbury. She gulped a deep breath of air. First, she must become the Countess, and to that end she must use her wiles against that hulking simpleton, who had not the wit to know when he was being hoodwinked.

She stalked out of the hall with its simpering horde of menials. By the time she returned to her chamber, she had hit upon a workable plan—indeed, it was her only hope.

Meg stood in the middle of the room with her arms full of colorful gowns. "Do...do ye wish me to start packing these, my lady?" she whimpered.

Isabel resisted the impulse to box the idiot's ears. "Nay, Meg. I am not going anywhere."

"But...I heard my lord say—"

Isabel interrupted her with a wave of her hand. "But he will change his mind very quickly, Meg. You will see anon. Soon I will be the true mistress of this heap of stones." She sat by the low fire, and stared into its red-hot embers.

"How so, my lady? Sir Thomas sounded—"

"He is like that great worthless dog of his—all bark but no bite." The more Isabel contemplated her plan, the more brilliant it shone in her mind.

Meg drew closer. "How now, my lady?"

Her mistress allowed a smile to curl her lips. "I shall plead my belly," she murmured, more to herself than to Meg.

The maid's jaw dropped. "Wh...what, my lady?"

Isabel looked directly into Meg's bovine face. "I will tell my esteemed brother-in-law that I am carrying William's child. Thomas cannot send me away from Wolf Hall if I am carrying the next Cavendish heir."

Meg's eyes grew rounder. "But ye're not expecting, my lady. Yer last monthly flow was but a fortnight ago."

Isabel cocked her head. Best to scotch this snake now

before it grew too big to contain. "I fear you mistook the date, Meg. 'Twas *two months* ago, before my husband sickened and died."

Meg shook her head. "Nay, my lady, I remember—"

Like a fork of lightning, Isabel reached out and slapped the stupid girl. "Think again, Meg, if you value your place as my maid. I would hate to have to send you from Wolf Hall for telling lies. Everyone knows that liars also steal. What would happen to you if one or two of my jewels went missing? 'Twould be the gallows for you, for certain sure."

Meg gulped. "I do not lie, my lady," she gibbered. "And all your jewels are safe and sound in your coffer. I swear by the cross, 'tis true." Two large tears rolled down her moon-calf face. "Please, my lady, do not turn me out. I have done ye no harm." She threw her apron over her head, and began to wail in earnest.

"Peace, you fool. Leave off your tears, and listen."

When Meg's sobs subsided, Isabel continued. "I tell you, I am pregnant by my Lord William, and none shall gainsay it. Do you mark me?"

The maid nodded. "Aye, my lady. You are with child."

Isabel smiled her satisfaction. She nurtured her little seed of deception. "I beg you not to mention this news in the kitchen, Meg. I have not yet told Sir Thomas. I have only just discovered it myself."

"Aye, I give you my word, my lady."

Ha! A vow as strong as water. By morning, the whole castle will know of the new heir. Now to seal the falsehood. Isabel stretched, then yawned. "By my troth, I have a most marvelous craving for some sweetened cream and wafers. Do fetch me a bowlful, Meg. I feel I must have it or die."

"Aye, my lady." The silly maid all but flew to the chamber door. "I will bring you the sweets in a trice."

Isabel held up her hand. "And mind you, not a word of my condition to anyone."

"My life upon it, my lady!"

Isabel laughed softly to herself as she listened to Meg's footsteps tripping down the passageway. She rubbed her stomach. It was true that her womb was empty. Isabel furrowed her brows. Nine years in bed with lusty William, and not even a miscarriage to show for it. Her father, the Earl of Bedford, had an army of children by Isabel's late mother. Even now, he filled the nursery with more puling waifs by his poor second wife. With such a sire, how could Isabel possibly be barren? She pushed away the very idea. It must have been William's fault.

No matter. She would get herself with child—and soon. She could be forgiven if the babe came a little later than expected. Thomas might know to the day when his bitch would whelp, but he had no idea of human female matters. He would believe anything she told him. His honor would force him to keep her at Wolf Hall—and, with the right prodding, his honor would convince him to marry her. The Cavendish heir must have a Cavendish father.

Isabel kicked off her slippers, then stretched out her toes to the warmth of the fire. Tomorrow, she would send a message to the Archbishop of York for a dispensation. Better to start the proceedings now. Ecclesiastical matters took a such long time. She sighed. *I must plant an heir.* She licked her lips as she thought of Launce, a groom whom she had seduced several months ago. Tall, sturdy and blond—like his Cavendish master, he swived well. The begetting would be fun in the bargain.

Isabel would lie with Launce on the morrow. She wiggled her toes at the pleasurable prospect.

The late-summer sun lingered in the western sky as Thomas led Alicia into the high-walled garden in the lee of the castle. She breathed in the familiar aromas of new-turned earth, roses in full bloom, and sun-warmed mint. Gillyflowers in pinks and whites, purple-headed irises, nodding, golden-eyed daisies and the ordered rows of the herb garden caught her by surprise.

"Your garden is lovely, and very well cared for, my lord. Isabel did not strike me as a gardener."

"She is not," he replied in a brusque manner. "'Tis Mary's."

Alicia's eyes widened. "Your little sister? I am amazed. She is so young, yet she has a skillful hand."

Thomas sighed. "Mary is young and old at the same time. She—" He stopped, looked at Alicia, then said nothing. Instead, he stared at his polished boots.

He can speak wisely, yet he chooses not to. Alicia thanked assorted saints in heaven for her conversation with Mary this afternoon. The girl had a good eye for the people around her.

Thomas withdrew his fingertips from her elbow, and clasped his hands behind his back. Alicia tried not to show her disappointment. She had been heartened by his undivided, though silent, attention during supper, and by his surprising rebuke of his sister-in-law. She hoped that this walk would initiate a discussion of their marriage. Yet Thomas acted as if her presence displeased him. She swallowed down her fear. At least, he had not sent her away. Pray God, he would honor his betrothal contract.

Alicia forced a smile to her lips. "The evening is my favorite time of day," she said by way of making small talk. "Everything is at peace with itself."

Thomas merely rumbled in his throat.

She ran her tongue across her dry lips, and continued the one-sided conversation in a bright manner. "Your sister must have a rare gift with growing things. The flowers are much larger than the ones my moth…my mother grew in her garden in York." She must not think of her abandoned home. The pain of parting hurt too much.

"Aye," Thomas muttered.

Alicia wondered what his deep voice would sound like when he whispered sweet words of love into a maiden's ear. Her cheeks grew warm at the thought. *Please, sweet Saint Anne, let him fall in love with me— or, at least, let him like me, just a little bit.* She could not bear the thought of living the rest of her life without the comfort of love. The Bramptons had given her their fullest measure of affection during her childhood.

Just then Georgie brushed past them. He sniffed along the path of crushed oyster shells until he came to a spot under a thickly flowering pink rosebush. He began to dig; the flying dirt just missed Alicia's skirts.

Thomas snapped his fingers twice. Georgie stopped his frantic activity, and gave them a look of reproach.

"Your pardon, Mistress Alicia. Did he foul your clothing?" Thomas reached out as if to brush away an offending clod of mud. Then he balled his fist, and jammed his hand behind his back again. He rocked back and forth on his heels, while he stared at a spot over her head.

He is afraid to touch me. Alicia found herself inordinately pleased with that possibility. *He must respect me, even a little bit.* Aloud, she remarked, "Nay, Georgie's aim was off the mark. Pray, what is he digging for? A badger or a hare?"

Thomas chuckled. The sound sung in her ears.

"Nay, Georgie's hunting days are past, I fear, though he does not know it yet. He buries his bones from the table scraps in the garden. Mary is at sixes and sevens over this little habit."

"Mayhap, Georgie hopes to grow a bone tree, and so never have to beg for scraps again," Alicia ventured.

Thomas laughed deep in his throat. The unexpected sound caught Alicia by surprise. She must try to get him to laugh again, and often. She suspected he was not used to expressing his mirth in such an open fashion, thanks to his older brother's torments during his childhood.

"Your little greyhound—do you know when she will deliver?"

"In a week's time, or thereabouts."

Alicia regarded Vixen. She noted how the sleek animal kept close to Thomas. "She is a beautiful creature. Did her other puppies look like honey as well?"

Thomas stared at Alicia, lifting his thick brows in surprise. "Very few look anything like their mother. I fear Vixen is too free with her favors. I never know who is the father until she whelps." He chuckled again. "'Tis always a surprise."

"Oh." Alicia searched frantically for something else to say. "Have you fixed her a nest for her birthing?"

He sighed. "Every time. And every time, Vixen finds her own spot. She had one litter in the laundry, right in the middle of newly washed linen. I had to pay the laundress two shillings to sweeten her temper. She was none too pleased at the mess."

"Methinks she liked your silver," Alicia observed.

He nodded. "Aye, she did. Silver is the way to all women's hearts—" With a stricken look, the rest of his words died on his lips. He strode down the path.

Alicia ran to keep up with him. "Do you think my heart is bought with silver as well, Sir Thomas?"

He stopped so quickly that Taverstock bumped into his boot. Thomas scooped up the little dog, and scratched him behind his ears. He did not look at Alicia.

"Your father paid my father a great sum of gold as your dowry," he muttered. "All women are bought and sold."

She put her hands to her hips. "Is that the truth?" she asked, cocking her head. "And what of your sister, Mary? I presume you will dower her?"

"She…" He chewed on his lower lip.

Alicia continued, heedless of where her tongue might take her. "My…my father may have bartered my body, my lord, but I assure you no stack of gold, nor mound of jewels can buy my affections. I am not Isabel."

"Thank God!" he murmured, still rubbing Taverstock's little brown ears. "You are…" He did not complete his thought.

"Aye, my lord?"

He took a deep breath. "You will be my wife. My father swore it, and I will do my duty to honor his word."

"Only duty?" Alicia gulped. Not even a glimmer of affection or desire?

Thomas put the little terrier down on the path. "Aye, well. We all have our responsibilities, mistress. I am newfound to mine, and I fear…"

Instead of finishing his sentence, Thomas turned on his heel, and practically ran back to the garden gate. Vixen and Tavie scampered after him. Georgie chose to stay with Alicia. With a sinking feeling in the pit of her stomach, she watched the new earl's receding figure in the half-moon's feeble beams. Sweet angels! Would he run out on her at the church door on their wedding day? Just before Thomas rounded the corner of the wall, he stopped.

"I am glad you have come to Wolf Hall, Alicia." Then he disappeared.

Her knees felt suddenly weak. She sank down on the path. Heavens above! Did he mean those words, or were they said for courtesy's sake? Georgie ambled over to her side. He licked her face. She rubbed his ears in return.

"At least, I know where your affection lies, Georgie." Alicia ruffled his neck fur. "To bed it is, and tomorrow I shall launch a quiverful of wiles at the bashful Earl of Thornbury—beginning with his meals. By my faith, Georgie, how could you stand to eat our supper this night? No wonder Sir Thomas is out of sorts. But tomorrow—aye, there's the challenge, Georgie. They do say that the way to a man's heart is through his stomach. Come!"

Rising from the ground, Alicia snapped her fingers as she had seen Thomas do. Georgie obediently followed her back to the castle.

That night, Alicia could not sleep. She lay in the middle of the huge ornate four-poster, and stared at the blue velvet canopy above her. Drawing the soft silken coverlet under her chin, she all but sank into the thick down ticking that was the mattress. Last night she had been in her own narrow cot under the eaves of the gold-smith's house. Below her gabled window, the city of York had hummed its night song: cats yowled, a dog barked in reply, and thick heels tramped on the cobble-stones as a late tavern guest wended his way home. Last night Alicia's mattress had been filled with sweet-smelling straw stuffed into a large bolster, and her cover had been a plain woolen blanket. Last night she had slept well.

Tears brimmed in her eyes as she recalled every nook and cranny of the only home she had ever known. What of her beloved guardians? Alicia said a prayer for their safe journey across the water to Flanders. She gripped the coverlet tighter as she willed herself not to give in to the sadness that gnawed within her.

This bed is too grand. She could get lost within its rich folds, and might never see morning's light again. Why had Andrew put her in such a sumptuous cham-ber? She did not feel at ease amid its silk and golden appointments. Even the maid, who had lighted the way for Alicia, knew that the goldsmith's daughter would have been far happier in simpler surroundings. Isabel might desire the pomp of velvet hangings and delicate carving on the headboard. Alicia only felt uneasy.

Just as the night watchman on the battlements cried the darkest hour of midnight, she heard a sound outside her door. Though she did not believe in hobgoblins or ghosties, she gripped the coverlet tighter. The closest weapon at hand was the brass candlestick on her bed-side table. She scooted across the mattress to be closer to it.

Toenails clicked on the floor in the corridor. Then something sniffed along the bottom of the door. Alicia released her pent-up breath. 'Twas Georgie, she was sure. She knew that Taverstock's little paws danced a faster pace, and Vixen made no sound at all. Alicia had never lived with a dog before now. She must get used to the sounds of their night wanderings—especially if she was going to be Thomas's wife.

A sharp snap of fingers halted the dog's investigation. Alicia froze. She stared at the door, trying to make out in the pale moonlight if someone lifted the latch. Her breath stopped in her throat. Thomas must be standing just outside in the corridor. What if he came into her room now, and demanded a sampling of the wedding night?

Alicia knew it was his right. She dug her fingers into the goose-down mattress. Katherine Brampton had reared her foster daughter to be a proper, modest girl. Alicia's sole experience with the opposite sex had been a kiss stolen by Peter Martext last May Day, and then his lips had merely grazed her cheek. Only this morning during a brief rest stop, Edward had warned her about the lusty appetites of the Cavendishes. His keen eyes had narrowed when he recalled his introduction to John and William. Thomas was bound to be just like them. Biting her lips, Alicia stared at the door latch, and waited.

Two more snaps, then she heard the sound of the dog's toenails recede down the passageway.

She crawled to the edge of the bed, then pulled back the covers and got out. The cold floor chilled her bare feet. She lifted the candle in its holder, then tiptoed over to the fireplace where the embers from the evening's fire glowed in its center. She lit the candle, then crept to the door, and pressed her ear against the stout oak panels. Not a sound outside.

Summoning all of her courage, Alicia lifted the handle, and cracked open the door. She held the candle above her head. No shadow leapt into its spilled light. With a deep sigh of relief, she closed the door and scampered back to the enormous bed. Blowing out the friendly light, she slid under the princely covers. Within a few moments she was fast asleep.

Just before the dawn, Alicia awoke to the unaccustomed cry of a rooster. At first she could not remember where she was. Then her gaze rested on the faded shield that hung over the fireplace. A fierce wolf's head glared back at her from a scarlet field—the Cavendish family crest. The promised morrow had come, and she was still at Wolf Hall. She rose, splashed chilly water from the pitcher on her face, then brushed the tangles out of her hair.

She must dress quickly and get to the kitchens before the cooks were too far along in their preparations for the noonday dinner. She vowed that Thomas, and the rest of the inhabitants of this dreary castle, would eat better today. He could not send her away if she pleased his appetite. Thank all the saints, Katherine had taught Alicia how to cook and care for a home. 'Twas a better schooling than that of a princess, she decided, as she tied the laces of her bodice together.

In her haste, she nearly missed the folded piece of paper that lay just inside her door. Alicia could swear she had not seen it in the middle of the night. The moonlight had spilled on this very spot. After opening the mysterious missive, she carried it to the window where the early light helped her make out the letters. Written in a large, bold hand, the words took away her breath.

To the peerless Alicia—
I take pen in a shaking hand to write you that
which I dare not speak aloud. When I laid down,
I could not sleep, for your sweet likeness danced
in my thoughts. I awoke this early morning with
your imagined kiss still moist upon my lips. Your
beauty steals me from myself, and I know not what
to say—save that I am ever thine.

No signature graced the bottom of the letter.

Chapter Five

Alicia reread the note. Its sweet words burned into her memory. She had never received a letter before now—and this one swept her away with its poetry. She furrowed her brows as she read the sugared words for a third time. An uneasy feeling stole through her—"I am ever thine." Whose desire had she awakened?

Certainly not Thomas. He had barely spoken to her, and their conversation had chiefly revolved around his dogs. Furthermore, he did not show the slightest interest in her as a person, let alone as a lover. "Duty," he had called their marriage. By now, Alicia knew enough of him to realize that duty and honor were everything to Thomas.

The door creaked open. One of the chambermaids poked her head inside.

"Good morrow, mistress," she began. "I came to help dress you—but I see you already have." A small frown of disapproval flitted across her expression.

Alicia stuffed the paper up her sleeve. The last thing she wanted was to become the object of gossip in the kitchen. "Good morrow. Your pardon, but I do not know your name."

"'Tis Audrey, mistress." She wiped her runny nose with the back of her hand.

Alicia made a mental note to introduce the use of handkerchiefs to the household as soon as she was married, and had become the lady of Wolf Hall. *If* that happy day ever came to pass.

She smiled at the girl. "I see you have a quick eye, Audrey," she praised her in a gentle tone.

"Aye, mistress." The maid shifted her feet. "My Lady Isabel says that I spy on her betimes—but I swear by the good book that I never done it."

Alicia smiled inwardly. No doubt Audrey observed Lady Cavendish a great deal, as well as the rest of the castle folk. The girl probably called eavesdropping "taking an interest." *Spying* was such an unpleasant word.

She studied the maid's pert expression. *I must watch out for Audrey and others of her ilk.* If Audrey knew that Alicia had a secret admirer, she would babble the news to all and sundry. Alicia would be banished from Wolf Hall in a trice. Sir Thomas Cavendish did not strike her as a particularly forgiving man. She could easily imagine him as a jealous husband if he suspected cause. *I must never give him reason to doubt my honesty.* She swallowed hard.

Audrey came a little closer. "Mistress, are you well? You look a bit on the pale side."

Alicia squared her shoulders. "'Tis a moment of sad fancy. See? 'Tis past now."

Audrey's smile returned. "Mayhap some morning ale will do you a particle of good. Aye, and a bit of bread to hold you until dinner. I will fetch some for you." She looked poised for instant flight.

Alicia held up her hand. "Nay, good Audrey. I was going to the kitchen myself."

The maid rubbed her nose. "Oh, aye? Wherefore, mistress?"

Alicia smiled in earnest. "To see to the dinner. I have a number of goodly recipes that my mother taught me. I would love to surprise Sir Thomas with some of them. What do you say?"

The young maid looked surprised at the question. Alicia surmised that she probably had never been asked to express her opinion.

"The cook may be willing, mistress. He is lazy and much given to drinking his ale. Methinks he would not mind a helping hand or two." She winked at Alicia.

"Good! Run along. I shall follow directly."

Audrey nodded. "Very good, mistress. 'Twill be a right pleasure to have you with us." With another wink, she skipped out the door, closing it behind her.

Perchance she thinks I am here as a housekeeper for Thomas and not as his betrothed. Mayhap that is all I will become in the end.

With a start, Alicia realized that she did not like that idea at all. Her sudden longing to become Thomas's wife caught her by surprise. Surely it was not for the protection of his name and title, though she desperately needed both. As a faceless member of his household, she would be safe enough from the upstart Tudor king amid the iron pots and straw brooms.

Alicia allowed her idle fancy to frolic in her thoughts. She recalled how fine Thomas had looked in the garden last night. He seemed to glow in the moonlight. His touch had been so gentle when they had chanced to encounter each other's hand under the table. She decided that his face was very handsome, and when he smiled, one could almost hear the angels sing for joy. Thomas should smile more often. He was made for life's enjoyments. Like a good dinner for a start, she reminded herself.

She fished out her mysterious letter from her sleeve, and read its contents one more time. Alicia did not yet know all the inhabitants of Wolf Hall, though they certainly knew who she was. One of them, more scholarly than the rest, must have found her to his liking. The situation bordered on utter madness. She must act as if she had never received this letter, pretend that its sweet words had not touched her heartstrings. She must assume an innocent mask to show whomever it was that she had not been beguiled by his penned poesy.

With a deep sigh of regret, Alicia crumpled the paper into a ball, then pushed it deep amid the feeble embers in the fireplace with the poker. She watched the pretty words burn to ashes.

Giving herself a shake, she tied on the apron she had brought from home, then opened her door. Georgie greeted her with a thumping tail and his tongue hanging out.

"Good morrow, my champion." Alicia caressed his ears. "Have you been sent to guard me, or did you hear the word *dinner?*"

Perking up, he regarded her intently with his deep brown eyes.

Grinning, she nodded. "I thought as much. Come, Georgie, let us see what miracles we can cook in yon kitchen."

Bowing his head, Thomas knelt before the altar in Wolf Hall's chapel, and prayed for guidance and strength. Blue light twinkled through the stained glass window, giving the holy chamber an unearthly glow. Over his head, the sanctuary candle burned in its suspended red glass globe.

Thomas squeezed his eyelids tighter, in an effort to block out the nagging distractions in his mind. He had never given any serious thought to marriage. Never saw the need for it. Now, as the Earl of Thornbury, one of his most pressing concerns was the continuation of the ancient title. If he did not produce a son and heir before he died, the line would die with him.

Who would have thought such a dire situation possible only six weeks ago? His father and two elder brothers had been in excellent health and spirits when they rode off to York, only to return to their ancestral home a few weeks later inside three oaken coffins. Now Thomas was alone in the world, and the burden of his responsibilities weighed down his shoulders.

His secular thoughts turned again and again to Alicia. She had looked breathtaking in the garden last night. He recalled the sparkle of her blue eyes, the golden sheen of her hair in the moonlight and her creamy complexion. He had been afraid to touch her, lest he frighten her. It was a good thing she could not read his thoughts and know his desires. One day he would dare to unbraid her hair, and run his fingers through its long gleaming tresses. He would unfasten the lacing on her gown, and allow it to fall to her feet, while he worshipped the fair Alicia in all her natural glory.

Thomas gulped as he felt himself harden below the belt. It must be a sin to think these wanton thoughts while kneeling in a chapel. Yet Alicia was the core of his current petition to heaven. How could he speak to her of their marriage agreement when he was mute as a fish in her company? Worse, how could he muster the courage to tell her how much he admired her looks, her voice, her every graceful movement? He hoped that his morning's letter to her had revealed something of his true feelings for her.

Thomas grinned when he thought of his predawn frenzy with quill and ink. By the rood, his penmanship must have been horrible to decipher. He hoped Alicia had been able to read his message. Reticent of the spoken word, he had always penned his secret thoughts in flowing prose. In times past, he had burned his work, lest one of his brothers find it, and badger him all the more. Now he could write to his heart's content without fear of discovery. He longed to know what Alicia had thought of his work. He wondered if she would mention it at dinner. It seemed a thousand years to the midday meal.

He finished his prayers with a hasty sign of the cross. Still deep in his meditations, he almost knocked over his sister-in-law, who skulked outside the chapel door. Her very presence renewed the anger he had tried so hard to curb.

"How now, Isabel? Still here?"

She smiled at his frown. "Of course, my lord. I knew you did not mean your command of yestereve. 'Twas the arrival of that...woman that put your good temper to flight."

Grinding his teeth, Thomas maintained his customary silence. Bolts and shackles! The shrew sorely tried his patience.

Isabel paused, waiting for him to say something. When he did not, she hurried on. "Indeed, Thomas, 'tis concerning Mistress Broom that I must speak to you. Hourly, she mimics the airs and graces that are not hers by right. When will you send the jade down the road?"

Thomas raised his brows very slowly. "Alicia stays at Wolf Hall."

He turned to go, but Isabel grasped his arm. Her claws reminded him of a cat's. "But the woman is so...common, Thomas. You cannot seriously think to marry the daughter of a goldsmith. The Earl of Thornbury should have a noble lady as the mother of his children."

He shook off her hand from his sleeve. "I will, and 'tis Alicia."

Instead of answering him, Isabel began to sway on her feet. "Thomas, help me, ere I faint," she murmured. She almost fell into his arms.

He held her against his chest, while he searched around for something on which to seat her. No bench nor coffer in sight. Where was his sottish squire at a time like this? No doubt, Andrew had experience with fainting women. He often bragged of his worldwide knowledge of the fair sex.

"What ails you?" He shook her.

She opened her eyes, and stared up into his. A soft smile parted her lips. "Oh, Thomas, you saved me from a nasty fall—and in my condition too." She fluttered her eyelids, and moaned a little.

A chill crept down his spine. "*What* condition?"

Stepping out of his arms, Isabel unhooked her fan from her golden girdle, and waved it back and forth in front of her face. She shot him a coy glance over the half circle of pierced ivory sticks. "Why, Thomas, do you not understand what a woman means when she speaks of her condition? Methought with the example of your dog, who drops a litter every few months, you would know."

A bitter taste of bile rose in the back of his throat.

His hands turned cold and clammy. Isabel couldn't possibly be breeding. After nine barren years had she managed to conceive at her last possible chance? "Explain yourself, madam!" he snapped.

She fanned herself even more. "By my troth, must I tell you every intimate detail? You costernoggin! 'Tis plainly this—I am with child, William's. Aye, you look amazed. Trust me, so am I. 'Tis a blessing I had often dreamed, but never realized—until now."

Blood roared in his ears. Sweet Jesu! Not now when he had finally met the one woman to whom he felt safe enough to give his heart. He looked down his nose at the simpering harpy. The devil take her! The mere sound of Isabel's nasal voice set his teeth on edge.

"Of course, Thomas, I pray that you and I become better friends—now. 'Twill be important for the child to have someone to look up to; someone to teach him the manly arts as he grows."

"Mummph," he muttered, his mind whirling like a weather cock in the north wind. Damn William! Why did he have to leave a belated reminder? Thanks to the tiny sprig growing within Isabel's belly, Thomas could be saddled with this harridan for years to come.

Closing her fan, Isabel tapped him on the arm with it. "And you would be a hard-hearted, cruel man to cast me out of Wolf Hall at a time like this. 'Twould be a great disgrace if I were forced to bear the poor babe in a ditch." She dabbed her handkerchief to her eyes, even though they appeared to be remarkably free of tears.

He wondered how many months a woman carried a child. He dimly recalled his mother's final pregnancy, and thought that Mary had taken a very long time to arrive. With a growing dismay, he realized that Isabel had him backed into a corner.

What of sweet Alicia? His sister-in-law will surely demand that he send her away. If Alicia stayed, Isabel would make her life—and Thomas's—a living hell. His throat tightened. The stone walls of the passageway closed in on him. He could not draw in enough air to breathe. He needed space and time to think through this horrifying dilemma.

Isabel stamped her foot. "Thomas! You have not heard two words that I have said. I asked you, what do you propose to do with me now?"

Send you to the devil! Aloud, he rumbled, "Go hunting!" He raised his voice to its full battle pitch. "Andrew! Andrew!"

His squire, who had been playing ball with Tavie down the corridor, ran at his master's summons.

"Aye, my lord?" Andrew replied, slightly out of breath. "Good morrow, my lady," he added to Isabel. "I wish you a safe and pleasant journey—"

Thomas cut off the squire's insipid remarks. "Tell the grooms to saddle our horses, and pack provisions for the day—nay, for several days. We go a-hunting."

A slow grin spread across Andrew's lips. "For hares or pheasant, my lord?"

"For whatever blasted thing we can find. At this moment, I could strangle a boar bare-handed. Quit gawking, loon! Get you gone!"

The lad glanced from Thomas to Isabel. His smile broadened. "I am ever at your service, my lord." Turning on his heel, he then raced down the passageway that led to the mews.

Isabel gave a cold little laugh. "True to form, as always, I see. When in doubt, run away and go hunting. I hope you find that boar, Thomas, and I hope he *eats* you. Just remember, I shall still be here when you finally decide to come home. Chew on that while you gallop over hill and dale."

With her threat ringing in his ears, she stuck her proud nose up in the air, and left him. Thomas swore several oaths under his breath. Then he snapped his fingers to the two canines who trotted after him. At the stairs leading to the kitchens, they encountered Georgie, who fell into place behind them.

Thomas didn't slacken his speed until he had locked the library door behind them. Then he knelt down, and lavished his attention on his beloved pets.

"My friends, I am trussed in a tight barrel, and that is no mistake. Isabel will surely try to chase Alicia away while I am gone, yet I must have time to think."

Vixen licked his hand. Georgie flopped down on the cold hearth. Tavie tried to scramble into Thomas's lap.

"A hard ride in the saddle is the only way I know to clear my head of cobwebs. Georgie, you must look after Alicia for me. Stay with her. Vixen, my sweet girl, do not have your puppies until after I have returned."

Thomas held the terrier out at arm's length, and smiled at his little brown-and-white face. "And *you* must be my watchdog, Tavie. I pray you three, do not harry Isabel—no matter how badly she treats you. Leave her to me. Above all, keep Alicia here. Understand? Keep Alicia safe." He stood.

Thomas glanced at his desk. His writing materials still lay where he had left them in such a hurry at dawn. He pulled the cork out of the ink pot, then dipped a fresh quill into it. Andrew knocked just as Thomas poured blotting sand on his latest note. He turned the key in the lock.

"Enter!" he bellowed.

The squire opened the door. "All is in readiness. We wait upon you."

"Good!" Thomas dripped a small blob of sealing wax on the flap. He blew on it until the wax hardened. Then he handed the letter to Andrew. "Put this in Mistress Alicia's chamber—somewhere where she alone will find it. I want no other prying eyes."

Andrew chuckled. "Another billet-doux? You have not done so much writing in a month of Sundays, my lord."

Thomas frowned at the boy's merry face. He knew the cheeky squire would probably tease him the entire day about this, but no matter. 'Twas better than thinking upon Isabel and her blasted condition. "Hold your prattling tongue, maltworm. Deliver my letter, and mind you, do not let anyone see you do it."

Andrew stuffed the paper inside his doublet. "Fear not, my lord. I will be as swift as a fox in a chicken coop, or—" He paused at the door. "Or as a lover stealing from a lady's bed."

"Out!" Thomas thundered.

With another chuckle, the lad disappeared on his mission. Thomas left the library and locked the door of his sanctuary behind him.

In the stable courtyard, his huntsmen already had the pack of lurchers out of their kennels; the hounds eager to be off. The falconer held his favorite peregrine on his thick leather glove. Several of the kitchen lads stuffed bread, cheese and cold meats into the saddlebags. Thomas adjusted his charger's girth while he waited for Andrew to return.

"Well?" he bellowed when the boy finally appeared. He noticed that his squire had made a hasty change of clothing, trading his fine satin suit for a more sturdy wool and leather hunting garb.

"Where do we ride, my lord?" he asked, as he swung himself astride his gelding.

"To the devil and back," Thomas replied. He kicked his gray stallion into a canter.

Chapter Six

Alicia blotted the perspiration on her forehead with the back of her hand. The large kitchens of Wolf Hall were far hotter and noisier than the simple cookhouse at her old home in York. A dozen loaves of parsley bread baked in the side ovens. Meanwhile, a brace of plump pigeons turned slowly on the spit while Alicia chopped dried cherries, and lentils for the stuffing.

Despite the heat and an ache in her low back, she hummed a tavern ditty—one that she had often heard her guardian sing. Master Konrad, the cook imported from Hanover, had been glad enough to let someone else do his work while he took his ease on a stool by the window that overlooked the vegetable garden. Now that the full menu had taken shape, he pushed his tankard aside and observed Alicia with growing admiration.

Someone clattered down the stone steps.

"My Lady Isabel commands ye to attend on her," a high-pitched voice announced over the kitchen din.

Alicia wiped her hands on her food-spattered apron before she turned to face the strident messenger. Everyone in the large room grew silent. She eyed the nondescript maid, who stood on the bottommost step as if the girl might be tainted if she came completely into the kitchen.

"Are you addressing me?" Alicia asked in her most formal manner.

The maid tossed her head. "Aye, that I am. My lady wants you in her room right quick."

Alicia stifled her impulse to tell the obnoxious wench what she thought of Isabel and her minion. Instead, she answered, "I will come by and by, after I have seen to this stuffing."

"My lady said this minute." The maid drew herself up in a poor imitation of Isabel's haughtiness.

The silence around Alicia grew even more profound than before, if that was possible. It seemed everyone held their breath at once.

The maid put her hands to her hips. "Have ye wax in yer ears, or are ye merely stupid? I said come *now!*"

Master Konrad cleared his throat. "Hush up your mouth, Meg. You are speaking to Sir Thomas's intended bride. He will not take it kindly to hear of your ill manners."

"Ha!" Meg tossed her head again. "Mistress Broom will have to walk many more miles afore she comes to her wedding day, methinks. Ye will see anon." She glared at Alicia. "Well? Hurry up, wench, and take off yer apron afore ye step upstairs. No need to bring the kitchen slops with ye."

"Mind how you—" Konrad began, but Alicia held up her hand. The cook fell silent.

"Tell your…lady that I am pleased to speak with her." Alicia forced herself to act more in charge than she felt.

She would not give in to any display of anger, no matter how much Meg provoked her. One day, Alicia might be the lady of Wolf Hall, and she wanted the servants to respect her when she was. She untied her apron, then hung it on a peg by the door.

Konrad picked up a basting spoon. "I will keep a sharp eye on your victuals, Mistress Alicia." Grinning at her, he rolled up his loose sleeves. "And do not fret yourself over these golden birds. I will finish the stuffing myself."

She flashed him a wide smile. "My thanks, good cook. Please do not forget to add two measures of oats. 'Twill add to the flavor and—"

Meg tugged at Alicia's skirt. "My lady hates to be kept a-waiting, mistress, and she has a short temper." The maid literally pulled her up the winding stairway.

In silence they hurried across the great hall. Alicia glanced about her as she went. The shabbiness and neglect of that noble chamber appeared more evident in the clear light of the morning's sun. Georgie looked up from the hearth where he had been dozing. Seeing her, he gave a deep bark of welcome. Then he rose and ambled after them.

"Ye must keep that cur away from my lady." Meg flapped her apron at the mastiff. He ignored her as if she were merely a droning fly.

Alicia slid her fingers through his short rough coat. "I am sure Georgie has no desire to renew his acquaintance with Lady Isabel."

"Humph!" the maid replied. They dashed up the main staircase to the gallery.

Meg stopped at Isabel's door and knocked. Out of the corner of her eye, Alicia noticed a shadow flit along the far wall. When she looked more closely she saw a light gray skirt disappear around the corner. She smiled to herself. 'Twas Mary. Good. Alicia might need a witness to the coming interview.

"Enter," Isabel replied in an imperious tone.

The maid opened the door. "Ye can go in now."

Alicia lifted one corner of her mouth in a half smile. "My thanks, Meg, for your kind attentions. I shall remember you anon—in my prayers."

The maid swallowed with a loud gulp that gave Alicia a small measure of satisfaction. "Stay here, Georgie," she commanded the huge dog. "Take your ease until I return."

Brushing a stray tendril of hair out of her eyes, Alicia sailed past Meg, and entered Lady Isabel's lair. The maid quickly shut the door behind her. Isabel sat on her armchair; red cushions peeked from under her voluminous black skirts. For a fleeting moment, Alicia experienced the uncomfortable feeling that she had just become entangled in the web of a poisonous spider.

Lady Cavendish lifted one raven brow. "You have kept me waiting long enough."

Alicia barely bobbed her head by way of courtesy. She drew herself up to her full height, and looked down her nose at the glowering woman.

"I was engaged in the kitchen." She chose not to mention her rude summons. That news would probably please the lady.

"Indeed?" Isabel flicked open her fan. "A useful occupation for...a certain class."

Alicia felt her cheeks grow warm. "The arts of simple cookery are useful to all. I intend to instruct my children, the boys as well as the girls, how to cook and sew."

Isabel continued to fan herself. A catlike smile appeared on her lips, though her dark eyes remained cold.

"How very useful! You will make some poor wheel-wright a good wife and mother to his brats."

Alicia dug her nails into the palm of her hand. *Tread carefully here. You still do not know which way the wind blows in this household.* "'Tis my hope that Sir Thomas will approve of my plans."

Isabel pretended to a yawn. "I pray you pardon my fatigue. I have just discovered that I am with child."

Alicia caught her breath, but said nothing. *That must be why she is still at Wolf Hall this morning.*

The woman chuckled in the back of her throat. "Surprised by this news? So was Thomas, and very, *very* pleased," she purred. "Now that he is the earl, he must produce an heir as quickly as possible."

Alicia felt feverish. She licked her dry lips. "You—and Thomas?"

Isabel smoothed her long black hair that hung unfettered below her shoulders. "Do not look so shocked, Mistress Alicia. Children have been conceived under all *sorts* of circumstances. What could be more natural than a loving brother-in-law comforting the grief-stricken widow of his dearly beloved brother?"

Alicia bit her lips to keep from crying out. She blinked back the tears that threatened behind her eyelids. When she managed to control the waver in her voice, she said, "I have been taught that such a union is a sin. The holy church forbids a man to take his brother's wife as his own."

Isabel snapped her fan shut. "How dare you, a common jade, lecture *me* on the laws of the church? I am amazed you even know them! Besides, a message has already been sent to His Excellency, the Bishop of York, to arrange a dispensation, so that our marriage can take place—soon. I am sure even you can understand the need for haste. 'Twould not do for the Cavendish heir to be born on the wrong side of the blanket, would it?''

Alicia did not trust herself to speak. A bastard herself, she felt a certain empathy for the unborn child. Why hadn't Thomas informed Edward of his liaison with Isabel when the Bramptons brought Alicia to Wolf Hall? His pride and shyness, no doubt. Thank heavens that he didn't know the dangerous secret of her royal lineage. Considering Isabel's unwelcome news, she decided that Thomas must never know. That way his precious honor would not be torn asunder. *Dear Lord in heaven, protect me now for I have no other guardian.*

"Cat got your tongue?" Isabel simpered. "I suspected my little surprise might give you a turn. In fact, methinks 'tis time that you yourself turn—and leave Wolf Hall."

Alicia gathered all of her reserves of strength and courage "I cannot go without first speaking to Sir Thomas."

"Ha!" The lady tossed her head. "'Tis too late for that. He has gone hunting, taking his entire company with him."

"Then I shall speak to him this evening."

"Tut tut, goldsmith's daughter, I fear you would have a long and fruitless wait. Thomas will be gone for *days,* perchance even weeks before he returns."

In the back of her mind, Alicia thought fleetingly of the marvelous dinner that she had been preparing most of the morning.

Isabel continued, "Therefore, in his absence, I am in charge of Wolf Hall." Her eyes narrowed. "You would be very wise to leave today, within the hour. You have no place here. Begone! I cannot bear to be upset at a time like this. 'Tis bad for the babe.''

Alicia drew in a deep breath. "Among my possessions, I have a copy of the betrothal contract between myself and Sir Thomas Cavendish, the third son of Sir Giles Cavendish, the late Earl of Thornbury. 'Twas duly signed, witnessed and sealed by Sir Giles and Sir Edward Brampton, my guardian. In addition, a handsome dowry in gold was paid to Sir Giles, who was glad to take it for his taxes.''

She stepped closer to Isabel. The smaller woman shrank down amid her velvet cushions. "In the eyes of the law and the church, I am legally Sir Thomas's bride. Money has been paid, the pledge of intent was made, and the kiss to seal the bargain was exchanged by us before witnesses. Until Sir Thomas—my bridegroom—breaks our contract before witnesses and returns to me my dowry, I will stay here where he has left me as a dutiful *wife* should. I wish you, and your babe, good health.''

Turning on her heel, Alicia marched to the door with her head erect. Though her eyes shimmered with unshed tears, she stared straight ahead. *Sweet Saint Anne, do not let me break down now. Give me the strength to wait until I am alone.*

"I did not give you leave to go!''

With her hand on the door latch, Alicia turned to face her enemy. "Good! Then I will stay in Wolf Hall, until Thomas returns—by your leave.''

She flung open the door, and nearly fell over Meg, who had been listening at the keyhole. Alicia lifted the woman up by her collar. "I pray that your ears are marvelous sharp, and that you heard *every word* that passed between your lady and myself. Be sure to retell this tale to all within these boundaries.''

"Meg!" Isabel screeched.

Alicia gave the trembling girl a shake. "Mark me, Meg, and do not mistake me for one like yourself. There is more to me than meets the eye." *Royal blood flows in my veins.*

She released the maid before she was tempted to blurt out her secret thoughts. Best to return to the kitchens, and lose herself in the preparations for the wonderful dinner that Thomas would miss. At least, it gave all the kitchen help good practice for another day.

Squaring her shoulders, she signaled for Georgie to follow her. She all but flew down the stairs with the lumbering animal in her shadow. Stokes, the castle steward, stopped her as she crossed the great hall.

"Your pardon, mistress." He bobbed his head by way of greeting. "I crave a word in your ear."

Pausing in her flight, Alicia regarded the earnest man before her. Stokes was tall, like many of the male population of Wolf Hall. Perchance the Cavendish family felt more comfortable being served by those of equal height. The steward's dark brown eyes looked very concerned.

"Aye, Master Stokes?"

He swallowed before he continued. "I just heard of your discourse with my Lady Isabel."

She arched an eyebrow. "News travels on winged feet, I see."

Stokes grinned and reddened at the same time. "Young Lady Mary has sharp ears and a quick tongue. But to the matter, mistress. Watch out for Lady Isabel. She had her eye on the new earl before her own husband was cold in the ground. She has been chatelaine at Wolf

Hall since the day my Lord William brought her home as his wife, and she will not easily relinquish her position.''

He glanced up at the soot-stained rafters, then at the piles of old rushes that had been swept into the far corners of the great hall. ''Not that my lady takes much interest in housekeeping matters. 'Tis the power that pleases her. And she has a sharp temper for such a small woman.''

Alicia's gaze followed that of the steward. From its appearance, she guessed that the hall had not had a proper spring cleaning for at least a decade. ''I care only for Sir Thomas's opinion, Stokes, but I welcome your fair warning. Pray, tell me, when was the fireplace last swept of its ashes?''

He blinked. ''I know not the exact day,'' he hedged his answer, ''but 'twas some time ago.''

She nodded. ''I thought as much. Stokes, the new Earl of Thornbury should not live in a pigsty.''

A slow smile spread across the man's good-natured face. ''Nay, he should not.''

''Do you think this day would be a fine one to set matters a-right before the master returns?''

He cast her a shrewd look. ''Aye, 'twas my very thought indeed.''

''And do you think that the maids would find a great deal of healthful employment in sweeping out the rushes, scrubbing the flagstones, dusting the cobwebs from the corners, and other such useful pastimes?'' Alicia hinted.

''''Twas on the tip of my tongue to say so,'' he replied with a cheerful wink.

She pointed to the limp red rag that hung over the fireplace. ''If 'twould not be too much trouble to take down yon banner from its pole, I could wash and repair it myself. Sir Thomas should be greeted by his family's crest in good order.''

Stokes chuckled. "I will have one of the kitchen boys attend to it for you straightway."

Alicia placed her hand on his arm. "And, Stokes, you have not heard me give you any orders, have you?"

He flashed her a broad smile. "Nay, mistress, none whatsoever. 'Twas all my own thought."

Alicia returned his smile. "Then my Lady Isabel's prerogative has not been challenged, has it?"

"Not at all, mistress," he assured her solemnly. "And we shall set upon the work within this half hour." He drew closer to her. "My thanks, Mistress Alicia, for I have grown a-weary of living in such poor surroundings."

"Wolf Hall is a noble house, and we shall bring back its luster in short order."

"Aye, mistress," he agreed with satisfaction.

Painting broad, red-orange strokes across the western sky, the sun began its evening descent. Thomas called a halt to the day's hard ride, and ordered his hunt master to set up a camp within a sheltering copse of fir trees. The pack of hounds sank to the ground with grateful thuds, their long pink tongues drooping from their mouths. Thomas eased himself off his horse, then gave Silver Charm an approving pat on his sleek gray neck. He loosened the girth, and pulled the heavy leather saddle from the stallion's damp back.

"Good boy," he crooned, wiping down the deep-chested charger with handfuls of dry grass. "We made many a long mile today."

Andrew joined him, massaging his lean backside. The

boy had no fat to spare in that particular area. "You mean, you put many a long mile between yourself and your problems, my lord." Ignoring Thomas's glare, the squire dropped down upon a welcome patch of springy green moss under a nearby tree. "Hell's bells, I ache all over."

"Aye, you will taste that truth, malt-canker, if your tongue continues to wag in that vein," he growled. By heaven, the stripling tried his patience on many an occasion. If it weren't for the boy's charm, good humor, common sense and knightly promise, Thomas would have sent him away long before now.

Andrew whistled in reply. "My tongue most desires a swallow of something wet. Would you care for some wine, my lord?"

Thomas checked Silver Charm's hooves before handing the horse over to his groom. Satisfied with the soundness of his mount, he answered Andrew's question. "Aye, a strop of wine and something to eat. By the book, I am near famished."

With a look between a grin and a grimace, Andrew pulled himself to his feet, then limped off to the packhorses. Thomas watched his squire's painful progress. With all the sudden responsibilities thrust upon him this past month, he had neglected Andrew's schooling in the arts of jousting and combat. He stretched, then kneaded his buttocks. Shackles and stones! He was getting soft himself.

In due course, the squire returned laden with provisions. A green wool blanket hung from his arm. He spread it on the ground, then laid out a loaf of yesterday's bread, a small crock of butter, another one of honey, several cold chickens from yesterday's midday dinner, apples, a generous wedge of fat cheese and a full wineskin. The lad broke the stale loaf into several pieces, spread one with lashings of butter, then offered it to his master.

"'Tis a sorry state of affairs to have to eat this simple fare when a finer feast awaited us at home this day," he remarked, cutting the cheese for his lord.

Thomas raised one brow. What bee buzzed within Andrew's bonnet now? "Explain," he muttered.

His squire expelled a dramatic sigh. "When I ordered the provender this morning, my nostrils were treated to the delights of fresh bread baking. Aye, and a sweet pastry of spiced apples, methinks. A number of fowls, plucked cleaned and trussed, lay on the chopping board, and a goodly joint of beef turned on the spit, basted with the most savory-smelling juices." He sighed again, this time louder. "It fair makes my mouth water to think of it."

Thomas chewed on a piece of the cold chicken before answering. The food in his mouth tasted a little off. His stomach rumbled at Andrew's enticing description. "Methinks you were woolgathering this morn, Master Storyteller. The cook is an able man—when he puts his mind to it—but his mind has turned more and more to the ale cask of late."

A grin lightened the boy's features. "'Twas not Master Konrad's doing, my lord, but Mistress Alicia."

Thomas blinked. "Methought she was still a-bed when we left Wolf Hall. Yesterday was a…long one for her." One that distressed her, no doubt. What sensible person would not be upset to be abandoned by her loved ones on his doorstep?

The squire shook his head. "Not so, my lord. She nearly caught me slipping your first note under her door. When I spied her in the kitchens, she had her hair braided, and piled on top of her head like a simple maiden. Her sleeves were rolled up to her elbows, and she had flour on her cheeks."

Thomas chewed in silence while Andrew's description danced in his imagination. The new Earl of Thornbury chided himself. What an ass he was! Sweet Alicia had risen with the dawn to prepare him a fine dinner—and he had run away. He allowed himself to consider all the charms of the goldsmith's daughter: her hair spun from the sunset; her eyes like crystal waters; her tall form, supple, bending to his touch; her full breasts like… He swore under his breath.

Andrew glanced at him. "My lord? What is amiss?"

"Me!" he snapped. Tipping the wineskin to his lips, he swallowed a long draught.

The lad gave him a look of wide-eyed innocence. "Are you ill, my lord?"

Thomas curled his lip at the squire. "Aye, and well you know it, scamp. I am plagued to death with women."

He nodded like a wise owlet. "Methinks you have hit the very core of your malady. And what is your remedy? Do we ride across the border to Edinburgh?" The squire shook his head. "I fear Silver Charm cannot outrun your thoughts."

With a growl in the back of his throat, Thomas hurled the hard-crusted heel of bread at his gadfly. The boy ducked it with a laugh.

"Tell me then, young physician, what would you recommend—since you claim great experience with women?"

Andrew regarded his master a moment before answering. "Truly would you know my mind?"

Thomas drank some more wine for fortification. "Aye. Out with it."

Andrew grew very serious. "'Tis this—on the morrow, return posthaste to Wolf Hall. If your heart turns toward the Lady Isabel, then write for a dispensation immediately—and send Mistress Broom to a convent."

The earl grimaced at the thought.

"But," Andrew continued, "if your heart has been touched by Mistress Alicia, then honor your father's contract, and make her your wife as soon as the banns have been proclaimed. For, in truth, my lord, 'tis a cruel torment you inflict on that sweet maid to leave her so unknowing of her fate."

Thomas flinched at his squire's just accusation. Mistress Alicia had come to him with open trust, and he fled from her like a hart from a hunter. Yet he didn't mean to shirk his duty—or his desires. He wanted to clasp her to his chest, and whisper his deepest feelings in her ear. *Then do it!* His guilty conscience prodded him like a thorn in his foot.

"I sent her two letters, if you spoke true when you say you delivered them," he mumbled.

Andrew dismissed that sop with a wave of his hand. "Pah! What are they but mere scratchings of ink on paper? A woman needs more than that. She needs your hands holding her close, your lips caressing hers, your—"

Thomas kicked at him. "Cease your prattling, magpie! We ride at first light."

"Where to, my lord?"

"To Wolf Hall, you ninny!"

That evening, when Alicia finally laid her weary head upon her pillow, she discovered another letter under it.

Torn between distress and curiosity, she hesitated before she broke open the seal.

> To Alicia, whom I would call my own—
> I have a most rare confession to make. I should have told you in person, but I feared that you would laugh at me. You might have even thought that I lied to win your favor, and thus misuse you. Trust me, sweet mistress, I am true. My confession? Tis this—I gave my heart to you the moment I first saw you. I pray you, warm it with your love.

The unsigned note kept Alicia awake most of the night.

Chapter Seven

Alicia rose long before the cock in the chicken yard crowed the start of a new day. Whomever had written the disturbing letter must be stopped! If Thomas suspected that she had a secret admirer, even if she had never encouraged another's attentions, he would expel her from Wolf Hall in disgrace. She lingered over the last line of the note. Its words warmed her lonely heart despite her anxiety about the anonymous writer. *Enough of this!* No matter how sweet the words were on paper, she must not fall prey to the temptation behind them. After stirring up the feeble embers in the fireplace, she crumpled the note, then thrust it deep into the heart of the red-orange glow. Within seconds, the missive burst into flame, then curled into a blackened feathery ash.

Pushing all thoughts of an ardent, anonymous lover out of her mind, Alicia donned her russet homespun skirt over her shift and petticoats. She tied the laces of her black felt bodice under her breasts. After vigorously brushing the night's tangles out of her hair, she braided it, then looped it around the top of her head. Her simple linen cap held her braids in place. After tying her dorneck apron around her waist, she faced another day in the kitchens, buttery, distilling room and scullery of Wolf Hall.

Before she left her sumptuous chamber, she examined the work she had done on the Cavendish banner. The material had washed cleaner than she had expected. Later this afternoon she planned to mend it. She smiled to herself as she envisioned how surprised Thomas would be when he finally came home. God willing, Alicia would have the hall, entranceway and kitchens shining to greet him. She did not dare to invade his bedchamber.

As for Isabel, that spoiled creature could do what she liked with her own apartments. Alicia hoped that Mary's lazy governess attended to her charge's appointments better than she did her charge. She sympathized with Mistress Genevieve. Mary was indeed a whirlwind. What the child needed was some useful employment that would challenge her bright young mind.

With a sigh and a shake of her head, Alicia shut the door behind her. She tried not to remember the honeyed words cooling in her fireplace. Musing upon the unknown author, she nearly tripped over Audrey, who scrubbed the stone steps that led down to the kitchens two flights below. Alicia studied her. Perhaps the inquisitive maid might know a thing or two about Alicia's mysterious letter-writer.

"Good morrow, Audrey!" She smiled warmly at the girl. "By my troth, you are very industrious for so early in the day. Have you broken your night's fast?"

The maid sat back on her heels, and wiped her soapy hands on her apron. "Aye, though I fear all the leftovers from yesterday's dinner are gone by now. 'Twas a princely meal you prepared. I have not tasted the like for a long time." She smacked her lips at the delicious memory.

Alicia glowed with pleasure at the girl's words of praise. "Many thanks. I will try a few more recipes for today's dinner—if Master Konrad does not object."

The maid's brown eyes widened. "Object? Methinks he is pacing the floor a-waiting for you this very minute." She giggled.

Alicia smiled. "Then I had best be going." She started down the first two steps, then pretended that she had just remembered something. "Oh, Audrey, a word or two more, if it please you."

The maid blinked. "Aye, mistress?" She gave her a wary look.

Alicia smiled to ease the maid's misgivings. "I still do not know everyone by name. Yesterday I saw someone near my door, but I am not sure who he was. Did you see anyone hereabouts yesterday?"

Audrey chewed her lower lip as she considered the question. Alicia held her breath. She prayed that the maid had indeed spied the mysterious author of the love letters. She also prayed that the girl would tell the whole truth.

"Is something of yours missing?" Audrey finally asked.

Alicia broadened her smile. "Nay, 'tis nothing of the sort. I was merely curious to know his name. 'Tis no matter." She pretended to lose interest. "I expect I shall recognize him by and by."

The maid relaxed her shoulders. "I saw only Master Andrew up here yesterday morn. And that was afore he went off a-hunting with my lord. Methought he was a-knocking at your door."

Alicia's heart plummeted. She managed to retain the

smile on her face. "In truth, it might have been Andrew, now that you mention it."

Audrey warmed to her tale. "Aye, 'twas he. I told him you were already in the kitchens, and he laughed, and tweaked my—" She stopped, and flushed a bright crimson.

Alicia contained her rising indignation. She could well imagine exactly where the lusty squire might tweak a pretty serving maid. She pretended sorrow to cover her ire. "Alas alack! I never saw Andrew in the kitchen."

"'Tis no matter," Audrey soothed her in innocence. "He said he did not need to speak with you directly. Then he kissed...I mean, he wished me a good day, and was gone." She giggled. "Master Andrew is a fine piece of work, mistress, if you do not mind me a-saying so. He is always so pleasing to the girls."

Alicia gritted her teeth. "Aye, he did strike me as a merry scamp. My thanks, Audrey, you have served me well." Not trusting herself to say another word, she virtually ran down the stairs.

She paused on the first landing, and waited until her heartbeat had resumed its normal rhythm. Of course it had to be Andrew Ford. No doubt, he had penned many a love letter, despite his youth. The churl dared to woo her behind his master's back, even as he dallied with Audrey. Clearly the lusty youth had too much time on his hands, and not enough gainful activity to occupy his mind. Alicia shuddered to think what Thomas would do if he discovered his squire's perfidy. She had already witnessed one outburst of his temper at Isabel, and she hated the idea of it being unleashed upon Andrew—no matter how much the boy richly deserved it.

Alicia massaged her temples. She must nip Andrew's

lovesickness in the bud, and she must do it quickly before Thomas found out. She would corner the squire as soon as the hunting party returned to the castle. In the meantime, she must begin preparations for today's dinner. Afterward, she would inspect the bed linens to see what needed to be cleaned and repaired. Something bumped against her knee. She looked down into the mastiff's dark brown eyes.

"Good morrow, Georgie," she murmured as she knelt on the cool stone floor to rub his ears. "Methinks I must attend to you as well. When was the last time anyone brushed your coat?"

He licked her cheek in reply.

"Methought as much. Today you and the others will have a bath, and a brushing with a treat afterward. Would you like that?"

The mastiff merely wagged his tail, as he followed her down the next flight of stairs.

Mary held her breath as her governess waddled past the girl's hiding place.

"Lady Mary, where are you?" Mistress Vive wheezed. "Lord have mercy, child. These stairs will be the death of me yet. Mary! 'Tis time for your music lesson. Nay, 'tis twice past time. The little wretch!" she muttered under her breath.

Mary stifled a giggle. In a few more minutes, her governess would be around the corner, and she could skip away, as free as a meadowlark. She didn't mind her lute lessons. In fact, she loved to play the beautiful stringed instrument that Tom had given her this past New Year's Day. What bored Mary to tears was the continual fingering exercises that Mistress Vive commanded her to practice. The girl much preferred making up her own tunes, or playing by ear any melody she had heard. This particular musical gift drove her governess to distraction, though Tom quite enjoyed it.

Mary peeked around the edge of the tapestry. The corridor was empty. Humming a tune she had heard Alicia sing, she tiptoed down the passageway to the stairs. Should she go up, and see what Isabel was doing? Mary wrinkled her nose. The lazy woman was probably still abed. Now that she had announced her pregnancy, she slept until the midday dinner hour. Mary snorted. Isabel breeding was a tale of fancy, if ever there was one. She didn't believe the truth of it for a minute. She knew a thing or two about the making of babies, and their birthing nine months later.

A person learned a great deal by staying in the shadows, and watching the goings-on in a large castle such as Wolf Hall. Mary would wager her new pearl earrings that her sister-in-law was as barren as ever. Time would tell. She wondered if Isabel would stuff her gowns with a bolster to give proof to her lie. No doubt about it— the woman would bear close watching, lest she pull the wool over darling Tom's eyes.

Mary chose to descend to the kitchens, where all the really interesting events happened. She heard a piteous howling even before she saw what took place in the scullery. With her skirts pinned up to her waist, Alicia held Georgie firmly by the scruff of his neck in a large tub of soapy water. When the ancient dog spied Mary, he gave another mournful howl.

"By my troth, Georgie, you act as if I was boiling you in oil!" Alicia turned her head away, just as the dog started to shake. Water droplets and soap suds flew in every direction, much to the amusement of an assembly of pot boys, scullery maids and laundresses.

"Hoy day, Alicia!" Mary laughed. "Old Georgie has never let anyone bathe him except my brother. What magic do you possess to soothe such a great beast?"

"Sweet words and a wealth of honey cakes," she answered as she dodged yet another vigorous shake. "By all the saints, methinks he is as clean as he is going to get. Pray, someone hand me those rags. Quickly," she added as Georgie stood up in the tub, and looked as if he would leap out.

Mary tossed her the worn clothes, then tucked up her own skirts. She took a step toward them, but her foot slipped on the wet flagstones. Flailing her arms, the girl skidded against the wooden tub. With a joyful bark, Georgie leapt at her. The next moment, Alicia, Mary and the dog found themselves in a large wet, wriggling heap on the soapy floor. Laughing, Mary wiped loosened locks of wet hair from her eyes.

"Larks and sparks! I had no idea that we could make the floor slippery with plain soap and water. We can go sliding all year round, and not wait for the north winds to freeze the cow pond to ice."

Still firmly gripping Georgie, Alicia gave the old dog a brisk toweling. "Methinks Master Konrad or Steward Stokes might have an objection to that plan, Lady Mary," she said, in between telling Georgie to hold still. "Please, give him another honey cake. They are on the bench by the pump. Sit, Georgie! Stay! There's a good boy."

Mary fed the dog a cake, then helped herself to one of her own. They tasted better than anything Konrad could bake. She allowed Georgie to lick her fingers clean of crumbs. "When you marry Tom, you will be in charge of the house, Alicia," she observed. "Then I can slide on soapy floors and eat honey cakes all the livelong day.''

Alicia rubbed the mastiff harder. '''Tis unlucky to count on things before they happen, Lady Mary,'' she murmured.

"Tom said he would marry you."

Alicia bent her head to inspect Georgie's paw pads. "Aye, if that is his duty as he sees it. But now there is Isabel." She did not look up, but Mary detected a faint glimmer of tears in the young woman's pretty blue eyes.

She wrinkled her nose. "The devil take Isabel! Tom will never marry her. He hates her."

Alicia brushed Georgie's short coat. The dog closed his eyes and assumed an expression of pure bliss.

"Thomas may have to." She sighed.

The child stamped her foot. "Never!"

Alicia looked up at her. "There are reasons—" she began.

Mary cocked her head. "The babe in her belly? If there is one there, 'tis not Tom's, I can assure you. He's never—" She caught herself in time before she spilled her brother's deepest secret. He didn't suspect that his little sister knew he had never been with a woman.

Alicia stopped brushing Georgie. "Forsooth, Mary, how do you know of such things?"

She grinned at the other's amazement. She loved to surprise people. "I know a great deal more than most folk realize. I am not a child anymore, no matter what everyone thinks."

A little smile curled Alicia's lips. "Ah, I had forgotten. You are the mistress of the keyhole."

She giggled. "Just so."

Returning her attention to the patient Georgie, Alicia

sighed. "As to Lady Isabel's fate, we will have to wait for Thomas to decide."

Mary groaned. "That will be until doomsday—unless you can hurry him along a bit."

Alicia shook her head. "I have no power over him. If he does marry me, 'twill be for his honor's sake—not for love." She whispered the last three words into Georgie's black ear.

Mary heard her. "I would not wager a pair of wet stockings on that."

Alicia gaped. The younger girl bit her tongue. She had better shut her mouth before she revealed all of Tom's secrets.

"You have almost finished with Georgie, and he looks better than I have ever seen him. I will capture Taverstock for you. I fear he will give you more trouble than Vixen. He *hates* water."

So saying, Mary bolted from the scullery. She hoped she had not said too much. Angels in heaven, please make Tom marry Alicia, she prayed as she ran across the courtyard. Then she sighed. Wishing will not bring horses to beggars, Mistress Vive had often told her.

"Here, Tavie!" she called inside the stables. She whistled two long and three short notes—a special signal that all three dogs recognized.

With a short bark in return, the little brown-and-white terrier scrambled around the horse trough. Racing to Mary, he leapt into her arms.

"Ugh! Your paws are muddy, Tavie. What did you bury now?"

He licked her ear.

"Nay, I do not need a bath, but *you* certainly do. Alicia will make you clean all over. Bathtime, Taverstock!"

At the word *bath*, Tavie pricked his ears. Before Mary had time to get a firmer grip on him, the little dog wriggled out of her arms. With his little bandy legs churning, he raced for the old south tower—a favorite hiding place for his bones and other treasures.

"Taverstock, come back here this minute! Tavie!" Lifting her skirts and petticoats above her ankles, she dashed after him.

By the time she reached the open door at the bottom of the tower's spiral staircase, the dog had disappeared. Mary paused to listen for him. His toenails scraped against the stone steps as he climbed toward the second floor.

"I have got you cornered now," she said to herself as she followed him on light feet.

At the first landing, Mary stuck her head inside the rounded chamber. She listened but heard nothing. The sacks of wheat that were stored there made her nose itch. She closed the door, then continued up to the next landing. She checked the second storage room, but found only casks of oil and boxes of tallow for winter candle-making.

Mary opened her mouth to call Tavie, but a human moan from above stopped her voice in her throat. She crept up the final set of stairs, where she found Tavie running back and forth in front of the closed door. Every so often, he stopped, and sniffed under the wide crack. Inside the storeroom, Mary could hear the very audible sounds of two people engaged in a passionate coupling. Just then, Tavie barked.

"What was that?" the woman croaked in a loud whisper.

A man chuckled. "Nothing, my lovely. 'Tis only one

of the dogs. The door is bolted.'' He ended with a low growl.

Tavie cocked his head.

The woman moaned again, then she urged, "Yes, yes, now, my stallion. Fill me up—now!"

Mary giggled into her handkerchief. She burned to know who was swiving in broad daylight. All of the other trysts she had stumbled upon had taken place under the concealing cover of night. She eased back down the stairs to the second landing. There, she slipped inside the storeroom, leaving the door a little ajar. Seating herself on a upright cask, she peeked through the crack, and waited.

More thumping overhead. Mary wondered if they were doing it on the bare floor. She wrinkled her nose. They should have gone to the hayloft. At least, it would have been softer there.

The woman cried out with a mixture of triumph and animal frenzy. Mary chewed her lower lip. She knew that someday, some strange man would do that same tussle with her. She hoped that he would at least have the decency of doing it in a bed, preferably one with clean sheets.

In the middle of her pondering the mysterious mechanics of lovemaking, a muted hunting horn sounded across the wide moor beyond the home park. Again it blew, this time closer, its deep brass notes clearer. She grinned. Tom was returning earlier than she had expected—and in the middle of the day. Taverstock barked several times. Above her, the amorous couple ceased their odd noises.

"Hell's bells, 'tis my lord!" the man rumbled.

"Nay, he will be gone—" the woman began, but the man cut off her further speech.

"'Tis he, for certain sure. I will be damned."

Just then, the door of the third-floor storeroom crashed open. Mary flattened herself against the wall of her hiding place.

"The devil take it!" the man swore at the top of the stairs. "'Tis my lord's dog a-spying on us. Away with you!"

Mary saw Taverstock practically fly down the steps. The man followed after him. As he passed the second floor, she saw him tying on his leather codpiece. His rough dorneck shirt hung outside the back of his high-waisted hose. She recognized it was Launce, the loose-limbed groom with hair the color of wheat in the sun. Not a bad-looking man, Mary conceded, but she judged that he might be very heavy if he laid on top of one.

"Launce," the woman called after him. She still spoke in a broken whisper.

He stopped, and turned to look back up the stairs. Mary held her breath, and prayed that she would not be discovered.

"Aye, my lady?" he replied. Behind his back, he snapped his fingers with impatience.

"Remember, this meeting is our little secret," the woman cautioned.

Launce looked at her as if she had gone stark mad. "God's teeth, my lady! Do you think I was kicked in the head by an ass? Of course, I will say nothing. Sir Thomas would flay me alive if he even suspected."

Mary's eyes grew rounder. Besides herself, there was only one other lady in Wolf Hall. Just then, Isabel rounded the curve of the stairway. Her raven hair was completely unbound, and she carried her black satin slippers with white rosettes in her hand.

"Be at ease, good Launce. No one knows, nor even

suspects our meetings. Put on a cheerful face, and whistle in the stables.''

The hunting horn sounded a third time. Mary heard the jingle of the horsemen's spurs, and the thudding of hooves as the company drew closer to the gates.

Launce tucked in his shirt. "I must be gone, my lady."

"Thomas will go to bed early tonight, worn out by the chase. Come to me when the watchman cries out midnight."

Launce blinked. "In your own chamber? Is it wise, my lady?"

Isabel's face grew darker. "I must have a babe, and soon." She softened her voice. "Trust me, Launce. All will be well. Adieu." She leaned down, and kissed him on the lips. Launce took her fully in his arms. Their kiss deepened. It appeared to Mary as if he was trying to chew off Isabel's lips. Her own heart beat faster. She prayed that the couple would not hear it.

Launce broke off the kiss and, casting a final hot glance at Isabel, clattered down the stairs. The woman remained where she was. With a catlike smile on her face, she took her time to pluck stray bits of straw out of her hair. Then she combed through her tresses with her fingers before gathering them under her widow's headdress. She slipped her feet into her shoes, shook out the creases in her gown, then slowly descended to the ground floor. She hummed a little tune under her breath.

Mary sagged against the wall with relief. She wondered what she should do and whom she should tell. Perhaps she should put the fear of God into Isabel. That idea appealed; however, Mary realized that she was still too young and insignificant in the household to be able

to cow her sister-in-law. Her best course was to bide
her time, and see what happened.

She peeked out the chamber's lancet window, and
saw Tom ride into the courtyard. Silver Charm and the
other horses were lathered to a froth. Andrew looked as
if he would fall out of the saddle with fatigue. Mary
hoped that he would. She would love to see the fastid-
ious boy get his fashionable garb muddy—just once.
The packhorses carried several fine-looking deer. One
wore an admirable rack of antlers—another trophy to
mount in the great hall.

Tom should have looked pleased with his success,
but Mary noted the deep furrow in his brow. What news
had brought him home so early? She gasped as Launce,
acting like a dutiful servant, caught the reins that his
master threw to him. He even wished his lord a good
day. What a false face the varlet wore!

Just then Isabel ran up to Tom, and attempted to
throw her arms about him. The earl stepped out of her
intended embrace. His expression grew even darker. He
scooped up Tavie in his arms, then strode toward the
entranceway.

Mary nodded with satisfaction. Just let that minx try
any of her wiles on her brother. "I know your secret
now, my lady," she whispered to herself. "If indeed
you carry a babe within you, he is not a Cavendish."

Chapter Eight

Thomas hurried toward the sanctity of his chamber before Isabel could catch up with him. He was halfway across the great hall when he stopped in amazement. The high arched windows sparkled in the late-morning sunlight. The flagstone floor was not only swept, but scrubbed clean of its crusted filth. The twin fireplaces on opposite walls had been cleared of their accumulated ashes. Even the high rafters looked a little lighter in color than before. The cobwebs in the corners had disappeared. The family's battle flag was…missing from its pole!

"Stokes!" he roared.

The steward appeared immediately as if conjured by magic. "My lord?"

Thomas pointed to the empty spot above the fireplace. "Where?" he snapped.

Stokes grinned. "Mistress Alicia took it down, my lord. She—"

"What!" he bellowed. "How dare she meddle with my family's most prized possession!"

"To clean and mend it," the steward explained in a rush.

Thomas felt as if someone had punched the wind out of his stomach. "Oh." To hide his embarrassment, he glanced around the hall once more. "And all this?" he muttered, pointing to the polished armchairs, the gleaming high table and side benches.

"Mistress Alicia, my lord. She directed us to rub everything with beeswax." The steward looked positively enraptured. "She is a wonder, my lord."

Thomas admired his clean hall. It had not glowed like this since his good mother had died while bringing Mary into the world. "Aye," he agreed in a softer tone. "A wonder, indeed."

"I am glad the hall pleases you, Thomas," Isabel spoke behind him.

He wheeled around to stare at her. From the safety of his arms, Tavie growled at her.

"How now, woman?" he asked in a low, dangerous tone.

Ignoring the warning signals from both dog and man, she waved her arm as a dancer in the midst of a pavane. "The servants have worked long into the evening hours to ready Wolf Hall for your return."

"You say you ordered this?" Thomas asked, his incredulity mixed with his anger.

She folded her hands over her breast. The gesture of humility looked out of place with her character. "I am your chatelaine, Thomas," she reminded him.

"Humph!" He glanced at Stokes who stood behind Lady Cavendish. The steward shook his head.

Just then Georgie trotted into the hall from the direction of the kitchens. Spying his master, he gave a joyful bark, then broke into a trot. Tavie wriggled, wanting to be set down.

Kneeling, Thomas released the terrier, while he

rubbed Georgie's ears in greeting. "What's this, old boy? You are damp." He ran his hand along the mastiff's gleaming coat. "By the book, someone has bathed you—and you let them." He glanced up at his sister-in-law, a wicked grin on his face. "I suppose that you are responsible for this miracle as well?"

She covered her surprise with a toss of her head. "Of course. He was filthy."

A light patter of toenails on the flagstones caused him to look beyond Georgie. Vixen pranced across the floor, leaving a trail of water and soapsuds behind her.

"Here, Vixen!" Alicia called from the direction of the kitchens. "Where are you? Vixen, come back, girl. I have not done—"

She burst through the archway. Her skirts were pinned scandalously high, showing a goodly amount of her trim ankles and shapely calves. Her braid had fallen out from under her cap. Her muslin shift was soaked to almost a sheer transparency. Her full, round breasts pushed against the top of her simple bodice. The wet cloth revealed her nipples, their tips hardened by the cold water. Devouring the sight of her with his eyes, Thomas found it difficult to breathe.

She skidded to a halt, then dropped a charming, disheveled curtsy. "Sir Thomas!" she gasped. "I...we did not expect your return so soon." She laughed like silver bells on a May morning. "I fear I have not yet finished my surprise for you." She pointed to Taverstock, who sniffed at Vixen's soapy fur. "Indeed, methinks 'twill take a full day alone to bathe that one."

"Indeed," Thomas agreed with a smile. "Tavie was once thrown into the meadow pond by Wil—" He glanced at Isabel, who had turned very pale. "By my brother. Since that ducking, the dog has avoided any body of water larger than his bowl. Though I must admit he could use a good scrubbing.''

Alicia returned his smile. "Then I think I can manage the work with a wet cloth instead of a tub."

Thomas picked up Tavie, and held him out to her. The little dog tried to wiggle free, but Alicia gripped him firmly with both hands.

"Courage, Taverstock," Thomas admonished his favorite. "Cleanliness is an indignity that all of us males must suffer."

She paused, then laughed. "Indeed, my lord? Shall I order you a bath as well?"

It was on the tip of his tongue to suggest that she accompany his tub of water, when Isabel broke the spell.

"*You* tend to the dogs, Alicia, as befits your station. I shall minister to Thomas as befits *mine!*"

Alicia went very white, then blushed to the roots of her golden hair. "Your pardon," she apologized in a soft voice. "I mistook. Let us be gone, Tavie."

With a carriage that would befit a queen, she returned to the kitchens with Taverstock, who gave his master pleading looks over her shoulder.

Thomas took several deep breaths before confronting his brother's shrewish widow. "My *squire* will attend to my bath as he always has. Meanwhile, I suggest that *you* spend the hour betwixt now and dinner relearning your good manners. You have obviously misplaced them. Come!" he commanded Georgie and Vixen with a snap of his fingers.

The three of them climbed the broad staircase without a backward glance at the fuming woman.

After his bath, accompanied by much unsolicited advice from Andrew, Thomas whiled away the time until the dinner hour in his library. First, he reviewed the marriage contract between William and Isabel that had been drawn up shortly before his own. On William's death, his widow's dower house in Yorkshire reverted to her, along with the tenancies and rental fees belonging to it. Any children would inherit William's portion of the Cavendish estate. As the second son, he owned a small holding near the Scottish border, an inhospitable place where the family's cattle often fell into the hands of the lawless reavers.

Thomas furrowed his brow, then he consulted his almanac, wherein he jotted his personal notations. Sir Giles had died on the twelfth of June. Pausing, the son said a little prayer for his stern father's soul. Moving his finger down the page, he stopped at the sixteenth. Next to that date, Thomas had written a single word. *William.* John, who had become the Earl of Thornbury while fighting a raging fever, had died on the twenty-first.

Thomas rubbed the side of his nose with his forefinger. William was *never* the earl, not even for a day. At his death, his property had reverted to the eldest, John, though his wife retained an interest in the revenue until she remarried. He shuddered. The witch wanted it all—through him. The idea of Isabel as the Countess of Thornbury made him gag.

"She should be sent to a nunnery," he confided to Georgie and Vixen. "She has dower enough to lead a comfortable life there. Aye, but how to get her into one? There is the rub!"

The dogs wagged their tails.

He dreamed briefly of abduction: a dark cloth thrown over Isabel as she lay sleeping, a wild ride at midnight with his trussed sister-in-law clawing and spitting like a wildcat, and finally, depositing her, in her shift, at the convent doors.

He grinned. "The idea has a certain appeal, I must admit, though I have not the spleen to do it." He sighed. "Especially now that she carries a child."

One thing was certain. Since its father had never been the earl, the unborn Cavendish did not inherit Sir Giles's title. Thomas breathed easier.

He had never considered fatherhood. But when he became the earl, he had assumed a number of serious responsibilities, not the least of which was the begetting of the next generation. That meant marriage—and a wedding night.

Thomas's hands grew cold at the thought. How on God's green earth could he be a good lover? He was such a big man. He would hurt any woman brave enough to be his wife. Besides, he had only the vaguest idea how to woo, and so far, he had been a dismal failure with Alicia.

Her image swam into his memory. A radiance shone around her wherever she went. Her smiles beguiled him as no others ever had. Her soft voice thrilled his heart. Yet the whole idea of bedding a woman terrified him. The thought of giving his heart unconditionally to another made him break out into a sweat, like a horse that had been raced to the farthest end of the moor.

Thomas picked up the other paper on his desk. He slowly reread his own betrothal contract to one Mistress Alicia Broom, ward of Sir Edward Brampton. He sat up with a start, and reread the exact wording. Ward, not daughter. How had he missed that in his first reading? If she was not the daughter of a humble goldsmith from the city of York, whose daughter was she? And why did she have so noble a guardian?

"There is something that lies hidden betwixt these lines," he informed his four-footed companions. "My father was always a shrewd man," he mused aloud. "Methinks this goldsmith's daughter is much more than she seems."

He recalled William's years of painful taunting. The lackwit betrothed to a merchant's daughter—mayhap *she* could teach him to cipher. Thomas needed no instruction in that area. 'Twas William who could barely read or sign his name. All those years of cruel jibes about Thomas's bride-to-be—what if everyone was wrong?

He closed his eyes and rubbed the bridge of his nose. Why the deceit? If the goldsmith was a counterfeit, which was most evident when Brampton reappeared at Wolf Hall dressed as a gentleman, why didn't Sir Edward reveal the truth then?

Because I ran away too soon!

Thomas expelled a deep sigh. He was a dolt and a coward and much more. He suspected that he may have misjudged sweet Alicia. Not that he had played false with his own feelings toward her. In simple fact, he had adored her from the first moment he had met her ten years ago. Those feelings had deepened since her arrival.

Then why hesitate? Proclaim the banns this day, and marry Alicia.

A happy thought—and a terrifying one, as well.

He returned to the contract. The amount of the dowry astounded him. He had not noticed the sum before now. One hundred gold sovereigns was a princely dower for any man to give—far too much for a simple goldsmith, no matter how prosperous. Who had fathered Mistress Broom, and bestowed such a goodly fortune upon her?

Ask her.

Thomas shrank from the obvious. Perchance she did not know who her parents were. Then his question would sound petty, or worse, full of avarice. She would think he only consented to marry her for the gold that his father had already spent years ago. Thomas shook his head. She must never think that for a moment, because it was not true. He would marry her because he had promised to do so a decade ago—and because he had lost his heart to her.

Inspired by this resolution, he opened his writing case, and drew out paper, pen and ink.

To the angel of my dreams, Alicia— he wrote.

The dinner bell rang just as he sealed his note with red wax. He discovered his squire loitering outside the library's door. Thomas handed his letter to the boy.

"Put this where Mistress Alicia is certain to find it," he instructed him.

Andrew grinned. "My lord? Methinks you have—"

Thomas interrupted him. He had no desire to hear any more of his squire's sly observations of his master's love life. "Away with you, magpie. You talk too much, and think not at all."

Alicia hurriedly changed out of her wet clothes, and into a gown of light blue linen before going down to the hall for dinner. She grinned to herself in the huge gilt-framed looking glass. This morning's toil had been worth all her effort, she mused. She undid her loose braid, then brushed out her hair. Afterward, she covered her head with a plain wimple that allowed her tresses to hang freely down her back.

As she pulled on a clean pair of stockings, she heard the outer door of her suite open without a preliminary knock. She wondered who invaded her privacy. A chill gripped her. Perhaps someone knew of the treasure she had hidden under her mattress, and they had now come creeping into her room to steal it. Gathering her courage, she quietly lifted the iron poker from the side of the fireplace. Gripping it tightly, she peeked around the corner. To her surprise she spied Andrew putting something into her sewing basket.

"How now, Master Ford?" she inquired, coming into the solar. "Have you taken up embroidery as a pastime?"

It gave her a certain sense of satisfaction to see the boy jump, and flush with guilt.

He covered his embarrassment with a dramatic flourish and a low bow. "Ah, Mistress Broom, you have found out my little vice. I pray you, do not bandy it about the hall, or, I fear, I shall have more requests for my handiwork than I have time to stitch them." He started to back out the door. "Your pardon, but the dinner bell has rung, and I must attend my lord straightway. We awoke before the sun this morning, and barely paused to eat before returning to Wolf Hall. He is quite famished. And so am I," the squire added as he made good his escape.

Alicia ran to her workbasket. Nestled among her skeins of bright-colored floss, she found another note. She sank down on the stool beside the cold hearth. "Oh, Andrew! Not again!"

She broke open the seal. Once more the sweet written words plucked at her soul.

To the angel of my dreams, Alicia—

Methinks I have gone mad, though I appear to the world as if I have not. 'Tis a sham. I can no

longer think of anything but you. I cannot form
two words together without whispering your name
between them. You have quite overwhelmed my
heart, and have made your abode therein. Each
passing hour makes me desire you more and more.
I swear I shall be moonstruck before the next
month turns the calendar—unless I hear from your
lips that you love me.

She stared at the paper in her hand. "Oh, Andrew,
'tis folly indeed, and none of my doing. This green-
sickness of yours is truly madness, and must be stopped
today."

Since there was no fire in the grate, she tore the loving message into tiny pieces, then wrapped them in her
handkerchief. She pushed the little bundle up her sleeve.
As an afterthought, she withdrew a small blue velvet
bag from under the bolster of her bed. If the squire
could come and go in her chamber without risk, so
could anyone else. The contents of the bag were too
precious to leave unattended. She stuffed it up her other
sleeve, then went down to dinner with the firm resolve
to put a large flea into Andrew's ear.

This proved much harder to carry out than she had
expected. As before, Thomas seated her on his right,
and shared his trencher and goblet with her. How could
she possibly talk to Andrew about his ill-conceived in-
fatuation with her betrothed sitting a heartbeat away?
The squire's smirks as he served the courses to his master did not help her digestion either. She could barely
taste the food she had worked so hard to prepare.

"By the rood! What wizard has enchanted Master
Konrad?" Thomas asked, after he had finished a second
portion of pigeons stuffed with dates and mustard.

"'Tis the best victuals I have eaten in a year—nay, more.''

Alicia struggled to think of a way to claim responsibility without appearing vain or proud. Isabel laughed in a bright brittle manner. "La and a day, Thomas! Thank you for your kind words. I do believe that is the most I have heard you praise anything in too long a time to count."

Alicia gulped as she fumbled for the wine goblet. She wondered how she could denounce Isabel's false claim without giving offense to Thomas.

The lower table grew silent. Thomas placed his eating knife beside his trencher. "How now, Lady Isabel? Am I to understand that we should give *you* thanks for this delicious repast?"

His sister-in-law tossed her head. "Oh, 'tis but a trifle, I assure you, dear heart. As your chatelaine, I felt 'twas my duty to rectify the deplorable matters in the kitchen. I—"

"Hogwash!" Mary erupted from the other side of the table.

Alicia gave her a silent nod of thanks.

Thomas folded his arms over his broad chest. Alicia itched to pull up the mourning band that had slipped below his elbow. Instead, she clasped her hands together in her lap.

"How now, little minx?" He tried to look stern, but failed miserably.

Mary glared at her sister-in-law. "Isabel had nothing to do with the preparations of this dinner, Tom. 'Tis all Alicia's hard work. Ask any of the servants. Alicia does a lot more around here than wash dogs." She pointed to the dusted rafters.

"Tittle-tattle," Isabel rebuked the younger girl. "If

you wish to continue to dine at table with the adults, you must learn to keep your mouth shut when others are—''

Thomas slammed his palm down onto the board. The cutlery rattled on impact. "Silence!" he bellowed.

Turning pale, Isabel took a large drink of wine from her goblet. No one else in the hall moved, not even the serving wenches at the cupboard.

The earl leaned over his trencher toward his sister. "Pray, continue, sweetheart," he commanded in a softer tone.

Under the table, Georgie nudged Alicia's clenched fingers with his wet nose. Grateful to do something, she stroked the large head that he rested in her lap.

Sitting up straighter, Mary smiled. "Since you left yesterday morn, Alicia has had the entire household at work. Look about you at the hall. Have you ever seen it so clean? The kitchens, too, are spotless. And the food—great Jove, Tom! We have eaten like kings and queens since dinner a day ago. Alicia says they are some of her mother's recipes, and she has promised to teach me cookery—if you approve, that is." She ended her recitation with a hopeful expression.

Thomas raised his eyebrows, then turned his full attention to Alicia. She felt herself grow warm under his searching gaze.

"'Tis true?" he asked her with a surprising gentleness. "You are the wonder worker?"

She swallowed. "Aye, my lord. I hope it pleases you."

He said nothing. She held her breath. Perhaps he didn't like to have his home changed around without his permission. She should have thought of that, but he had left so quickly yesterday morning, and her mind had been otherwise engaged by Andrew's troubling love letters.

Thomas placed his large hand over hers. "It pleases me well," he murmured.

She looked up at him with words of gratitude trembling on her lips, but he turned away. "Bring on the next course, Andrew!" he roared down the hall.

"Aye, my lord! 'Tis roast salmon in an onion-and-wine sauce," the squire announced with a grand flourish, as he carried the steaming platter up to the high table.

The other diners cheered as he passed by them. The savory aroma of the sauce filled the hall. Thomas gave Alicia's hand a gentle squeeze before he picked up his knife, and returned to his dinner. She sighed with relief. Just then, she caught Isabel's expression over his shoulder. It was a look of pure venom.

Chapter Nine

Thomas did not speak to Alicia for the rest of the dinner, though he glanced often at her when he thought she wasn't looking. She tried to read his expression, but could not. Only his beautiful blue eyes seemed softer. As he had done during their first shared meal, he made sure that she received the choicest portions of everything. When he drank from their goblet, he always wiped the rim before offering it to her. Once she thought she spied a hint of a smile at the corners of his mouth, but he quickly turned away from her. She chided herself for giving in to idle fancy.

On the other hand, both Andrew and Mary kept up bantering one-sided conversations with Thomas. Mary made it a point to exclaim over every new dish, each new sauce and the novel methods of presentation. When the sweet course was served, she ascended into verbal ecstasies over the tansy cakes topped with mint cream.

Meanwhile, Andrew driveled nonsense about the food, the wine, the time of day, the month of the year, the weather, the swept hearth and the current phase of the moon. The jabbering squire associated each topic with its amorous connotations and lovers' desires. Alicia presumed that he directed all his suggestive remarks to her personally. The fragments of his letter grew heavier inside her sleeve. She couldn't wait to burn them, and to box Andrew's ears for his impertinence.

At last, Thomas grew tired of his squire's quips. "Tie up your tongue," he growled.

With a deep bow, the boy retired from the high table. Just before he exited into the kitchens, he winked broadly.

Alicia sighed with relief. At that moment, Thomas turned in his chair, looked at her, and cleared his throat.

"Come to the library," he muttered. "If you please," he added almost as an afterthought.

"Willingly," she replied. Apprehension rose in her throat. He looked so serious, it frightened her.

He means to discuss our betrothal, she thought as Thomas helped her from her seat. By his stern expression, she feared that his decision would not be in her favor. *Perchance he will let me stay at Wolf Hall as his housekeeper.* Casting a glance at Isabel, Alicia changed her mind. The earl might not object to having Alicia underfoot, but Isabel had made it plain that she would rather see her rival at the bottom of the well.

He led the way, attended by the three dogs. Isabel rose from the table.

"Thomas, wait!" she pleaded. Lifting her skirts, she ran after them.

Alicia felt her delicious dinner turn to a leaden weight inside her stomach. She steeled herself for an unpleasant interview. *Oh, Edward, you should have taken me to the Low Countries with you.*

Thomas halted, his hand on the library door latch. "How now, Isabel?"

The low tone of his voice, and the steely look in his

eye chilled the atmosphere. Taverstock bristled, and growled at Isabel.

She took no notice of Thomas's demeanor, nor of the little dog's unfriendly greeting. "I must speak with you upon an urgent matter. Now." She flashed Alicia a withering look. "You may deal with this servant later."

Before he could reply, Mary joined the group. Thomas directed his attention to his sister.

"Go plague someone else, Mary. 'Tis serious matters I must discuss with these two ladies."

Putting her hands on her hips, she cocked her head. "If it concerns our family, I will stay, Tom. I am old enough to understand."

"Go," he muttered, though he did not put his whole heart behind the command.

Isabel drew herself up, though she was still shorter than Mary. "You heard your brother, child. 'Tis not for you to thrust your nose where it plainly is not wanted."

Mary laughed in her face. "Very well, go to. Closet yourselves in secret conference. 'Tis a waste of time. I shall know everything that you say before the words are even out of your mouths."

Alicia could not help smiling at the girl's open defiance. "Mistress of the keyhole?" she murmured.

Mary nodded. "Just so."

Thomas looked at each of the three determined females before him, then he shrugged his shoulders with resignation. Alicia couldn't help feeling a little sorry for him. He might be a stellar huntsman, but he certainly was at sixes and sevens when it came to handling the women of his family.

He opened the door. The dogs scampered inside, and made for their accustomed places before he had even lighted the candles on his table. He offered the only chair to Alicia. Isabel started to object, but he held up his hand for silence. Alicia settled herself on the cushioned seat, grateful for this little consideration. She had a nasty feeling that her knees might give way under her. Once Mary got the hems of her gown and petticoats out of the way, Thomas shut the door behind her. Four people and three dogs made a tight fit in the small room. Thomas leaned against the mantel, crossed his arms over his chest, and stared at the assembled company.

The silence hung heavily in the room like a damp woolen cloak. Isabel tossed her head.

"Thomas, Wolf Hall is rife with gossip. The news of my pregnancy has spread like wildfire, no thanks to a certain long-eared person here present." She glared at Mary.

The girl narrowed her eyes. "I have kept that piece of motley news to myself. Look to your own maid Meg. Her tongue has not stopped wagging." She lowered her voice. "There is much that goes on around here that I keep to myself."

The sudden adult tone in the child's voice surprised Alicia. Isabel stared at Mary for a long moment, then dismissed her.

"To the point, Isabel!" Thomas snapped. He rubbed the bridge of his nose.

"The babe I carry needs a father. *You* are honor-bound to grant me your protection. Announce our marriage. Set the date." She took his free hand, and laid it against her cheek. "I will make you a good wife, Thomas."

His jaw dropped, though he did not snatch his hand away from her. Alicia saw her secure future evaporating before her eyes. Her patient waiting had achieved her nothing. If she did not open her mouth now, all would be lost.

She took a deep breath. "My lord, your father and my guardian signed and sealed a contract of marriage between us. I have been under your roof for some days now without the comfort of kith or kin. I beg of you, please honor that contract, before my good name is ruined."

Alicia bit her lower lip. She had said her piece, though only heaven knew what Thomas would say. She could find herself on the post road back to York before midafternoon.

Thomas stared at her, then at his sister-in-law. His face turned red. He brushed away Isabel's hand as if it were a firebrand. Then he exploded.

"Silence, all of you! Do not abuse my ears with any more of your mewling. 'Tis giving me a monstrous headache. Mary, you imp, hold your tongue until you are spoken to. Isabel, you are enough to drive a holy man straight into hell."

The little widow quickly recovered her composure. "But, dearest Thomas—"

"I am *not* your dearest anything! God shield me, I pray I never will be dear to you. I cannot marry you, Isabel, as you were my brother's wife, even though you seem to have recovered from the shock of his death in swift time. Our union would be against the holy church's law of affinity. As for you, Alicia—"

He stopped in midtirade as if he searched for the words he wanted to say to her. Though she trembled inside, she sat up straighter in the chair, folded her hands and tried to look composed. "Aye, my lord?" she asked, holding her voice steady.

He took a deep breath. "I fully intend to honor my father's agreement. We will marry within the week."

Alicia sagged with relief against the high back of her chair. She swallowed down the lump in her throat.

"Yahoo!" Mary clapped her hands with joy.

Thomas gave his sister a fierce look.

"But I did not say anything, Tom," she protested. "I think you have made the right decision," she added.

Isabel stamped her foot. "You are every bit the knotty-pated fool that William said you were, Thomas. The Archbishop of York can grant us a dispensation to wed. The bishop would quite understand your reluctance to marry a...a..."

"Be still, woman!" Thomas warned in a low voice.

Undaunted by his anger, she continued. "'Tis your duty to *me*. I carry the Cavendish heir. Your elder brother's child—the one who *should* rightfully be the Earl of Thornbury."

"Your tongue should be fed to the dogs," Mary sneered.

Her brother's eyes widened with surprise at her unusual outburst.

"How now?" he asked.

"Send this prattling child to bed this instant," Isabel screamed.

Mary put Tavie on the floor. "What a brazen-faced liar you are!" She advanced toward Isabel. The angry woman retreated until she bumped against the locked bookcase. Mary laughed out of the side of her mouth. "Look you, Tom. She turns pale at my words."

Isabel put her hand to her abdomen. "'Tis the babe..."

The child curled her lip. "Ha! You play your part

well, madam. Methinks we should hire you out to the mummers.''

"Thomas!" Isabel beseeched. "Are you content to stand there like a great staring oaf, and do nothing while I am maligned by this impudent mischief-maker? She should be tied to a bedpost and whipped for what she has said to me."

He shook his head. "Mary, what are you jabbering about? Be brief and to the point. My patience has flown up the chimney."

"Aye, Tom. 'Tis this. How do you *know* that this child of Isabel's is a *true* Cavendish?"

Before Thomas or Alicia could react, Isabel slapped Mary across her face. The sharp sound set Tavie to barking. The hair on Vixen's neck stood straight up. She growled, and bared her needlelike teeth at Isabel. Georgie hoisted himself to his great feet. The child winced at the pain, but did not cry or step back.

Thomas clenched his fists. "By heaven, I have never struck a woman before, but I swear to you, my fingers itch to do the deed now. I warn you, hell-hag, tread carefully with your next few steps, lest you be marked for my hot vengeance. Mary, child, come here." He held out his arm to his sister.

The red print of Isabel's hand stood out on her cheek. Her chin trembled, but she did not give herself over to tears. Alicia started to rise, but Thomas shook his head at her.

Isabel swelled up like a cornered cat. "The little chit should be sharply punished for the slander she has uttered against me."

"And you should be banished for the foul things you have done against this family," Mary retaliated. Then she looked up at her brother. "This very morning, before you returned from the hunt, Isabel lay with Launce, the groom, in the top-floor storeroom of the south tower.''

Isabel turned pale. "The devil take you straight to hell!" she yowled, her pretty face contorted with rage.

Alicia made a quick sign of the cross against Lady Cavendish's terrifying curse.

Thomas's silent anger filled the small chamber.

Alicia put her hand over her heart. "Oh, Mary, are you certain sure of this?"

Isabel clutched the bookcase for support. "Of course not. She would say anything to besmirch my good name. The little wretch hates me."

Mary held her ground. "I heard her call Launce her stallion, and she told him to…to fill her up," she related in a low tone. "Later, I saw them descend the stairs. Launce's codpiece was undone, and Isabel had straw in her hair, and her skirts were…"

Thomas sliced the air with the edge of his hand. "Enough, child! I do not need to hear the particulars of that disgusting scene—especially from your innocent lips."

Isabel formed her hands into claws. "Innocent, ha! She is as false as vows made in wine." She lunged at Mary.

All three dogs barked, as Mary sought safety behind Thomas. Alicia could not sit by and watch Isabel injure the young girl. As the angry woman dashed past her, Alicia rose, grabbed her by the wrist, and flipped her into the chair.

"There, my lady, you have a seat at last." Then Alicia sat on top of her. "And so do I," she added with a great deal of satisfaction.

"My babe!" Isabel cried, beating her fists against her back.

"Methinks it lives in your imagination and not your belly," Mary taunted.

"Damn your tongue!" Isabel shot back.

Thomas massaged his temples. "Peace!" he bellowed. The room fell silent. "Stokes!" He threw open the library door. The steward and Andrew literally fell flat over the threshold. As they struggled to their feet, their master gave them a cold smile. "I commend your promptness, gentlemen. Andrew, send for Launce, but he is not to know the nature of his summons."

The squire grinned like a sprite on All Hallows' Eve. "Aye, my lord. I will effect this dainty undertaking myself."

Thomas curled his lips. "Be brief in your words, and quick on your feet." After Andrew had departed, the beleaguered earl turned to his steward. "Find the wench Meg. Instruct her to start packing Lady Isabel's bits and pieces. They will be gone from Wolf Hall in two days' time."

Stokes attempted to hide his grin. "Aye, my lord. 'Twill be done as you command."

Thomas grabbed the man's arm as he turned to go. "Seal your lips about this affair. Give no answer to Meg, or to any other. The Cavendish name must not be dragged though the mud by idle gossip."

Looking more sober, the steward nodded. "Aye, my lord."

Thomas closed the door. Isabel bucked against Alicia's weight.

"Thomas! Tell this great broomstick to get off of me."

He raised an eyebrow. "Tsk, tsk, my lady. That is a most discourteous way to address my future *wife*."

Isabel made a rude noise with her lips. "Wife or broomstick, I care not! She is a great heavy lout, and is crushing me."

Alicia raised her eyes to meet his. "My lord," she asked softly. "What is your will?"

He snorted. "If I had my will, I would have the witch pressed flat. Since she still calls herself a lady, you may let her up. But, I warn you, Isabel, you are to sit quietly, and say nothing—or I will make you silent. Do you mark me?"

Isabel said nothing, but her expression communicated her anger. She drummed her nails on the arm of the great chair. Meanwhile, Mary retreated to the window niche.

Alicia did not know where to put herself. Thomas had not indicated that he wanted her by his side, and she certainly had no desire to be anywhere near Isabel. Feeling very conspicuous, she sank down on the hearth beside Georgie, and began to stroke his back.

It seemed an eternity of silent waiting until someone knocked on the door.

"Enter!" Thomas commanded.

The door swung open, revealing Launce. He pulled off his leather cap as he crossed the threshold. "My lord?" The tall man touched his forehead with his fingers. "Your squire said 'twas most urgent to see you."

Thomas nodded. "I have a question for you," he growled. "And I expect an honest answer."

Launce shot a quick look at Isabel, then licked his lips. "Aye, my lord?"

Thomas pointed to his sister-in-law. "Did you lie with her in the south tower this morning?"

The groom swallowed several times. He clutched his hat until his knuckles turned white.

The earl took a step toward him. "Well? Your answer?"

He cast another glance at Isabel. She ignored him.

"How could I do that? Lady Cavendish is much above my station," he muttered.

Alicia felt immediately sorry for the servant. She had no doubt that Isabel had duped him in some way in order to sate her wicked desires.

Thomas bared his teeth. "I quite agree. I will ask you once more, and I warn you think on your answer with great care. Did you have carnal knowledge of my late brother's *wife?*" He shouted the last words into Launce's face.

The man twitched, but did not back away. He swallowed again. "I am a servant, my lord. I do what I am bid."

Alicia saw a vein throbbing at Thomas's temple.

"And what did this fine lady bid you to do?" he whispered.

Isabel studied the coffered ceiling. Launce looked first at Mary, then at Alicia. He flushed.

"I have no wish to offend the innocent, my lord."

The groom's response surprised Thomas. He considered his reply for a moment, then he drew out his dagger.

Launce's eyes grew wide with fear. He held up his arm to shield his face from the expected blow. Thomas drove the point of his dagger deep into the top of his desk. The weapon quivered upright. The earl gave his groom a severe look. "Swear by the cross, here represented by the handle of my knife, that you have never slept with my sister-in-law."

Launce dropped to his knees. "Your pardon, my lord. I regret everything I have done. Aye, I did take pleasure with the Lady Isabel."

"Um." Thomas rubbed his forehead. "And what prompted you to this shameful act?"

The man blinked several times before he answered. "The lady requested my…services."

"How often? When did you first make bold with her?"

Isabel sucked in her breath through her teeth. She coiled in the large chair as if ready to spring at her accuser.

The man stared down at the floor. "Since this past May Day, my lord," he mumbled.

Thomas gripped him by the collar. "While my brother still lived?"

Alicia barely heard Launce's response.

"A…aye, my lord."

Thomas grew very red in the face. He glared at Isabel. "Then any child you carry is indeed a bastard by this stable boy," he thundered.

The groom gave Isabel a look of surprise. "Babe? Nay, my lord. The lady is not breeding, so far as I know. That is why she lies with me—to get her with child."

"Ah-h-h," Thomas drew out the word.

Isabel suddenly spat, "The varlet lies! He threatened me. He held his knife to my throat. Tell my brother-in-law the *whole* truth, Launce. Tell him how you forced yourself upon me."

The servant broke into a sweat, like a rabbit cornered by a fox.

Thomas arched an eyebrow. He studied the man's belt, then asked softly, "Where is your knife, Launce?"

"In the stables, my lord. I have spent the day mending one of the saddle girths."

Isabel glared at the groom. "So you say, Launce, but this morning your knife was at my throat!"

Mary shook her head. "Nay, I saw no knife in his hand. Nor did Isabel appear frightened. I watched them kiss most lovingly on the stairs."

Launce slumped his shoulders. "Such sights are not for a young girl's eyes, Lady Mary," he muttered.

"Such sights are not for anyone's eyes," Thomas snarled. "What promise did the Lady Isabel give to entice you to lie with her? Did she admire your manly parts? Did she lust for your touch? Or did she offer to pay you?" he roared.

"I was taken by force!" Isabel shouted. "This churl should be flogged, then hanged for daring to touch me."

Launce looked at his master squarely in the eye. "She came to me on May Day. I was befuddled with new wine. She kissed me in the stables, and stroked my—" He glanced at the child, then continued. "'Tis God's own truth. She promised me the position as her chamberlain when she became the Countess of—"

"Liar!" Isabel shrieked. Blue veins stood out on her neck.

"Thornbury," Thomas finished. "My...wife. The one who would give birth to the Cavendish heir. And the child would look like a member of my family, would he not, Launce? You are tall, well made and have hair the same color as my own. Was that her plan?"

Isabel jumped to her feet. "How can you believe this villain? He would say anything to save his precious neck."

Launce dropped his hands to his sides. "You speak the truth, my lord, in all particulars."

Isabel opened her mouth, but Thomas denied her the chance to speak. "Save your tongue, madam. You will need it when you arrive at your father's house."

"Never!" she shrieked.

The earl continued as if he had not heard her. "I will write to him this evening and tell him that you are coming. He will receive my message by the time you and your baggage have cleared my lands."

Isabel fell back onto the chair. "You cannot do this to me."

He gave her a cold smile. "I can, and I will. At last, I can wash my hands of you with a clear conscience. Furthermore, you will get nothing from William's estate. Once again, you will be your father's burden. If he asks you why, be sure to tell him the truth." He loomed over her. "Be thankful that I will not denounce you in public, nor take you to court to be tried for adultery and fornication. The circuit judge is a just man, but harsh. He does not take kindly to wayward women—especially ones who were unfaithful to their living husbands."

Isabel paled. "But, Thomas—"

He turned his back on her. "I do not wish to have any further conversation with you. Take yourself back to the Earl of Bedford, with my compliments—or without them. I care not. You are to be gone within two days—after my wedding. Now, leave us."

Isabel looked as if she might attack her brother-in-law. She rose slowly out of her seat. With a great show of smoothing her skirts, she walked to the door with her nose in the air. As she passed Launce, she hissed. "I wish to speak with you in my chambers."

He shook his head. "Nay, my lady. I will have nothing more to do with you."

"Fool!" she snarled. She grabbed at the latch, flung open the door so that it slammed against the library's wall, then sailed out.

Thomas's shoulders visibly sagged. Alicia, who had not moved from her spot on the hearth, wished she could do something to soothe the headache she knew he must be suffering.

"Methinks you have had enough amusement for one afternoon, Mary," he told his sister. "An hour or two of French lessons would do you no harm."

She made a face behind his back, then flashed a grin at Alicia. "Very well, if it pleases you, Tom, but after supper, will you play a game of chess with me?"

He kissed her on the forehead. "We shall see, poppet."

The girl left the room more quietly than Isabel. Thomas studied the dejected Launce for a few minutes. Alicia made a move to retire and leave the men alone, but Thomas shook his head, then pointed to his chair. Giving Georgie one last rub, she slipped back into her original place.

Thomas crossed to his desk, and opened his writing case. "You realize that I must send you away from Wolf Hall, Launce?"

Squashing his cap in his large hands, he nodded.

The earl took out a piece of paper, his bottle of ink and a quill pen. "You are not entirely to blame in this matter," he remarked as he dipped his pen, and began to write. "Still, you should have known the penalty of the law for debauching your lord's wife."

"Aye." The man trembled. "As God is my witness, I am most heartily sorry for what I have done. What will happen to me?"

Thomas scribbled across the sheet. "I am writing to

a friend of my father's, Sir William Jefferson, who lives near Coventry. I am recommending you to him as a stable groom. I will tell him that I have too many servants at the moment, and cannot keep you in food or livery.'' He glanced up from his writing. ''One look at your proportions, and Sir William will understand my predicament.''

Launce sagged at his master's generous mercy. ''Bless you, my lord! Thank you, sir! Upon my soul, I swear that I will never disgrace myself again.''

Pausing midletter, Thomas regarded him. ''Do not be overhasty in making such a vow, Launce. Temptation comes in too many pretty disguises.''

Staring at the letter on the desk, Alicia clutched the arm of the chair. Though she could not read his upside-down words, she recognized the bold, looping handwriting. Touching the little bundle of torn scraps still hidden in her sleeve, she wondered at the possibility that Thomas could have composed her letters. Her reason rebelled. The earl was not a poet. Andrew must have counterfeited his master's hand. The squire's perfidy loomed larger in her eyes.

Thomas folded the letter, melted red sealing wax over the candle's flame, then applied it to the fold—exactly like the missives Alicia had received. Then he pressed his signet ring into the hot wax. After he blew on the seal, he handed it to Launce.

''See that Master Konrad gives you enough provisions for your journey.''

The groom rose shakily to his feet, then again touched his fingers to his forehead. ''Many thanks, my lord. God's blessing be upon you—and your new lady. I am much obliged to you.''

Thomas massaged his temples. ''Stay out of tower

rooms and haylofts, Launce. Get yourself a good wife—and be faithful to her.''

He nodded. After blessing his master several more times, he backed out of the library, and disappeared. Thomas sighed, then hunkered down to stroke Vixen. Seeing that he had forgotten her, Alicia got up quietly, and eased toward the door.

Thomas did not look up from Vixen's face. "How now, Mistress? I have not yet done with you."

She froze. "Do you mean me, my lord?"

He stood, then stretched his arms over his head. Alicia could not help marveling at his physical power that seemed to fill the chamber.

"Aye, Alicia. Please return to your chair. We have much to discuss before our wedding day." He closed the library door.

Quelling a sudden stab of panic, she perched herself on the edge of her seat. "Aye, my lord?" she asked. She wondered which man was going to speak: the stammering dullard who had hidden himself in the forest or the lord of the castle who had ordered Isabel out of Wolf Hall.

Thomas paced up and down before the fireplace for some minutes. Once or twice he rubbed his fingers on his temples. He needed to lie down with a cool compress of witch hazel, Alicia thought. Perhaps he would allow her to banish his pain.

"You have a headache?" she finally asked.

He waved his hand as if swatting flies. "A trifle. I am subject to them when I am distressed. 'Twill go in time."

"I have a recipe for voidee. 'Tis a soothing drink of spiced wine. I could prepare it for you this minute." She started to rise again.

He held up his hand. "Nay, my head will wait. My questions will not."

Alicia sank back into the chair. Her mouth went dry. "What questions, Sir Thomas?" she asked in a low voice.

He stared at her as if he tried to look into her very soul. His eyes appeared to turn bluer.

"Tell me the truth, Mistress Alicia Broom. Exactly *who* are you?"

Chapter Ten

Hovering outside the library door, Isabel stiffened. Thomas's unusual question and the tone of his voice sparked her interest.

After her degrading dismissal, she had waited for Launce to emerge from the scene of her downfall. When the knave saw her, he turned on his heel, and hurried out to the courtyard without a second glance. Isabel ground her teeth at his craven retreat. How differently he had acted only this morning. Then he could not get enough of the charms that she had bestowed upon him so lavishly.

Quelling her rising panic, she decided to throw herself upon Thomas's mercy. She could not return to her father's house, and once again be lost amid that flock of sisters. If necessary, she would barter her dower lands for the privilege of remaining at Wolf Hall. As for Mistress Broomstick, Isabel would find a means to disgrace her in the simple earl's naive eyes.

Thomas had not shut the door securely. It swung open a crack when Isabel touched it. Glancing up and down the corridor to make sure that her eavesdropping would not be observed, she peeked through the opening under the hinge.

She saw Alicia sitting in the chair as if she already owned the castle and all its chattel. The sight of her rival made her seethe with renewed anger at her own humiliation. She prayed that none of those idiot dogs would betray her presence.

Inside the library, Alicia blushed at Thomas's question. She licked her lips. Isabel pressed closer against the wall to hear the wench's answer.

"I am amazed, Sir Thomas, and know not what to say." Her face clouded with uneasiness.

He drew closer to her. "You are not the daughter of a goldsmith from York, are you?" he pressed her.

The sudden vibrancy of his voice caught Isabel off guard.

Alicia gave a little nervous laugh. "Are you a soothsayer, my lord?"

He took a seal-encrusted document out of his strongbox, and held it up in front of her face. "This is a copy of our betrothal contract. I reread it, and found some very interesting wording that I had missed the first time."

Alicia smoothed out her skirts. "Oh? Which words in particular interested you?"

"That the so-called goldsmith, *Sir* Edward Brampton, was not only a gentleman, but he is also your *guardian*—not your father, as I had believed."

Biting her lip, the tall girl looked away. "A fascinating point, Sir Thomas."

He rattled the paper at her. "Furthermore—"

She shot him a quick glance. "There is more? I had not noticed."

He chuckled without humor. "I am surprised, Alicia.

Mayhap a hundred gold sovereigns is nothing out of the ordinary to the daughter of a goldsmith. I assure you, 'tis an unusually large sum to dower a poor maid to the lackwit third son of an earl—a peer who happened to live far away from the intrigues of court. Methinks there is more to you than meets the eye, eh?"

In the corridor, Isabel pressed her hand over her mouth to muffle her gasp of shock. The Cavendish family was wealthy in properties, cattle, sheep and rents, but never had she seen even a quarter of that sum in cash since the day William had brought her to Wolf Hall as his bride.

Avoiding his penetrating gaze, Alicia knotted her fingers together.

Aha! Isabel thought. *This wanton is from a family of brigands, and the dowry was stolen from noble folk.* She smiled to herself. Thomas will *have* to turn Alicia over to the high sheriff—his honor would demand it. Then he would *need* Isabel to keep his house in good running order.

The broomstick cleared her throat. "I knew this moment of reckoning would come, though I did not think 'twould be so soon." She sighed. "There is also a second part of the dowry."

He scanned the paper in his hand, and furrowed his brow. "Aye, you are correct, mistress. It says that the second portion will be given to the earl on your wedding day." He ran his fingers through his sun-spun hair. "In other words to me, your...your husband." His voice grew weaker on the last word.

Alicia raised her chin with a cool stare in his direction. "I was told to ask you to display your family's portrait of King Edward IV. Do you know of such a painting?"

Thomas stiffened. "Aye, what of it?"

"'Twill prove the tale I must relate to you."

Isabel barely breathed.

He rubbed the bridge of his nose. "We once had such a portrait of the late king," he answered slowly. "It hung in a place of honor in the great hall. I remember it as a child. My father and John fought for his youngest brother, King Richard, when Henry Tudor invaded England in 1485. Even William went as squire to my father. After the debacle on Bosworth Field, the painting...disappeared."

"Oh!" Her eyes clouded.

He cleared his throat. "My family have always been staunch supporters of the House of York. Since the Tudor took the throne of England, my father thought it prudent to hide all appearances of our loyalty to the Plantagenet family."

Outside the library door, Isabel mulled over this dangerous episode of Cavendish family history. William had never spoken political matters to her, and, until now, she had cared very little who sat on England's throne. She realized that Thomas's words bordered on treason. The very idea made her heart pound with a mixture of fear and excitement.

Alicia's eyes gleamed with expectation. "Do you know where it is?"

Isabel tensed, prepared to leap away from the door in case Thomas came out. Instead, he moved to the hidden portion of the room, out of her line of sight. She heard a low, rumbling noise. Intense astonishment colored Alicia's expression.

"There are a number of hiding places in Wolf Hall," he said from the unseen corner of the chamber. "I still do not know all of them. My father did not think it necessary to reveal the family secrets to his third son.'' He paused while he moved around a few heavy-sounding things. ''He thought I had a great poverty of wit.''

''Parents do make mistakes,'' Alicia remarked with a tight smile. She craned her neck to see what he was doing.

''Aye, they do indeed,'' he agreed.

Isabel cursed under her breath. She would love to know what was hidden inside the library's secret room. She made a mental note to investigate the chamber later tonight when the rest of the household was abed.

He reappeared holding a large painting. The front of it faced Alicia. Though Isabel could not see the image on the canvas, she found the girl's reaction more than intriguing.

Putting her hand to her mouth, Alicia turned a shade paler. ''Is that truly King Edward IV?'' Her voice held an awed tone.

Thomas nodded. ''Aye, 'tis a fair likeness, I am told. There is the painting—what is your tale?'' He propped the portrait against the side of the fireplace.

Alicia rose, and stood before the portrait as if enchanted by the painted visage. Thomas watched her with one eyebrow raised. She reached out as if to touch it, but held her hand in midair.

''I have never seen what he looked like,'' she murmured with a faint tremor in her voice.

''Then gaze your fill, for I will have to return the portrait to its hiding place.'' Leaning closer, he asked, ''What of it?''

Her eyes shimmered. Isabel could not understand what had touched the girl's emotions. The portrait's face was handsome, but not enough to bring tears to the observer.

Alicia pointed to the cap on the king's head. "Mark the brooch that he wears," she said. Then she fumbled inside her sleeve for something. She drew out a small blue velvet bag, and laid it on the desk where Thomas's dagger still impaled the oaken top. Untying the strings, she took something out. Then she stepped back to allow him a closer inspection.

Rising on her tiptoes, Isabel tried to spy the thing that had struck the young earl completely dumb. Whatever it was, it winked in the light coming from the library's single lancet window.

"God save me!" Thomas breathed in wonder.

Alicia grinned. "Pick it up," she invited him. "'Twill not bite."

Isabel's curiosity nearly burst as Thomas gingerly held the mysterious item to the sun. A splash of blood-red light danced on the whitewashed wall next to the fireplace. Isabel's mouth dropped open. The ruby must be the size of a pigeon's egg. She moistened her lips with her tongue. She had nothing in her own jewel box to compare with such a gem. The pearl drop that dangled from the gold setting would be perfect to wear on a black velvet ribbon around her neck. A wave of greed engulfed her. She must have that royal bauble, come rack or ruin.

"Do you recognize it?" Alicia asked Thomas.

The dull-witted simpleton acted stunned as he turned the jewel this way and that. Even at her distance, Isabel recognized it as the same brooch that graced the cap of the great king.

"Aye," he answered at last.

"'Twas my father's," Alicia replied as she caressed the portrait with her gaze.

"'Twas the king's," Thomas muttered low in his throat while he compared the painted brooch with its original.

"They are one and the same." Her voice faded away to a reverent stillness.

He stared at her as if she was some angelic creature that had just materialized before him. In the hall, Isabel's breath caught in her throat. Then she turned away from the door, lest her muffled laughter be heard inside. What a stupid girl! Alicia had condemned herself out of her own mouth. By nightfall, she would be locked within York's grim gaol. Once again, Isabel would be the undisputed mistress of Wolf Hall. 'Twas too rich a jest by half.

"Explain, I pray you," Thomas commanded Alicia in an odd but gentle tone.

She drew herself away from the painting, then resumed her seat. She folded her hands in her lap. "You are correct, Sir Thomas, my guardian was not a goldsmith, though he became quite skilled in that craft. Edward assumed that disguise for safety's sake after the battle of Bosworth Field. You see, King Richard had entrusted him with the care of the Plantagenet children."

"What children?" He gave her a sidelong glance of utter disbelief. "Richard's only son was Edward, and the child died the year before his father."

Alicia nodded. "You speak the truth, but there were four other Plantagenets. John and Katherine were Richard's natural children, begotten when he was a young man before he was married."

"I have heard of them," Thomas agreed. "Methinks they are grown now."

She sighed. "Aye, grown—and gone away. The third was young Richard, the former Duke of York."

He furrowed his brow with bewilderment. "He died in the Tower as a boy."

"Nay." She gave him a smile of triumph. "His elder brother, little King Edward V, is the one who died of a fever. King Richard feared for his other nephew's life. I was told that there were many rumors of murderous plots flying about London at the time."

"Humm," muttered Thomas. He fingered the beautiful brooch in a distracted manner.

Alicia continued with her outlandish tale. "King Richard spirited Dickon out of the Tower under the silence of night, and sent him north to Middleham Castle where good Queen Anne reared him with his cousins, Katherine, John and poor little Prince Edward. Then, there was me—I was only a babe." She paused before she continued in a quieter tone. "I wish I could remember that time, but I cannot."

Gripping the fabulous jewel, Thomas touched the cruciform of the dagger. "On your most solemn oath, Mistress Alicia Broom. Tell me again. Who was your father?"

Isabel leaned closer to the door's crack in order not to miss Alicia's next words. Under her tight bodice, her heart beat with a wild cadence.

"Your father?" he repeated with desperate firmness.

Alicia pulled back her shoulders, and lifted her chin a notch. She stared directly into his eyes. "I have the honor to be the youngest child of his most gracious majesty, King Edward IV—and may God have mercy upon his soul."

There was not a sound in the small room. Isabel pressed her forehead against the cool plaster wall by the doorjamb. *The wench is lying!* The thought pounded in her brain like a desperate prayer.

Closing his eyes, Thomas rubbed his temples. Alicia did not alter her position. An expression of pride and wonderment lighted her face.

"And your mother?" he finally asked.

Her lips parted in stiff smile. "Edward told me she was named Jane Shore, one of the king's favorite mistresses. I know very little about her."

Isabel shook her head with disbelief. How could Thomas possibly think of marrying the daughter of a whore, even if she was a by-blow of a king?

He returned to the narrow window, and stared out of it while he stroked the quivering greyhound with an absentminded air. "What happened after Bosworth Field?"

"Edward and Katherine established our little home above the goldsmith shop in York. I lived happily with them and Dickon. Everything changed ten years ago when the Tudor king's claim to his throne was challenged by a young pretender named Lambert Simnel."

Thomas rubbed his forehead. "I have heard of him. He was eventually caught, and was sent to the royal kitchens as a turnspit boy. My father remarked that Henry Tudor must have been seized by a fit of mercy to act so generously to the lad. Simnel could have been hung, drawn and quartered for treason despite his tender years."

Alicia cast him a quick look. "Aye, the boy kept his life—but not John Plantagenet. Did you know he was executed?"

Thomas said nothing, though his face mirrored his disbelief.

"Both he and his legitimate cousin John, Earl of Lincoln, suffered death for their parts in the Simnel deception."

"Why did they dirty their hands with this lie?" he croaked.

Alicia snorted. "Edward said 'twas to test which way the wind blew with the new king. Henry Tudor feared that his throne was threatened by a son of Edward IV. He reacted against the pretender's party with swift violence. Meanwhile the real Richard of York was safe."

Thomas frowned. "But only a few men died."

She curled her lips. "True, but the king tightened his net around the other members of the Plantagenet family. For instance, my gentle cousin Katherine was wed to an illiterate farmer by the king's express order. The Tudor himself picked out the man. I heard that Katherine's husband beat her almost daily, and made her life a hell on earth."

Thomas closed his eyes. "Mother of God," he whispered.

"Edward could not protect his two older wards for they had come of age by then," she continued. "He grew most anxious for the safety of the true heir—and me. One night my guardian took Dickon away. Several days later he returned without him. Edward told me that he had sent the boy overseas to his aunt in Burgundy. At the time, I did not guess the true reason why. All I knew was that I had lost my dearly loved older brother. I have never seen him again." She released an audible sigh.

Isabel darted another glance along the corridor in

case someone happened by. *Do not stop now, Mistress Broom. Tell all.* She chewed her lower lip.

Thomas perched on the edge of the desk. "Ten years ago we were betrothed. Was that part of your guardian's plan?"

Alicia nodded. "Edward knew your father's loyalty to the Yorks. He told my true parentage to Sir Giles, and swore him to secrecy. My guardian thought that the strength and respect of the house of Cavendish would give me the protection that I needed."

"How old are you now, Alicia?" he asked, his voice smooth but insistent.

With a slight smile of defiance, she replied, "Seventeen this past March, but my guardian said I was mature for my years."

"Ah." Thomas stared at the ceiling. "Methought you were not to wed until you turned eighteen."

She clenched her jaw. Her eyes flashed blue fire. "I am old enough. May I remind you that your own brother was married at sixteen?"

He nodded. "Aye, because he needed the steadying influence of a wife in a hurry. William had already sired several bastards in the village."

Isabel swallowed down a sob of frustration. All those years of vigorous bedding for nothing? William had children by peasant girls, but never one by his wife. No wonder the old earl had grown impatient with her. Hot tears of mortification and self-pity ran down her cheeks. She wondered how long she had been the laughingstock of the kitchen and stables.

Alicia had the decency to blush. "Oh! I see." She cleared her throat. "My brother, Dickon, returned to England several years ago, using the name Perkin Warbeck. He was able to rally a number of supporters to recognize him as Richard Plantagenet, and to fight for his claim to the throne.''

Thomas blinked. ''Warbeck is the true heir?''

''Aye,'' she whispered. ''Two weeks ago, Dickon was captured, and imprisoned once again in that dreadful Tower of London. We heard that he was lodged with his first cousin, the young Earl of Warwick, son of Dickon's ill-fated uncle George, Duke of Clarence. My guardian feared that his own arrest was imminent, since he had generously financed Perkin Warbeck's bid for the crown. The Bramptons made immediate plans to escape to Flanders, but they needed to settle my future. 'Tis why we arrived at Wolf Hall without prior warning.''

Thomas pinched the bridge of his nose, as if he sought to block a sneeze or a pain. Alicia studied his face.

''Now I understand why my father's death must have been a severe shock to your guardian,'' he remarked. ''Of course, I knew nothing of this.''

''Aye, but there is more,'' she replied. '''Tis your right to know the danger you face.''

He raised one golden eyebrow. ''How now?''

''King Henry has a vast network of spies throughout the kingdom. I am sure he knows of my existence by now. As I told you, the Tudor hounds anyone with a drop of Plantagenet blood.'' A tear rolled down her pale cheek. ''Thomas, you could lose all of your estates if you marry me. Mayhap even your own life. Henry will purge England of Plantagenets to make his crown safe for his children to inherit. Your wedding gift to me is the noble title of Thornbury. My gift to you will be a life of constant fear and deception. Do you understand?

Dangerous blood flows in my veins. Ponder this, Thomas—if we wed, you could be sleeping with your executioner.''

Her words fell like February icicles against cobblestones.

Isabel leaned back against the wall, and hugged herself with joy. Her fortune lay within her grasp. No need to pine to be the Countess of Thornbury, and live the rest of her life with a pack of flea-bitten dogs, when she could find richer pickings in the court of King Henry VII. She imagined how grateful the Tudor sovereign would be when she handed him, not only another Plantagenet sprig, but the certain knowledge that the young man imprisoned under the name of Perkin Warbeck was in fact the living heir of Edward IV. Perchance Henry would reward her with marriage to a duke.

This heady prospect made her feel quite giddy. Fie on Thomas Cavendish and his revolting curs! Let them all rot here in the wilds of Northumberland. The fabled city of London beckoned Isabel with visions of all its wealth and glitter.

Lifting the hems of her skirts, she raced through the hall, and up the stairs to her chamber with the lightest heart she had ever felt inside the walls of Wolf Hall. A plan had already formed itself in her mind. She found Meg slowly folding her clothes, and putting them into her trunks.

Isabel clapped her hands, which started the maid out of her daydreaming. ''Make haste, you slug! I want to quit this gloomy tomb before next Christmas.'' She began to pitch her shoes willy-nilly into an open coffer.

Meg gaped at her. ''Yer pardon, me lady?''

Isabel danced a little jig on the hearth. ''Aye, Meg,

mark what I tell you. We are off to bustle our own way into this wide, wonderful world.''

Meg shook her head to herself. ''Horn-mad, she is,'' she muttered in an undertone.

Chapter Eleven

Alicia crossed her fingers for luck under the folds of her skirt. She felt much better now that she had revealed her dangerous secret to Thomas. She prayed that he would not send her away, or put her into a nunnery. She did not think he would turn her over to King Henry's minions. At least, she could trust the unswerving loyalty of the Cavendishes to her family.

It was a strange experience to name aloud her true father and mother. She herself scarcely had time to assimilate all that the Bramptons had told her before their hasty departure from their shop in Micklegate. She still could not quite believe that she had come from such an ancient, highborn line. She held her silence, and wondered what Thomas would do.

When she finished her story, he stared at her, while his eyes turned bluer by the second. Then, massaging his temples, he paced the floor before the fireplace. In such a small chamber, he crossed the width in four of his long strides.

As the silence lengthened, Alicia steeled herself for his repudiation. What man, newly come into his title and estate, would gamble everything, including his own life, for a tall, willowy girl whom he barely knew? Considering her situation from Thomas's point of view, she concluded that her hopes for lifelong protection hung by a very slender thread. That she had grown fond of him during her brief time at Wolf Hall was beside the point.

Thomas halted, pried the dagger out of the desktop, then studied the weapon with deep concentration.

Watching him, an icy fear twisted around Alicia's heart. *Sweet Jesu, he is going to kill me!* That dreadful solution had never occurred to her before now. She pressed herself against the back of the chair. An unfamiliar panic welled up in her throat. He could dispatch her as easily as paring an apple, then toss her remains into the river that flowed past the castle's walls. If anyone should find her body downstream, no one would know who she was, or who had killed her. Considering how plainly she was dressed, no one would even care.

He stood before her, balancing the knife in his hand. The rays of the afternoon sun glinted along its sharp blade. His massive shoulders stretched the black velvet doublet he wore until the seams looked as if they would burst. The expression in his eyes was unfathomable. His steady gaze impaled her. She clutched the chair's arms until her knuckles stood out white under her skin. She wanted to ask him to at least give her a decent Christian burial, but her words solidified in her throat. In this final moment of her life, she marveled how handsome her murderer looked.

Without a flicker of an eyelash to give her warning, Thomas dropped to one knee before her. Alicia froze, benumbed in body and soul. Bowing his head, he lifted her dusty hem to his lips, and kissed it with a deep reverence. She lowered her gaze, totally bewildered by his startling behavior. The beating of her heart throbbed in her ears.

Then he raised his eyes to her. His expression was as soft as a caress. "I am a man of few words, sweet lady." His deep melodious voice trembled with barely checked passion. "When we quit this chamber, neither of us will ever speak of what happened here so long as we live."

"Thomas, I—" she began, but he shook his head.

"Prithee, allow me to continue while the words are still fresh on my tongue." He cleared his throat. "In this private place and for this moment only, I will call you princess, for you are royal indeed."

Alicia refused to accept the significance of his words. She glanced at the hard calluses of her work-worn hands. "Oh, no, Thomas, not that. I am only a…a bastard." She flinched inwardly as she said the degrading term.

His free hand cupped her face, and held it gently, while the beginning of a smile tipped the corners of his mouth. His touch was almost unbearable in its tenderness. Her skin tingled.

"You are indeed your royal father's daughter, and well named."

She blinked in surprise. "How so?"

He grinned. "Broom. 'Tis the name of a little yellow field flower."

She shrugged. "Aye, common enough."

"Nay, not common at all. The French call it plantagenet. In truth, you have always borne your father's name," he told her in a tone of respect. "And you are like him. You need only to look into the glass to see the resemblance."

Alicia's mouth went dry. She found herself extremely

aware of Thomas's virile appeal. She moistened her lips with the tip of her tongue. "I never saw my reflection until I came to Wolf Hall. I am still not used to the experience."

With infinite tenderness, his finger traced the line of her cheekbone and jaw. "Then let me be your mirror, my princess." A strange, faintly eager look flashed in his eyes. "Your hair is the same red-gold color as the king's, and your eyes are the Plantagenet blue. You are tall and graceful, as I have been told your father was. You know that the Plantagenets are known for their height."

"Aye," she whispered. She quivered under his gentle stroking.

"You have his cheekbones, his nose..." Thomas hesitated, then placed his finger to her lips. "Your mouth is the image of the king's. 'Twas made for laughter and merriment."

His touch upset her balance. A rush of heat flooded her cheeks. "You...you are kind to say so, Thomas." A strange inner excitement filled her.

His expression stilled, and grew more serious. "I am deeply privileged that your guardian entrusted your person to my care." He held the dagger aloft by the blade. The sunlight cast the shadow of a cross on the white wall opposite them. "I hereby vow upon my honor as a knight, and upon the cross of our Redeemer, to uphold this trust so given to me."

She felt a warm glow of joy flow through her. Now he would tell her that he loved her. His touch, his voice and the gleam in his eyes sent shivers of delight through her. She waited with happy expectation for the words of his love to tumble from his lips.

He sheathed his weapon, then he took her hands, and

placed his large ones within the cup of hers in the ancient act of allegiance. The fire from his brilliant blue eyes pierced the distance between them.

"Know this of me, Alicia Plantagenet, that I, Thomas Martin Cavendish, ninth Earl of Thornbury, do swear to become your liege man of life and limb and of earthly worship, and, with the faith and truth that I will bear unto you, to live and die against all manner of folks that threaten you." Then he bowed his head, and sealed his vow with a kiss on her palm.

The warm brush of his lips against her skin set her blood on fire. Alicia was very thankful that she was seated, for her legs had grown uncommonly weak. A soft gasp escaped her, causing him to look up at her. The intensity of his expression shocked her. It made her nervous to have this powerful man on his knees before her. How did one answer to such a solemn oath? Nothing that Edward or Katherine had taught her prepared her for anything like this moment.

She cleared her throat, pretending not to be deeply moved. "My thanks, Thomas," she murmured, hoping that her voice did not reflect the surging tide of her feelings. "Please stand, I pray you. I am not used to such formality."

He rose in a single fluid motion. Taking her by the elbow with surprising gentleness, he raised her up from the chair. A muscle quivered in his jaw. Nervously Alicia again licked her dry lips. He was so close, she could feel the heat from his body. His steady gaze bore her into silent expectation. A nameless desire consumed her. Her pulse quickened at the anticipation of his next move. The very air in the chamber seemed to crackle like a fire leaping in the grate.

Without uttering a word, Thomas gathered her into

his arms. He clasped her body tightly against his. She inhaled sharply at the contact, intoxicated by his warm, manly scent. She felt her blood coursing through her veins like a flooding mountain brook in springtime. His broad shoulders heaved as if he had just run a footrace. His hard-muscled thigh brushed against her hip, sending a thousand sparks dancing up her leg. The touch of his hands on her spine, firm and persuasive, invited more intimacy. Abandoning her shyness, she wound her arms around his neck, and locked herself within his embrace.

"Alicia." He murmured her name like a prayer. His warm breath fanned her face.

Her thoughts spun.

She felt herself weaken as his lips slowly descended to meet hers. Parting her lips, she raised herself to meet his kiss. He brushed hers, then gently covered her mouth. His featherlike touch was a delicious sensation she had never before experienced. He kissed her with a slow thoughtfulness. His tongue traced the outline of her lips before venturing inside. She melted in his embrace, and returned his kiss. Her eager response momentarily shocked her. His tongue sent shivers of intense pleasure racing through her. He tasted as warm and sweet as summer wine.

She moaned in the depths of her throat.

Raising his mouth from hers, Thomas gazed into her eyes. Cobalt fire leapt within the depths of his. She panted lightly between her parted lips, silently pleading for his return. His mouth again took hers with a new hunger. She answered his deeper kiss with a passion that belied her calm exterior. His ardor transported her to a soaring mountaintop. His kiss sang in her veins.

The dogs, who had been very quiet since Isabel's departure, now barked and leapt about. Taverstock dropped to his forepaws, and stuck his backside into the air, uttering a series of commanding barks. Vixen added an unexpected yip or two, as she circled the entwined couple.

With a sigh of resignation, Thomas dropped his arms, and stepped back. "Be still!" he ordered his furry chaperons.

Georgie and Vixen obeyed him at once. Tavie continued to protest his displeasure with growls low in his throat.

"Your pardon, sweet lady," he mumbled, not looking at her. "My dogs think you are attacking me. I need to school them better in their manners." He glanced down at the bulge that was clearly outlined by his black knit hose. His face turned red. Clearing his throat, he swept up the terrier into his arms. "By your leave, I will remove them hence, and take them for a long walk in the forest. They...um...need the exercise."

He picked up the king's brooch from the desk, and placed it in Alicia's hand. "Wear that at our wedding on the day after tomorrow. 'Tis fitting that you keep it."

Grasping the struggling Tavie in a tight hold, he leaned over and brushed a final, gentle kiss across her forehead. His lips touched her skin like a whispered promise.

Taverstock barked with renewed indignation.

Thomas rapped him on the nose with his finger. "Enough, you loudmouthed knave. You offend my lady's ears with your noise." He snapped his fingers again. "Come, you two, let us be gone."

Georgie and Vixen trotted out into the hallway ahead of him. In the doorway, he executed a court bow without dropping the protesting terrier.

"My princess," Thomas addressed her. "Now and forever more." Without waiting for her response, he closed the door behind them.

Alicia heard his footfalls receding down the corridor. She collapsed into the chair, and sat quietly while she waited for her heartbeat to slow to its normal rhythm. Tracing her swollen lips with her finger, she relived the velvet warmth of his kiss. A sweet sense of well-being enveloped her. He had accepted her, even with the danger of her Plantagenet blood. He had sent Isabel away, not her. Two days from now he would marry her.

And yet...

A niggling worry wormed its way into the pleasurable contemplation of her wedding day. Alicia had been surprised—overwhelmed—by Thomas's dramatic acceptance of her lineage. He had called her a princess in tones usually heard before the high altar during the mass. His kiss, so unexpected yet so desirable, indicated that he was a man full of passion. She furrowed her brows together, and wondered if that passion was for the House of York, whom she represented, or his ardor was for her, that noble family's lowliest member. He had extolled the virtues of honor and duty—but not of love.

She touched her sleeve, and recalled the scraps of the latest love letter hidden there. She fished out the little bundle, then smoothed each of the tattered pieces of paper. She fitted the bits together until the complete message lay on the desk. Rereading the loving words, she drank in their meaning. Then she studied the handwriting with its large loops and bold dashes. Truly they were the same as she had seen him write earlier this afternoon, yet the man and the message did not fit together.

Cease your woolgathering! Take what has been offered, and pray 'tis true. Her tongue touched her lips, still warm and moist from Thomas's kiss. She squeezed her eyes shut. Startled by a sudden truth that flashed through her mind, a tiny gasp escaped her lips.

I love him!

The admission sprang from a hidden place beyond all her common sense. Its verity shook her to her very core. Moreover, she realized that she desperately wanted him to love her in return. She swept up the slips of paper, and returned them to the protection of her handkerchief. She would make a paste of flour and water, and bind the pieces together again.

Alicia rose, and stretched. Though she had not done any physical exercise for the past hour or two, her limbs felt as heavy as if she had washed and wrung dry the castle's entire inventory of bed linens. She needed activity at once. The kitchen would have started its preparations for the evening's supper by now.

Opening the library door, she breathed in the coolness of the passageway. She felt her flushed cheeks with the back of her hand. It had been close in that little chamber. Or was it Thomas's kisses that had made her feel so warm? She tossed her braid over her shoulder. Of course not! 'Twas the strain of telling her secret, nothing more. She closed the door. The latch clicked into place.

The usual noise and bustle in the large kitchens stilled when Alicia came down the steps. The assembled spit boys, scullery maids and assistant cooks stared at her with expressions that ran the gamut between surprise and awe. Even Master Konrad regarded her with a new look of respect in his eyes. No one said a word, nor coughed, nor even shuffled their feet. She swallowed back her unease, though she held her head high. She fought the urge to flee to the sanctuary of her overly splendid chamber.

The cook took a deep breath. "Good afternoon, my lady," he intoned, touching his fingers to his forehead. "We did not expect to see you down here again, now that you are to wed my lord."

She smiled, and prayed that her trembling lips did not reveal how frightened she suddenly was at the prospect of becoming the chatelaine of Wolf Hall. "Why would I not come? My…mother taught me that a good housewife knows every inch of her kitchen, and what goes on there. We worked well together yesterday. Why not now?" She laughed lightly, though her heart banged against her rib cage. "And I am not yet a lady until Sir Thomas marries me. Now, good Master Konrad, I am in urgent need of some flour and water, for I have torn a paper of my lord's by mistake, and must mend it."

A wide grin split the cook's face. "'Tis a pleasure to have you here, my…that is, Mistress Alicia. You know where the flour is kept. I will clear a spot on the cutting board for your work." Then he turned upon the rest of the servants. "What ho, you gaping rascals? Back to your duties, and be quick about it." He shot them a fierce glare.

The usual hum of activity stirred again in the kitchen. Alicia sighed with relief as she lifted down the heavy flour crock from the pantry shelf. She poured a small amount into a bowl, then added some water from the bucket by the drain board. Using a whisk made of peeled twigs, she mixed the paste until she was satisfied with its consistency. She cut a piece of kitchen parchment approximately the size and shape of her note, then she positioned the scraps on the table beside her. Settling herself on a tall stool, Alicia bent over her work. She hoped that none of the curious servants could read.

Despite Master Konrad's prodding, most of the boys and maids managed to wander by Alicia to look over her shoulder. She pretended not to notice their open interest. If she made light of the ticklish task, she hoped they would grow tired of watching her.

She smeared the paste on the back of the first scrap— the top left-hand corner—then positioned it on the parchment. Next she added the neighboring bit, making sure to align the loops and dashes together into a seamless whole. Most of the servants grew bored with the tedious process, and meandered away until only Audrey remained. Alicia glanced at the maid out of the corner of her eye.

"Do you know your letters?" she asked, hiding her dread behind a cheerful smile.

Audrey shrugged. "One or two, but not when they are all run together like this." She squinted at the half-finished letter. "Are you certain sure that this paper was writ by Sir Thomas?"

Alicia shifted uneasily on her stool. "What do you mean?" she asked with a bantering tone. "Who else would make such large, strong letters?"

"Master Andrew," the girl replied at once.

Alicia's former misgivings increased a hundredfold. Her hands grew cold. She feigned a complacency that she did not feel. "Aye? How could that be?"

The maid scratched the tip of her nose. "Sir Thomas schooled his squire in his letters. I remember it well because Master Andrew protested that he had already learned a fine hand from the Duke of Buckingham. 'Twas no matter. My lord told him to start again."

The nagging suspicions in the back of Alicia's mind

refused to be still. She wiped her fingers on her apron, then gave her full attention to Audrey. "Why would Sir Thomas wish that his squire should copy his hand?"

The maid shrugged. "I do not know, Mistress, but Andrew once bragged to me that he could now imitate my lord's script so well that he could pen a letter to the sheriff of Northumberland, and that worthy man would be none the wiser."

Alicia felt a heavy weight drop onto her shoulders. She stared at the partial note. Its sugared sentiments mocked her in its swirling loops and elongated dashes— just like Thomas's. Under the table her hands shook. She clutched them together. Her initial suspicions had been correct. Andrew *was* the true author, either to tease Alicia, or to fulfill his own lusty desires.

Her lighthearted gaiety veered abruptly to hot anger. She couldn't wait to get a hold of that stripling. She would box Andrew's ears so soundly, he would hear ringing bells for a week. She slid off the stool, then gathered her half-finished work in her paste-crusted hands.

"My thanks to you, Audrey. You have been most enlightening. Pray excuse me, I have a headache."

Biting her tongue to keep from blurting out her true emotions, she fled the kitchens. She did not draw a deep breath until she was safe behind the door of her chamber. She glared at the pulpy mess she clutched. How could she have possibly thought that Thomas had written these beautiful lines to her? Until a short hour ago, he had thought of her only as the goldsmith's daughter. A hot tear of humiliation trickled down her burning cheek.

Alicia crossed the room, and pulled back the tapestry that concealed the narrow garderobe. With a bitter sob of dejection, she dropped the partially-mended note down the noisome privy shaft. The rest of the missive fluttered after it. Then she rinsed her hands in the basin, and threw herself across the wide luxurious bed. She sank into the down mattress, without noticing its comfort.

In two days, I will be Thomas's wife—honored, respected, but never, ever loved!

For the first time since she had come to Wolf Hall, Alicia allowed herself the release of a good cry. Afterward, she fell into an exhausted sleep, and completely missed supper.

She awoke in a night-filled chamber with a number of firm resolves etched in her mind. She would be the perfect mistress of Wolf Hall, and bear Thomas whatever children God would send them. She would treat her husband with all the dignity and honor that befitted the Earl of Thornbury. She would be grateful for the protection of his name, and the loyalty that he had pledged to her Plantagenet family.

But she would never be silly enough to allow Thomas to touch her heart again.

Chapter Twelve

Thomas immersed himself in a frenzy of preparations for his nuptials. That way, he didn't have time to contemplate the new life that lay after the wedding day. The prospect terrified him.

He cornered the castle chaplain, told him that he would marry Alicia at eight o'clock in the morning the day after tomorrow. He brushed aside the reedy priest's stuttered objections to the hasty ceremony.

"Proclaim the banns at the three masses tomorrow." With that, the young Earl of Thornbury left his confessor gasping in his wake.

He ordered Stokes to send messengers with invitations to the neighboring nobility—even to his near neighbor and frequent enemy, Sir Roger Ormond of Snape Castle. At least, there would be one day Ormond could not poach Cavendish game.

Thomas plunged the kitchens, buttery and scullery into total chaos by demanding a large wedding breakfast prepared for all the tenants, villagers and guests. Master Konrad mopped his broad brow when he scanned the menu prepared by the bridegroom.

"Sturgeon, my lord?" The cook frowned. "I do not know if I can procure such a rare fish in time."

Thomas turned on his heel. "Send a boy to York within the hour," he advised over his shoulder.

By the time he sat down at the high table for supper, he had used up much of his excess energy. He felt fatigued, and longed for hours of blessed sleep, when he could block out the frightening event-to-come. When Alicia did not appear at the meal, Thomas cursed his clumsiness. One of the maids reported that the lady had retired to her chamber pleading a headache, but he knew the true cause of her distress.

He had frightened her this afternoon with his heavy-handed, bumbling attempt at lovemaking. Never before had he allowed himself to lose control as he had done in the library. The depth of their kiss had shocked him as much as it did Alicia. The extreme pleasure of touching his betrothed and tasting her sweet mouth had completely overwhelmed him, making him forget his vow to treat her with the highest respect. He trembled inwardly when he relived that disgraceful scene in his mind. In his heart, Thomas knew that if Tavie had not interrupted them, he would have taken Alicia's virginity on top of the desk—mounting her like an animal. No wonder the poor girl had trembled in his arms! He must have terrified her with his blind lust. A true knight did not ravish a princess.

After supper, he gave into Mary's pleadings and played a drawn-out game of chess, but his mind could not focus on the queens and rooks. Instead he thought of his own beautiful princess hiding in her chamber. He thought of her cheeks, soft as a downy chick. She fit so well within his arms—as if she had been created especially for him. He recalled the enticing curves of her body, especially when he had placed his hand against the small of her back, and pressed her against himself....

His manroot stirred, then grew stiff at the memory. He shifted in his chair, crossed and recrossed his long legs in an effort to ease the ache between them.

"Have you got fleas, Tom?" Mary asked, sweeping her bishop into an offensive position.

He blinked. "Go to, imp! Neither my dogs nor I have the vermin. Ouch! Where did that bishop of York come from?"

His sister giggled. "You were not paying attention. Shame on you! 'Tis fleas, I warrant, no matter what you say. You are wriggling more than Tavie when he wants a bone."

Thomas crossed his legs for a third time, then mopped the perspiration from his brow. Warm for this late in the season, especially here in the cold north. He wet his lips—and tasted Alicia's honey mouth once again in his imagination. The troublesome ache increased.

"Mayhap you have bridegroom jitters," his little sister observed as she waited for his next move. "You have been quiet since supper, and itchy as a bed of nettles. Hoy day! *Now* I know what I shall give you for a wedding present."

Her brother shot her a stern look. "*Not* a bed full of nettles, you little gadfly, or I will apply them to your backside."

Mary wrinkled her nose. "You would not dare. Besides, you would have to catch me first, and methinks you will be busy elsewhere."

The picture of Alicia lying naked in his huge bed flashed across his mind. He could practically touch her lush breasts with her pink nipples rising to meet his fingers. He mopped his brow with his sleeve. He desperately desired to take a long walk. He moved his king into an absurd position.

Like a duck capturing a water bug, Mary attacked his castle with her queen. "Check, Tom! Try to escape my clutches now."

He imagined Alicia's delicate hands, stroking his bare chest. Her long supple fingers coaxing his— He moved an inoffensive pawn in a haphazard fashion. He had a pressing need for some vigorous exercise.

"Checkmate!" Mary surrounded his king with her queen, bishop and knight. "I have won, and you owe me—"

Thomas stood up so quickly that he nearly upset the board. "I will pay your forfeit, whatever it is, but not now." He snapped his fingers to the dogs. "Come, gentlemen and lady. You need a run. Andrew!" he shouted across the hall.

His squire looked up from his game of dice with Stokes and the chaplain. "My lord?"

"Stir your stumps, knave. Saddle our horses!"

Andrew gaped at his master. The boy looked like a fashionably dressed trout. "Now, my lord? The moon has already risen."

Thomas strode across the flagstones of the hall toward his squire. "Good! Then we will be able to see where we are going."

Not waiting to hear his squire's further protests, he hurried out to the courtyard. As he pulled on his leather gloves, he inhaled the cool night air. A faint scent of woodsmoke and hay tickled his nostrils. The harvest hinted its arrival. He tried to remember what he had been doing last year at this time, but all he could think about was what he was going to be doing two nights hence.

Much to Andrew's vocal disgust, Thomas rode them hard over the heather-tipped moor. The moon was high overhead by the time the exhausted horses, dogs and men returned to Wolf Hall. Thomas fell into bed. Surrounded by his beloved dogs, he fell instantly asleep with his boots still on his feet.

The next morning, he roused his squire, huntsmen and grooms for a hunt to provide game for the feast. He urged Silver Charm to a full gallop in his effort to escape the black fear that loomed larger as each brief hour slipped by. He did not see his bride until they met at supper. In less than a day, she would share this meal—and his bed—as his wife. The expectation of his husbandly duties turned his stomach into a lump of ice. He sent a silent prayer of thanksgiving that Isabel had chosen to take her supper in her chambers. One less woman to torment him.

Alicia watched him push his pigeon pie around their trencher with his eating knife. "The food does not please you, my lord?" she asked.

"'Tis good," he muttered, not daring to look at her. Every time he did, her beauty took his breath away.

She cocked an eyebrow. "I am sure that Georgie agrees with you since he has gobbled down most of yours. I am glad to see that my recipe finds favor with *someone* in this household."

Thomas stabbed a large chunk of the pastry, then shoved the whole thing into his mouth. "Good." He spoke through the crumbs, though he could barely taste the juicy morsel.

She inclined her head in a regal manner. "My thanks for your compliment, my lord."

He waited to hear her laugh as she had often done in the past, but instead, she turned away from him, and engaged Mary in a conversation concerning ribbons and lace. I repulse her, he thought. He had trouble swallowing the meat, and drank a deep draught of wine to ease the food on its downward path.

"Wine, sweet lady?" he asked, offering the goblet to her.

She started to reach for it, then dropped her hand to her lap. "Nay. I thank you." She did not look at him, but stared at some distant part of the hall.

Thomas ground his teeth. How could he have let himself attack her like that? More to the point, how could he make amends for his beastly behavior?

After supper, he suggested a stroll around the garden where he planned to beg her forgiveness.

Her lips trembled, then she shook her head. "Nay, my lord. I am quite weary from the wedding preparations. By your leave, I will go to bed now, so to be fresh for...for the ceremony in the m-morning."

Without waiting for his permission, she dropped him a formal curtsy, then all but fled his presence. He stared after her, missing the sunny smiles and gentle teasing that she had favored him with in the days gone by. He strode out of the hall, followed by the dogs.

Andrew tagged behind him. "My lord? Pray, a word with you." He broke into a run to keep up with his master.

Thomas did not slacken his pace. "What now, clodpate?" he said out of the side of his mouth.

The squire circled around him, blocking his way. "Methinks you are in sore need of some wise counsel."

Halting, he curled his lip. "I presume you mean from yourself, jackanapes."

The boy grinned. "I am at your service, my lord."

Thomas pointed to the garden door. "Out there, before you utter one more word." He had a very good idea of the nature of Andrew's advice, and he did not want the whole population of the castle to overhear it.

The youth darted ahead of his master and undid the latch. When the squire opened the door, the terrier dashed out first, running down the path to the stone bench in the far arbor. Vixen followed at a more sedate pace. Thomas studied her thick middle. He calculated that the pups would come any day now. He closed his eyes. Not tomorrow, he prayed.

Then he glowered at Andrew. "Well?"

Far from being cowed by his master's look, the stripling grinned at him. "What finery do you intend to wear for the ceremony?"

Thomas blinked. In all the activity of the past two days, he had given no thought to his clothes. He rarely did. "I have no need of frippery. I am still in mourning for my father and brothers."

Andrew shook his head. "Nay, 'twill never do. You have asked all the shire to attend your wedding, you must shine like the morning sun."

He bared his teeth. "I am no peacock like you. Feathers and furs look better on their proper owners."

His squire ignored his master's pointed remark. "Methinks your red satin surcoat will fit the occasion. We can add a gold chain or two, as well as your cream silk shirt, and the red and gold cape with the high-standing collar."

Thomas stared at Andrew as if the lad had grown a set of horns through his gray velvet bonnet. "Crows

and daws, boy, I am not entertaining royalty—" He
stopped abruptly, when he realized that he was about to
do exactly that. Not only would royalty be present tomorrow, but he was marrying her. Thomas coughed.
"Very well, the red it is, but I will still wear the black
armband."

Andrew's brown eyes widened with surprise. The expression on his face gave Thomas a measure of satisfaction. The boy was getting much too full of himself
these days. He needed to be overbalanced on occasion.

"You will cut the finest figure there, my lord," he
said.

Thomas sighed. "Nay, I will be but a shadow to my
lady wife."

Unfortunately, the squire's sharp hearing caught what
he had said. "Aye, speaking of Mistress Alicia—" he
began.

Thomas turned so that he towered over his slim
squire. "If you speak of my lady, mind your rattling
tongue, knave."

Andrew swallowed, and took a step backward. A
white rosebush with especially long thorns snagged his
thin woolen tights. He cursed under his breath as he
disentangled himself. "I speak with all due respect, my
lord. After all, the lady will become my mistress tomorrow."

Thomas ground his teeth. "Aye, that she will." Even
though the evening was warm, his hands grew cold.

The youth gave his master a shrewd look. "And she
will become your bedfellow tomorrow night. Have you
given much thought to *that?*"

He was tempted to tell the little maltworm to mind
his own business, but prudence stopped him. His squire
had often boasted of his own wide experience in the

matters of bedsport. Perhaps the boy could be of some help. At any rate, it was no use to pretend that the idea of making love did not scare the wits out of Thomas. Andrew read his master like a book.

He allowed his shoulders to slump. "Aye, I have thought of it. Indeed, it plagues me hourly."

Andrew nodded. "So I suspected. Do you know if Mistress Alicia is a virgin?"

He nearly struck the insolent pup. "Of course she is!"

The squire held up his hands, palms out. "I crave your pardon, my lord. 'Twas a base question from a twittering fool."

"Humph."

"My point is that she will be frightened. More than yourself."

Thomas flashed him an evil glare.

Unperturbed, Andrew warmed to his topic. "Take heart. She probably thinks you have plucked many a young flower in your time."

Thomas made a fist. "Take heed, boy, lest you burn yourself by your heat."

Andrew sat on the bench. Tavie leapt up into his lap, and curled himself into a fur ball. The boy rubbed the dog behind his ears. Tavie closed his eyes with contentment. "Your lady will expect you to lead her down the pathways of love."

Thomas sank down beside his squire. He hung his head. "Aye, you have hit the nut and core of my problem."

"At least Mistress Alicia likes you. 'Tis one point in your favor."

Thomas recalled her coolness at supper. The memory

of his lustful groping in the library sickened him. She might have liked him—at first, but not now. "Go on."

"Do you love her?"

Thomas snapped his head up. The boy had voiced the truth that had kept Thomas wakeful night after night since Alicia's arrival. He licked his cracked lips. His hands began to sweat.

Andrew cocked his head. "I perceive that you do. You must win her heart, as well as her hand. Then you will have a marriage made in heaven."

Thomas sighed down to his toes. Had he already lost his chance with Alicia? "Tell me how, soothsayer."

The squire leaned closer to his master. "Take her gently. Do not rush things."

He digested this piece of wisdom, and tried to understand it. "Explain!"

Andrew reddened about the ears. "You will be tempted to take her the moment you are alone together."

Thomas stared openmouthed at him.

The boy cocked an eyebrow. "Tell me that you have not imagined what she looks like without her shift on."

Thomas recalled his conduct in the library, and how close he had come to doing just that. "Aye, I confess that I have. 'Tis a base instinct, and not respectful of a virtuous lady."

Andrew puffed out his cheeks before replying. "Do not berate yourself. 'Tis a natural thing for a man to do. But, my lord, you cannot tear her clothes off of her immediately."

"I had not planned to do so," Thomas remarked. He tried not to think of Alicia, standing naked amid the tatters of her gown.

The squire chuckled softly. "A great many things

happen in bed that you may not plan. But more to the point, you must be gentle, unhurried and, most particularly, very understanding when she cries.''

Thomas clenched his jaw. "I will not do anything to make her cry. Do you think I am a hard-hearted villain?''

Andrew gazed up at the gathering twilight before he answered. "Mark me, my lord. Your lady will cry—at least, a little bit. After all, you will pierce her maidenhead with your shaft, and I understand that it hurts. Expect a few tears and some blood.''

Thomas shuddered at the thought of spilling sweet Alicia's blood. "Then I will not do it.''

Andrew placed his hand on his master's shoulder. "You must. 'Tis your duty, and your right, as her husband. Be of good cheer. 'Twill be over in the twink of an eye. If you are gentle and loving, she will forget all about it before morning.''

He stood up. "You have given me much cold comfort, squire.''

Andrew merely laughed at his rebuke. "Treat your wife with all your love, my lord, and the rest will fall into place. You will see anon.''

His master grimaced. "I feel like I am going into battle with one arm tied behind my back—and naked to boot.''

The scamp's eyes twinkled. "Start with naked, my lord.''

The night watchman on the battlements called the hour of two in the morning. Thomas lay on his back, and stared at the dark canopy overhead. He had not slept a wink since he had blown out the candle four hours ago. With a sigh of resignation, he pulled himself into a sitting position and rested his back against the carved headboard. Tavie and Vixen inched closer to him, one on each side. At the foot of the bed, Georgie slept, undisturbed by his master's anxiety.

Thomas stroked Vixen. "'Tis a rough night. Alicia will be as close to me as you are now. And she will expect me to perform my duty toward her." He ran his fingers through his tangled hair. "God shield me! How can I do *that* to her, and not hurt her?"

Vixen thumped her tail against the coverlet several times, then licked his hand. He smiled down at her. "You have been my only lady until now, Vixen. What do I know of women? Isabel?" He grimaced. "Lewd minx! She cannot claim one womanly virtue as her own. And Mary? My little sister is as sweet as springtime, as light as a breeze—and will drive her husband to drinking strong ale within an hour of their wedding. On the other hand, Alicia is like one of God's own blessed angels." He stared at the dagger that lay on his chest. The moonlight made the jewels on the handle glow with an unearthly fire. "She faces the world with nothing but her own courage as her shield. Her royal father led his army into battle at the age of eighteen. By my troth, I believe that Alicia could do the same. She is a woman without peer. Aye, there's the rub! How can I make a worthy husband for such a great lady? Do I dare profane a princess with my body's lustful desires?"

He held his head in his hands. "God save me, but I do ache for her!"

Bored with the subject, Tavie went back to sleep. Vixen followed suit. Surrounded by his snoring friends, Thomas watched the moon's light creep across the floor, until it faded away hours later in the pearl gray dawn.

He had still not resolved his dilemma when Andrew came to dress him for his wedding.

The squire grinned as he shook out the red surcoat. ''I see that you spent last night in prayerful contemplation of your nuptial day, my lord.'' He lowered his voice. ''Your eyes are bloodshot.''

Chapter Thirteen

Alicia did not expect to fall asleep on the eve of her
wedding, but sometime after the midwatch she did. The
muffled sounds of horses stomping on the cobbles, and
their drivers swearing woke her in the predawn. Rubbing the sleep from her eyes, she got out of her great
bed, and padded over to the window. At first she
thought that the noise must be some of the guests, who
had arrived very early for the festivities. Then she heard
Isabel's shrill voice above the general din.

"Take care, you shambling bear! 'Tis a piece of Venetian glass that you carry—not a load of firewood."

Alicia peeked out the window. Several of the castle's
lackeys loaded a large wagon with boxes, trunks and
even some pieces of furniture. Standing on the bottom
step of the entranceway, Meg held aloft a lighted torch.
Beside her, Isabel alternately chided and cajoled the
men as they carried her enormous amount of baggage
out of Wolf Hall.

I wonder if Thomas knows what she is taking. Alicia
decided not to worry if a few pieces of the silver turned
up missing. What did a cup or a spoon matter if it meant
that she would never see Thomas's sister-in-law again?

"Make haste! You are nothing but slugs and worms! I wish to be gone before daylight."

Alicia breathed a sigh of relief. Thank heavens Isabel did not intend to stay for the wedding. The ceremony would be trying enough without her angry face and wasp's tongue to curdle the festivities. Over the rim of the horizon, the sun's rays painted the sky with a wash of pink and peach colors. Not a cloud in sight. It would be a beautiful morning to start a marriage.

Sounds of heightened activity in the hallway seeped under the bedchamber door, scattering Alicia's serenity. When someone knocked, she clutched her nightshift tighter around her body. It couldn't already be time to dress?

"Come in!" Her voice caught in her throat.

Wreathed in smiles, Audrey stepped inside. "God give you a blessed morning, mistress. I have brought your bath."

Alicia blinked with surprise. She did not recall asking for a bath, and certainly not one this early in the morning before the day's work had begun.

The maid giggled. "Did you forget 'tis your wedding day?"

Alicia shook her head. "Nay, 'tis been on my mind all night, but—" Then she remembered that Katherine had explained the ritual bath to her. She blushed. The maid must think that she was reared by gypsies. "Your pardon, good Audrey. My mind has gone quite giddy this morning."

The girl giggled again as she opened the door wider. In the hall, Alicia saw Stokes at the head of a long procession of maids and men from the kitchens. Each one bore two steaming pails of water. Stokes himself staggered in with a large wooden tub.

Alicia grabbed her night robe, and held it in front of her as the servants invaded her chambers. The steward put the tub before the fireplace, then he knelt to stir up the embers, and to add fresh wood to the new flames.

"Stokes?"

He looked over his shoulder at her with a friendly grin. "Aye, Mistress Alicia?"

"Methinks the tub is wet."

Still smiling, he nodded. "My lord just finished with it."

"Oh."

Alicia turned away so that the steward would not see her blush. Through the curtain of her unbound hair, she watched the servants slosh the bathwater into the tub. *How on earth had Thomas fit into such a small container?* She pictured him wedged in it, with his knees almost touching his chin. She imagined the water flowing down his broad shoulders, and across the wide expanse of his chest—his *naked* shoulders and chest.

Wanton! she scolded herself. *He will behave in a proper manner toward you—no more, no less. He will give you his body, as Katherine had described the marriage act, but he will not give you his heart.*

Alicia shook herself. She would make the best of it, and be grateful. In a few hours Sir Thomas Cavendish would marry her as his father had promised her guardian many years ago. What more could she expect?

Once the tub had been filled to almost overflowing, Audrey shooed everyone out of the chamber, then shut the door behind the last grinning pot boy. She turned to Alicia. "Now, Mistress, jump in quick afore it turns cold."

Alicia slipped out of her shift, then stepped into the warm water. Closing her eyes, she gave herself over to the pleasure of having her back scrubbed by the enthusiastic maid.

Without the preamble of a knock, the door opened again, and Mary skipped inside. She carried a wealth of flowers and greenery in her arms.

"Good day! Good day!" The girl danced about the chamber like a fairy sprite. "'Tis the best day in all the year!"

Alicia could not help smiling at the child's infectious spirits. "How now, morning lark? You have been gamboling in the gardens, I see. Take care your governess does not spy the mud on your hem."

"Pooh!" Mary dismissed the threat of Mistress Vive's ire with a roll of her eyes. She spread her floral gleanings across the window seat. "I have brought you roses for your bridal wreath, and more for you to carry." She sniffed a branch of an herb before holding it up for approval. "See? Here is a sprig of rosemary for you to wear."

Alicia tried to remember if her foster mother had mentioned rosemary as part of the nuptials.

Catching her puzzled expression, Mary laughed. "Ha! Have I cudgeled your brain? No matter! Rosemary is for remembrance. We will tie it on your sleeve, so that you will remember the joy of your girlhood home, and will bring that joy here to Wolf Hall." She grew a little wistful. "We need joy around our hearth, Alicia, and I cannot fashion it all by myself. I am so glad you will soon be my new sister." She gave Alicia a quick hug, then laughed as she flicked away the clinging soapsuds.

A small lump formed in Alicia's throat when she remembered the Bramptons. She wished they could be here with her. She owed them more than she could ever repay. "I will bring joy into this house, Mary. 'Tis my most solemn vow."

The girl pranced about the tub, nearly slipping in the puddles that dotted the floor. "You cannot be solemn on this day, Alicia. 'Tis all gladness and frolic—and food! Mmm! I passed by the kitchens on my way from the gardens." Her voice sank into an excited whisper. "Did you know that there are gingerbread and sugared almonds? Oh, joy and rapture!"

The news took Alicia by surprise. "We had no almonds two days ago."

The girl tossed one of the pillows up in the air, then caught it on the way down. "Tom sent one of the lads to York with a shopping list as long as your arm. We *never* have gingerbread except on Twelfth Night. Huzzah! Three cheers for good old Tom!"

Audrey poured rinse water over Alicia's long hair. "'Tis true, mistress. My lord has ordered up a feast fit for a king. You have ne're seen the like before."

Alicia's heart rose within her breast like a bubble. Quelling her excitement, she told herself that the lavish preparations were not for her, but for Thomas's noble guests. "I am glad. 'Tis proper for the Earl of Thornbury to offer his friends the best he can afford."

Mary paused in midcaper. "Tom does not care a pin what our neighbors think. In fact, they consider him muddled in his head, and have only come to his wedding out of idle curiosity. You silly goose! Tom has done it all for *you!*"

She wanted to believe the child's words. Despite her best intentions to protect her heart, she still craved his love. She opened her mouth to object, but Audrey dropped a thick piece of toweling over her head, and began to rub her hair with great vigor.

*Take what is offered, and do not look behind the gift.
You will be happier that way.*

The trumpets on the battlements above the courtyard blew cheerful notes, announcing the wedding procession. In her chamber, Alicia fidgeted under Audrey's and Mary's last-minute adjustments. Her blue brocade gown shimmered and crinkled with the newness of the material. Katherine had made it in the spring for Alicia, not suspecting that it would be first worn on her fosterling's wedding day. While they had sewed the tiny seed pearls on the long, pointed sleeves, Katherine had instructed Alicia in all her wifely duties, beginning in the bedroom. The physical activities sounded indecent. Alicia pushed them out of her mind. She would think about them later, when she could not avoid it.

She smoothed her hand over the bodice, then remembered what she had planned to wear there. Alicia went to the bed, fumbled under the mattress, and drew out the blue velvet pouch. Mary and Audrey emitted gasps of surprise when she displayed Edward IV's ruby brooch.

"'Tis a princely jewel!" Mary touched the dangling pearl. "'Tis a good thing that Isabel did not spy this, or I would not wager you a farthing that you would have kept it past midnight."

Though she agreed with Mary's assessment, Alicia gave her a look of disapproval. "'Tis wrong to accuse someone of covetousness."

The girl made a face. "'Tis wrong to covet, and that Isabel did in extreme. Why, she left this morning with much that was not hers. When Tom finds out, he will—"

A knock on the door interrupted her.

Alicia pinned the brooch to the neckline of her gown so that the pearl hung between her breasts. "Come in," she called when the ruby was in place.

Stokes, resplendent in a flowing black cloak with wide sleeves ornamented in gold thread, bowed his head in courtesy. When he looked fully at Alicia, his jaw dropped. "Mistress…my lady, I…I have the honor— the supreme honor—to escort you to the chapel." His dark brown eyes shone with pride.

Grinning, Alicia returned his bow with a curtsy. He started to object, but she shook her head. "Nay, good Stokes, I am not yet the lady of anything, but only the poor daughter of a merchant. You do *me* the honor to lend me your support, for, in truth, my legs are shaking."

He patted his black velvet cap as if to make sure it had not flown somewhere else. "'Tis natural for a bride to quake a little on her wedding day, my lady, but poor you will never be."

The trumpets, sounding more insistent this time, cut off her rebuttal. Stokes held out his arm to her.

Mary snatched up a length of pale blue ribbon from the window seat. "Wait! I have not yet tied on the rosemary." As she spoke, she made a quick love knot around Alicia's upper arm. She tucked the sweet-smelling herb under the ribbon. "For luck," she whispered to Alicia. Then she kissed the bride's cheeks.

Touched by Mary's open affection, Alicia tried to frame her thanks, but Mistress Vive bustled into the already crowded chamber, and whisked out her charge with barely a nod to the bride. While Stokes led her down the corridor to the stairs, Alicia promised herself to replace Mary's governess at the first opportunity.

The steward cast a quick smile at her as they crossed

the great hall where the kitchen servants paused in their preparations for the wedding breakfast, and bowed to the bride. "You look right comely, my lady," he told her in an undertone. "Smile for everyone. Do not let them see that your lips tremble."

"My lips are not trembling." Alicia moistened them with her tongue. "In sooth, they are numb."

She had not expected to be this nervous. After all, she was going to marry the man she had dreamed about for almost ten years. Yet the grown-up Thomas Cavendish with his handsome face and the body of a Viking warrior had surpassed all the idle fancies of her girlhood. That he made her heart flutter every time he came close to her was an added surprise, and one that intrigued her. If only he loved her as much as she had grown to love him! She curled her fingers into the broadcloth of Stokes's sleeve. He patted her hand. They stepped out into the brilliant sunlight of a perfect August morn.

She blinked as her eyes grew accustomed to the brightness. Then she beheld the huge gathering of smiling folk, all dressed in jewel-colored silks, velvets, brocades and damask. She had never before seen so many noble personages in one place. She nearly tripped on the cobblestones of the yard, but Stokes steadied her in time. By the ill-concealed tones of envy that she overheard as she passed by, Alicia knew that many of the guests gazed, not on the bride, but upon the fabulous jewel that she wore.

"Is that real?"

"Look how the ruby catches the light!"

"How could Thornbury afford so costly a bride gift?"

"I am amazed that the simpleton even thought of one at all."

Alicia's ears flamed. How dare they make such disparaging remarks about her husband-to-be? She lifted her chin a notch higher.

"Smile!" Stokes whispered again as they neared the chapel door.

Alicia could only manage a wobbly grin when she first laid eyes on her waiting bridegroom. Thomas Cavendish, the ninth Earl of Thornbury, completely captured her attention with his arresting good looks. He had doffed his usual black-and-gray garb. Instead, a surcoat of bloodred satin encased his powerful shoulders. The Cavendish emblem of a snarling wolf's head was embroidered across his chest. Alicia barely noticed that Andrew wore a tabard in matching colors and motif. For once, the knight outshone his peacock squire. The young man smiled broadly at her, then winked.

Alicia ignored the boy completely. She had eyes only for her bridegroom. He drew himself up to his fullest height, towering over the castle chaplain at his side. His stance emphasized the strength of his hard-muscled thighs and the slimness of his hips encased in gold-colored hose. Alicia felt her blood surge from her fingertips to her toes. She gripped the stems of her bouquet of white roses that Mary had arranged for her. She took no heed of the sharp thorns that pressed into her palms. Her gaze drank in Thomas with greedy pleasure.

Stokes disengaged his arm from her fingers. With a bow to his lord, he withdrew into the crowd around the bridal couple. Trying to remember everything Katherine had told her, Alicia sank into a deep curtsy before her groom. She thanked her guardian angel that she rose without mishap. She could not possibly embarrass

Thomas in front of all of his friends. *How serious he looks! Mayhap he is as nervous as I am.*

Without moving a facial muscle, Thomas bowed to his bride. Instead of a simple bend from the waist that was customary, he swept her a deep court bow as if they were at Westminster Palace. The crowd murmured at this apparent odd behavior, but Alicia guessed the reason. *He is honoring my Plantagenet blood.* Her cheeks colored under the intense heat of his gaze when he again looked at her. A delicious shudder heated her body. *Please smile at me, Thomas.*

At her feet, Taverstock uttered a few sharp barks. Tearing her gaze away from her bridegroom, she looked down at the little terrier. She could not stifle her surprised laughter.

The three dogs wore beautiful collars around their necks.

Thomas cleared his throat. "Had to dress them up," he explained in a gruff tone. "For their new mistress."

Alicia smiled at him. "They are the handsomest trio here," she whispered, hoping none of the onlookers could hear her.

A faint smile hovered around his lips. Then the chaplain coughed. Thomas's smile vanished, much to Alicia's regret. They turned to face the priest.

He launched into rapid Latin, as if he was afraid that the couple might change their minds before the ceremony was completed. The ritual blurred out of Alicia's focus. She responded automatically when asked if she willingly took Thomas as her husband. As she listened to her groom's responses, she thought of the Bramptons in faraway Flanders, and wished that they could have witnessed the completion of all their hopes for their beloved ward. Closing her eyes, she prayed for sweet

Dickon, the only sibling she had ever known, now a prisoner inside the thick, rough walls of the fearsome Tower. *That could have been my fate as well, if it was not for the man who stands at my side.*

She returned to reality when Thomas took her left hand in his. He held a circlet of gold between his thumb and forefinger. Echoing the priest's words, he blessed each of Alicia's fingers with the ring, before sliding it firmly onto her fourth. The ring was too big. He slipped it back to her third.

"Must fix that later," he muttered in her ear. He enfolded her hand within his, taking her with gentle authority, but he did not look at her when the priest uttered the final amen.

Silence wrapped the courtyard, as if everyone held their breath. Alicia flashed a quick glance at Thomas out of the corner of her eye. She realized that the guests were waiting for the husband to kiss his new wife. Clearing his throat, the chaplain gave the groom a meaningful stare. Alicia shifted her feet. She wondered if she should make the first move, but decided that it would be too bold of her.

"For God's sake, kiss her, my lord," Andrew hissed out of the side of his mouth.

Thomas gripped Alicia's hand. With a low rumble in his throat, he turned to her. Before Alicia could catch her breath, his lips brushed against hers for an instant, then were gone before she could even return his salute. The guests applauded, though some snickered. She buried her nose deep into her bouquet lest anyone see that she blushed with shame.

The priest threw open the chapel doors, and escorted the newly wedded couple into the house of God. Thomas held her hand in a death grip, as if he feared she would run away from him. Alicia didn't know exactly how she felt toward her new husband at this moment, but flight was the last thing on her mind. The guests filed in behind them for the nuptial mass. All during the service, Thomas stared straight ahead at the altar, not once looking at his bride. However, he never let go of her hand.

Afterward, the Earl and new Countess of Thornbury were congratulated on all sides by friends, neighbors and castle inhabitants. The throng escorted the bridal couple up the outside stairs, and into the hall for the sumptuous feast that Master Konrad and his minions had prepared. Pulling Alicia behind him, Thomas mumbled his thanks to well-wishers as he worked a passage to the head table.

As he helped her into a large armchair next to his, he whispered, "Tavie would not have liked it."

Alicia stared at him, a small frown knotted her brows. "What, my lord?"

Thomas did not reply until after he had seated himself. Filling her goblet with wine, he muttered, "Kissing you out there. Jealous, you know."

She glanced under the table at the little dog. Taverstock stared back at her. The hair on his neck bristled around his ornate collar.

She gave Thomas as bright a smile as she could muster under the circumstances. "What do you think we should do about him…Thomas?" she asked.

His eyes turned bluer. He tapped his finger on the table for several minutes. "Have to fix that, too." He took a long drink of wine.

Mary popped up behind them. Like a friendly angel, she hugged them both, kissing her brother first.

"You dear old thing, Tom! Thank you, thank you, a million times over!"

He bestowed a precious smile on his little sister. "How now? What mischief have you devised?"

Mary laughed. "None—yet. But the day is not over." Then she turned to Alicia. "My thanks is for giving me the most wonderful sister in the world—and for sending the sour one away. Welcome to the family, Alicia Cavendish!" She kissed her on the cheek.

Stunned by the girl's loving acceptance, Alicia stuttered her thanks. If only Thomas would treat her as warmly as his sister did. Mary flitted away to greet other guests at the high table.

One of the lords, a bearlike man with a black patch over one eye, pounded on the board, raised his goblet, and roared a toast. "To your bride, Thornbury. May she keep you busy—and out of the forest!"

The company stamped their feet, and cheered with mounting good humor. Thomas gripped his eating knife. A small muscle twitched in his jaw.

Alicia touched his arm. "Thomas, what ails you?"

He narrowed his eyes. "Sir Roger Ormond yonder turns my stomach." His anger unleashed his tongue. "His jest was rude, and an open taunt. My fingers itch to flay his mottled hide."

"Mayhap he has already drunk too much wine." She massaged the tense muscles under his silken sleeve.

"Aye, the villain is a preposterous ass, and no mistake. He wants you to keep me occupied in the marriage bed, so that he can poach my deer without fear of my retribution."

Alicia bit her lip. "Oh." For a moment, she had hoped his anger was for *her* sake and not his own honor. She should have known better.

Ormond slammed his fist on the table, again calling for attention. He jerked his thumb at the little whey-faced woman seated next to him. "My lady wife admires your bride gift, Cavendish. Where did you steal the bauble?"

The hall erupted with more laughter. Thomas half rose out of his chair. Alicia held tight to his arm. She could not permit a brawl on their wedding day.

"Nay, Thomas, he is nothing but an annoying fly. He is not worth your ire."

Her new husband ground his teeth, then eased himself back into his seat. When Andrew offered the first course, a veal omelette, Thomas stabbed the food with venom. The squire almost dropped the platter.

"More wine," Thomas growled.

As the long meal progressed, Alicia watched him sink deeper and deeper into a foul mood. She plastered a wan smile across her face so that their guests would not see how upset she was. *He cannot stand me. He wishes I were dead, but now that I am a Cavendish, there is nothing he can do.*

At the end of the feast, Master Konrad entered the hall carrying his masterpiece—a spun-sugar subtlety depicting a golden wolf surrounded by white roses. As the cook paraded down the aisle to the high table, much applause followed his artful confection. He presented it to Thomas.

"Felicitations, and long life to the bride and groom," Konrad said. He smiled broadly.

Thomas's black humor lifted a little. He turned to Alicia, and cocked an eyebrow. "Does it please you, my lady?"

Tears of happiness pricked her eyelids. "Aye, my

lord.'' He had remembered that the white rose of York was her royal father's family badge.

Thomas leaned closer to her so that only she could hear his next words. ''Which piece do you choose?''

His warm breath tickled her ear. She fought her over-whelming desire to kiss him in front of the entire shire. ''The wolf. I will always choose the wolf.''

A faint light twinkled in the indigo depths of his eyes. Using the point of his eating knife, he pried the sugar creature loose from its base. He presented it to her as if the figure were made of pure gold. ''Take good care of him, my lady.'' A faint tremor in his voice indicated that some strong emotion boiled within him.

''Always, my lord.'' Their fingers touched. Her skin prickled pleasurably.

He broke off the largest of the roses, and put it on his trencher. ''I am partial to these,'' he murmured, then he raised his voice and addressed his cook. ''Outdone yourself, Konrad.''

The man basked in his lord's appreciation.

Alicia opened her mouth to add her thanks, but Mary called out, ''Do not take all the flowers for yourself, Tom! Please let me have one—or two. I have never seen such a treat. I utterly *long* to eat one!''

Her brother chuckled. ''Serve the young minx her fill, Konrad. She will plague me otherwise.''

The cook bowed, and took his platter down the table. Thomas turned in his chair, and gazed at Alicia. He studied her face as if he would divine her most secret thoughts. She grew warm under his scrutiny.

''When will you eat your wolf?'' he asked, his ex-pression a mask.

''When you eat your rose, my lord.'' She held her breath.

Again he leaned closer to her, his face almost touching hers. He smelled of wine, leather and some exotic scent that surely must have been imported from the mysterious east. His nearness kindled a burning deep within her.

"Feed me." His command was a caress.

Alicia's toes curled inside her slippers.

Thomas put the sugar rose in her hand. She could barely contain her trembling. Without another word, she touched his lips with the sweet. He opened his mouth. She placed the flower on his tongue. His closed his lips over her fingers before she could withdraw them. He laved each one with his tongue. She wanted to yield to the burning sweetness that had captured her. Their gazes locked as their breathing came in unison. A hot ache rose in her throat.

Her mouth went dry. "Thomas, please, people are watching."

Slowly he pulled away, releasing her. The air felt very cold on her wet fingers. She experienced a sudden sense of loss, and wished she had not spoken.

He picked up the wolf. A mischievous look flashed in his eyes. "Open, my lady."

Alicia eyed the figure. "He is three times the size of the rose, Thomas. I fear he will not fit." she whispered.

His left eyebrow lifted a fraction. "Take the head for now."

A spark of desire spiraled through her. Her reason counseled restraint, but her heart paid no attention. She parted her teeth, and bit off the wolf's head with a wanton hunger. The sugar melted in the heat of her mouth, filling her with sweetness. Her lips quivered with her unspoken passion.

Please, say it now, Thomas. Tell me that you love me.

He sat back against the cushions of the chair. His gaze dropped from her mouth to her shoulders, then settled on the brooch between her breasts. Within a heartbeat, his demeanor changed. His eyes narrowed, and his back became straight as an arrow's shaft. He knotted his fist, then banged it on the table several times. The hall froze into silence.

He rose, and bellowed, "I am going hunting!"

His words cut Alicia. Her eyes widened. "Now? This minute?"

Thomas ignored her question. "Any man who wishes to accompany me, meet at the stables in ten minutes," he told the company.

Applause and cheers greeted the host's unusual announcement. Alicia felt faint. What had she done wrong?

Sir Roger Ormond slammed down his goblet. His wine slopped over his hand. "I wager I will kill more deer than you, neighbor!"

Thomas hooded his eyes like a hawk. He clenched his fist behind his back. "You will ride on my nearside, Ormond, so that I can keep my eye on you."

Sir Roger merely laughed at the steely tone in Thomas's voice.

Alicia took his hand in hers, and attempted to soften his tense grip with her touch. "I had thought there would be dancing anon," she suggested. Her new husband felt like a man made of marble.

He glanced down at her. "You ladies can dance. We will hunt."

She blinked back her tears. This was not how she had envisioned her wedding day. "But why *now*?"

His blazing stare bored into her like a dagger. "Because I must. Trust me," he whispered.

Then he was gone from her side. Thomas marched down the hall with lengthening strides. Barking, baying and yipping, his three boon companions scampered out from under the high table. Andrew tossed his serving cloth to a nearby wench, and hurried after his master and the excited dogs. He cast a sympathetic look over his shoulder to Alicia.

I must not cry or whine or scream like a fishwife. I will pretend that this shock was planned as part of the day's festivities. I will smile to all these noble ladies whom I do not know—but later, Thomas Cavendish, I will give you a wedding night you will never forget!

Chapter Fourteen

Thomas could not erase the memory of Alicia's stunned expression when he announced his intention to go hunting instead of spending the day with her. His breath caught in his throat when he recalled how he had caressed her long, supple fingers in his mouth when she fed him the sugar rose. If they had been alone, he would have taken her to his bed then and there.

Behind him, he could hear his male guests preparing themselves for an unexpected day of excellent hunting. Good-humored shouts rang across the courtyard as grooms and stable lads hurried to saddle several dozen horses at once. Thomas knew that his neighbors thought him to be mad—especially to leave his beautiful bride alone while he rode off to the forest. He didn't care. There was a higher purpose to this expedition than mere entertainment. Only Alicia mattered. When he returned, he hoped he could make her understand his motive, and win her forgiveness.

Stuffing his leather riding gloves under his wide belt, he stepped into his library. He would write his new wife another letter to ease her mind until they met again. Andrew found him just as he finished his note. He started to sign his name, then paused. Surely she knew who her mystery correspondent was by now, even though she had never once mentioned his other letters. He folded the paper, then sealed it with a dab of wax.

Andrew gave him a jerky bow. "Your horse awaits you, my lord," he said in a cold tone. He did not look at Thomas.

The knight glanced at his ruffled squire. "How now, Andrew? You do not approve of the noble sport of hunting?"

The boy's face hardened. "'Tis not my place to give an opinion. I am only your lordship's humble squire."

Thomas blew on the waxen blob. "Aye, yet you look like the angel of doom. Speak!"

Andrew glanced at his master out of the corner of his eye. "If the fair Alicia was *my* wife, I would not stir from her side on my wedding day."

He nodded. "I agree."

The squire's flinty expression dissolved into one of surprise. "Then why—if I am permitted to inquire?"

Thomas regarded his young companion. He suddenly felt much older than his four-and-twenty years and very world-weary. "Because I have forgotten to give the lady a gift for our wedding," he replied in a soft tone.

Andrew crossed his arms over his chest, and attempted to look cynical. "Oh? So you think running away to your forest is exactly what she wants?"

He shook his head with a little smile. "I am not running away at all, but running *for* something. Pray that I find it."

"I will, for if you do not, methinks Lady Alicia will flay you alive upon your return—and I will gladly hand her the knife."

Thomas whistled through his teeth. "I will engrave

your threat upon my memory, Master Avenger. In the meantime, please leave this where my wounded lady will find it." He gave Andrew the note. "Then attend me. Georgie will go with us. He has grown too slothful and needs a good run. Put Tavie in my saddlebag as usual, for he will be underfoot, and in danger of trampling if he remains here among the ladies."

The squire took the letter, and stuffed it inside his jerkin. "And Vixen?" He still did not unbend his self-righteous stance.

Thomas sighed. "Let her choose what she will. Methinks she will want to stay close to home, but would resent it if I chained her."

Andrew sniffed. "You seem to give more thought to your dogs than to your wife." He stuck out his chin.

Thomas curled his lip. The boy sometimes pushed his limits. "I think of Lady Alicia every moment of the day—particularly this one!" He turned on his heel, and went out the door. "Come, young Lancelot. We burn daylight!"

Muttering under his breath, Andrew hurried past him on his errand. Thomas locked the door behind them. His squire would understand when Thomas found what he sought—if he found them. For the sake of his new, fragile marriage, he prayed that hunter's luck rode with him.

Alicia discovered that the abandoned wives did not miss their husbands' company at all, but instead took the unexpected opportunity to exchange news and gossip with each other. She led everyone outside to the gardens. Enjoying perfect weather, the ladies divided into little groups of twos and threes, then settled themselves like so many colorful butterflies on the stone benches that dotted the garden's paths. Alicia instructed the castle minstrel to wander among them, and play sweet ballads upon his lute. She instructed other servants to pass around cups of watered wine, and platters of the sugared almonds and gingerbreads. Since Thomas had ordered the delicacies for the wedding, they may as well be eaten before they turned stale.

The bride spoke to each of her guests, taking care to memorize their names and titles. To every lady, Alicia gave a warm smile and words of greeting. She laughed in a carefree manner when one or another of the finely dressed women questioned Thomas's sudden idea of a hunt. She knew they considered her husband an idiot, and perhaps they pitied her. No matter. Thomas had asked her to trust him, and she would try her best to do so.

Lady Margaret Palmerson flashed Alicia a patronizing smile. "Husbands! What does one do with them?"

I do not know, but I suspect I shall soon find out. Alicia dimpled in her most charming manner—an expression she had often used in the past to win over the customers in Edward's gold shop. "La, my lady! Thomas is a great one for the hunt. Methinks he will die in the saddle someday." *If I do not kill him first.*

Lady Katherine Francis fluffed out her red-and-cream silken skirts. "Do you not think it strange for your new husband to abandon you on your wedding day, my dear?"

Before Alicia could reply, Lady Martha Bolton answered for her. "How can the poor girl possibly know what is strange or not strange about Thomas Cavendish? She has only been married to him for three hours." She smiled at Alicia like a cat in the sun. "What we *really* want to know is, where did Thomas find such a beautiful brooch? By my troth, I have never set eyes on anything so fine.'' She inspected the jewel like a connoisseur.

Alicia fumbled for an answer. How could she say it was her father's? The next question would be how could a mere goldsmith have afforded such a costly ornament? Instead, she shrugged. ''I know not, my lady. Thomas continually amazes me. Do you think it might be an heirloom of his family's?'' She crossed her fingers behind her back.

''A king's token, I would wager,'' Lady Margaret judged.

Alicia's heart almost stopped. Despite the warm sunshine, she felt icy cold.

Lady Katherine nodded her head in agreement. ''No doubt some Cavendish ancestor rendered a service for one of the Plantagenets, and was well rewarded for his trouble.''

As the day wore on, Alicia looked around for Mary. At least the girl's company would be more wholesome. Following the sounds of squeals and laughter, she found her new sister-in-law in the courtyard. Mary had engaged a number of the village girls in a game of hoodman-blind. Alicia was tempted to join them, but then she remembered she was now the Countess of Thornbury and should conduct herself with dignity—especially with all of the shire's gentry watching. Someone touched her shoulder. When she whirled around, she saw Stokes gazing down at her with a wise look in his gentle brown eyes.

''Methinks you are tired, my lady.''

She nodded. '''Tis been a long day.''

The steward squinted at the sun. ''Aye, but there are a few hours yet until evening.''

She sighed, and wondered how long Thomas intended to go roaming around the woods.

As if he read her thoughts, Stokes continued, "'Twill be neigh suppertime afore my lord will return. He often hunts ten or twelve hours."

She felt her courage dissolving. "Oh."

The steward lowered his voice. "I mean you no insult, my lady, but you need to rest. Tonight will be…that is…" He reddened to the roots of his dark hair.

"Tonight I must please my husband in all things," she finished for him. "Aye, my mother instructed me well in this matter."

He looked relieved. "No one will think ill if you retired for an hour or two. Audrey has turned down the master's bed for you. I will attend these ladies, and see that they stuff themselves with ample sweetmeats."

She flashed him a grateful smile. "You are a good man," she said. "I hope Thomas pays you well."

The steward bowed. "Aye, my lady, he does."

With another word of thanks, Alicia stole away from the merrymakers. As Stokes had observed, none of her guests noticed her leave-taking. As she mounted the entranceway stairs, Vixen emerged from the shadows. The dog looked up at her.

Alicia dropped to her knees, and caressed the pregnant greyhound. "Did he leave you, too, girl?" She stroked the dog's smooth flanks. "Does he think we females are a bother? Come, Vixen. You look as if you could do with a nap."

Together they walked in silence through the now-empty hall. She noticed with satisfaction that all the trestle tables had been taken down and put away. Not a scrap of the wedding feast remained on the sideboards. She blessed Stokes for his efficiency.

Together, they climbed the wide staircase. Each step seemed higher than the one before it. Alicia covered a yawn with her hand. She waited while Vixen negotiated the last stair. The dog's limp appeared more pronounced as they continued down the gallery toward Thomas's bedroom.

"Methinks the load you bear has become too troublesome for you," she observed. "Tomorrow I will make an ointment, and rub it on your leg. Perchance 'twill ease some of the stiffness."

When they arrived at the master's chamber, Alicia hesitated before crossing over the threshold. She had never seen the inside of Thomas's lair. She discovered that his room and its appointments were less lavish than those in the chamber she had been given, yet she liked this one better. It looked more comfortable with its simple furnishings and unadorned coverings. With only the dog for company, she felt like a child sneaking into a forbidden place.

On the other hand, Vixen appeared quite at home. Giving a little run then a graceful leap, she landed in the middle of the huge, canopied bed. She circled several times before she plopped down next to one of the bolsters. She yawned, then looked at Alicia with an expectant air.

"Are you inviting me to join you?" She crossed the floor, then sat down on the edge of the bed, and gave a tentative bounce on the thick mattress. *Thomas must like his bed ropes pulled tight. So do I.*

She kicked off her new kid slippers, and wriggled her toes. The shoes had not been broken in yet, and they pinched. She lifted her flower wreath from her brow with care. She already had a number of thorn pricks from her bouquet. She found that she couldn't unlace the back of her gown by herself. Praying that the rich material of her skirts would not wrinkle too badly, she lay down next to Vixen.

Alicia rubbed her companion's velvet-soft ears. "My thanks, Vixen. I am very grateful for your company."

The greyhound closed her eyes, and appeared to fall instantly asleep. Alicia relaxed against the bolster. She caught sight of a piece of paper lying on the small nightstand. Its red wax seal looked all too familiar.

She reached for it, then hesitated. Perhaps it was a note for Thomas instead. A horrible thought flashed through her mind. Maybe he had a mistress who had sent him a letter on his wedding day. Alicia had never considered that possibility, though she realized that many men took a mistress. Thomas had been a bachelor for a long time, and he was not unattractive to women.

Alicia chewed her lower lip. Who was she hoodwinking? Thomas was more than handsome. He looked like the golden god of the dawn. He probably had no end of women vying for his attentions. She touched her lips to the fingers that he had caressed so intimately at the feast. Her skin tingled at the delicious memory. No doubt, Thomas was a master in the art of lovemaking. She hoped she would not disappoint him tonight. She thanked the sweet angels that Katherine had taught her so much about pleasing a man.

Alicia stared at the note. Her curiosity ate away at her reluctance. She picked it up. If Thomas had a mistress in the village, the wench probably couldn't read or write, she told herself. Her heart almost stopped. In the familiar bold penmanship, she read her name on the flap. With trembling fingers, she broke open the seal.

My own Alicia—
Mere words cannot tell you of the joy you have
given to me this day. For the past two nights, I
have asked myself if my happiness is not an idle
dream. The feelings that I have do not belong on
this earth, but in heaven. My heart overflows with
such emotion that I do not know where I am. A
hundred thousand kisses I give to thee, my
sweetest joy. I look forward to being with you soon
again.

    Trust me.

Alicia started to rip up the note when the last sentence, written at the bottom as an afterthought, stopped
her.

She collapsed against the thick bolster, and stared at
the blue velvet canopy above the bed. Those were the
very words that he had whispered before he left her.
Could it be? Alicia refused to be gulled again. Thomas
was too spare of words, especially sweet ones. This was
Andrew's idea of a wedding prank—to plague her with
endearments of love.

She read the letter again and tried to think of what
she should do. A heavy drowsiness crept over her. Her
eyes fluttered in mild protest against the invasion of
sleep. Just before she drifted into that sweet cloud of
oblivion, she pushed the note down between the headboard and the mattress. She did not want any curious
servant to stumble upon it while she slept.

The lamplighter had already begun his rounds when
Isabel and her travel-stained retinue lumbered into the
stable yard of the Black Dog Inn at Ainsty, just outside
the walls of York. She glared at the creaking sign that

hung over the doorway. Would she never be rid of those flea-infested creatures?

Though her servants dripped with weariness after the bone-shaking trip over rough roads, Isabel herself felt wide-awake and anxious to set her plan into motion. While her bodyguard made lodging arrangements with the greasy-faced landlord, Isabel sought out the stable boy.

"You look like an intelligent lad," she remarked to the hulking oaf. She held her scented handkerchief to her nose to ward off the boy's foul odor.

The costernoggin grinned, displaying a lack of front teeth. He tugged his forelock until Isabel expected his dirty hair to come away in his hand.

"Aye, lady. I am, so please ye."

She stepped into a darker patch of shadow. She did not want the boy to get a good look at her face. "I fear I am in distress."

The dullard's expression changed to concern. "Can I help ye, lady?"

Isabel clasped her hand to her heart. "Oh, if you only could, good youth."

He practically drooled with eagerness. "Tell me what you want, and I will do it!"

She grinned into her handkerchief, then affected a deep sigh mixed with a sob. "Alas, alack, I am in such trouble." She lowered her voice. "I am being pursued by an evil man."

The idiot looked over his shoulders. "Where?"

"Up the road apiece. I am a poor widow with only a few sticks of furniture and a few rags of clothing, yet I fear for my life."

The boy gripped the handle of his hay rake. "I will defend ye!"

She gave another sigh. "Ah, you are too kind—a real gentleman, even though you work in a stable. But you are a little young for the dire villain who is my enemy. I need two grown men with strong arms and sharp knives. Do you happen to know of any like that around here?"

The lout nodded so vigorously that his cap slipped off his filthy head. Isabel stepped away from it lest its vermin leap onto her gown.

"Aye, lady, I do! But they are rough, and not used to gentlefolk."

She could barely contain her glee at this news. *Exactly what I need!* "No matter. The brigand who endangers me requires rough handling. Can you fetch these friends of yours, and bring them to the taproom within the hour? 'Twill be worth a…a silver penny to you." Best not to let him know how much hard money she carried under her skirts.

His eyes widened at the mention of a fee. "Aye, lady. I will. But my friends will want to be paid for their trouble, methinks."

"Of course," she purred. "Tell them that if they do my work well, they will be royally paid." She chuckled at her little jest—royally paid for royal blood.

The lad tugged his forelock again. "I will this minute!" He dropped the hay rake on the spot. Isabel jumped as it clattered at her feet.

She ground her teeth at the lackwit's behavior. At least he could run fast enough, she mused as she watched him race down the street, then duck into an alley. She hoped the men he knew were what she wanted. She would have a devil of a time getting rid of them if they proved to be as addle-brained as the stable boy. Isabel shrugged to herself. If one was going to prosper in this world, one needed to take a few risks. Humming to herself, she joined Meg, who had been waiting by the courtyard's pump for her mistress.

The maid yawned. "By Saint Sebastian's arrows, I am sore, and could sleep for a week."

Isabel shook her by the shoulders. "Do not think of it yet, Meg. We will be entertaining company anon."

Meg screwed up her face in protest. "In this dingy place? By our larkin, my lady! What manner of folk would come a-visiting us at this hour?"

Isabel swept past her toward the inn's back door. "An excellent question. We shall see in good time."

An hour later, Isabel discovered just how unsavory her guests could be. She thanked her good sense that she had decided to meet with the stable lad's friends in a corner booth in the crowded taproom. These two brigands would have slit her throat if she had entertained them alone in her chamber. Her hands grew clammy while she regarded the two villains who sat opposite her, quaffing their second jacks of ale at her expense.

The leader called himself Flash. "Handy with a knife, see?" He wiped his mouth with the back of his hand, and leered at her. Tall, though not like the Cavendishes, he had long powerful arms, and huge hands, that looked as if they could strangle her in a trice. "What be your pleasure, lady?"

His companion, introduced as Demon, merely belched and signaled for another round.

Goose bumps dotted Isabel's bare neck and shoulders. She wished she had worn her cloak, but the room was very hot and smoky. Under the table, she clutched the small leather bag full of gold marks. She tossed her head, then looked squarely into Flash's watery gray eyes.

"I wish to have someone abducted."

He coughed, then spat on the floor. "Sprout told me that a man was after you. *That* I can understand." He openly appraised her, his gaze lingering on the swell of her breasts.

She narrowed her eyes. This ruffian made her skin crawl. She almost wished she had not been so anxious to implement the deed. No doubt, she could have hired someone less coarse by light of day. Too late, she realized. *Let us see what mettle these churls are made of.*

"I seek to have a lady stolen away from Wolf Hall."

Demon whistled under his breath. "'Tis the Cavendish roost, or I will dance in hell."

Flash brayed a laugh, then slapped his friend on the back. "You will dance there anyway, my friend. But he speaks the truth, lady. Wolf Hall belongs to a family of powerful lords."

She allowed them a superior smile. "Your news is old. All the lords you fear died of a fever just two months ago. There is only one Cavendish left—Thomas. He should give you no trouble at all. He is lacking most of his wits. He prefers to wander through the woods with his dogs, than to protect his home."

Demon snarled at her, baring his teeth like an animal. "I a-fear no one on this side of the grave."

She smothered a squeal of fright. She knew she would have nightmares tonight. "I am glad to hear that. Then stealing one lone woman will not tax you at all, will it, Master Flash?"

He hooded his eyes. "Do not say 'steal,' lady. 'Tis a foul word, and could hang a man. Me and Demon—we *convey* the goods."

Demon chortled into his ale. "Aye, that we do!"

Flash leaned across the table toward her. "Myself—

I am the best of cutpurses, or cutthroats, in these parts. Who is the coney?''

She blinked. She had no idea what the ruffian had asked.

He grinned. ''Your pardon. I forgot I was conversing with a lady of quality.'' He crooned the last word. Then he smacked his lips.

She pressed her back against the dingy wall. If he so much as laid a finger on her, she would scream the very rafters down. She leveled her gaze at him.

''You will abduct Alicia Cavendish, Sir Thomas's wife. You cannot mistake her, for she is as tall and thin as a stripling boy, and her hair is the color of firelight.''

Demon nudged his companion. ''Sounds like a bit of fun.''

Isabel hurried with her instructions before her courage gave away completely. ''You are not to kill the woman, nor Sir Thomas—but you may keep whatever jewels or money you might find on her person.''

Flash cocked an eyebrow. ''I had intended to do just that with or without your permission. 'Tis my right.''

Demon nudged Flash again. ''How about this Alicia's honey pot, eh? Can we take that, too?'' He laughed amid a series of hiccups.

I do not care a groat. She shrugged. ''Take whatever you will. You can deliver her in her shift if you wish. Just do not kill her, or 'twill come down on your head, I promise you.'' *Two can play their nasty little game.* She leaned forward, and whispered, '''Tis king's business, so do it well, and you will be amply rewarded.''

Demon's dark skin turned a shade paler at the mention of the king. Flash stroked his bristly chin for a minute or two in silence.

''Why does the king want this woman?'' he asked.

Isabel gripped the coin pouch tighter. "She is the sister of Perkin Warbeck, who tried to claim the throne. He pretended to be Richard of York."

Demon scratched his filthy head. "Who?"

Flash gave him a cynical smile. "Last son of King Edward—the one who died years ago in the Tower."

His companion crossed himself. The reverent gesture took Isabel by surprise.

She pursed her lips. "Warbeck is a traitor to our gracious king, and so is his sister."

Flash narrowed his eyes into slits. "How much for the lady?"

Isabel plopped the leather purse on the table. The coins jingled faintly inside. "Ten marks now. Twice that when you have delivered the woman to me here at the inn. And, good masters, know that you will be watched. His Grace, King Henry, does not like to have his money ill spent." She prayed they could not hear the pounding of her heart.

Flash eyed the pouch as if it might suddenly leap up and bite him. Demon showed no such qualms, but pulled it open, and plucked out one of the golden coins.

His black eyes gleamed. "By the cross, she speaks the truth!"

Flash covered Demon's hand with his own. "Put it away, you clodpole. Do you want to have your belly slit afore you can spend it?"

Under the table, Isabel knotted her hand into a fist. *Take the money, you pigs, and leave me. Your stench sickens my stomach.*

Flash swept up the pouch, then stuffed it in his filthy shirt. "We will undertake your piece of work, lady, and we will discuss further payment afterward."

She gritted her teeth. "Bring Alicia Cavendish here

as soon as you can. His Grace does not like to be kept waiting.''

Rising from the booth, Flash gave her a snake's smile. ''Nor do I like to wait, lady. Remember that.''

He pulled up Demon by the collar of his jerkin. Without a backward glance, he strode through the crowd, dragging his henchman behind him.

Isabel expelled a deep breath of relief. A wave of elation washed over her. Soon Alicia would be in her clutches. She could not wait to hear that upstart beg for her freedom. *The king will reward me well when I deliver the last Plantagenet bastard to him. Why go home to my father's madhouse when I can find a better place in court?*

Buoyed by that enticing prospect, Isabel rose from the food-encrusted table, and made her way up the stairs to her chamber, where simpleminded Meg awaited with warm rose water and clean sheets.

Dream sweet dreams tonight, Alicia. 'Twill be your last night of freedom!

Chapter Fifteen

The muted sound of a hunting horn woke Alicia from a deep sleep. She rubbed her eyes, then glanced around at the unfamiliar chamber. The horn sounded again in the darkness outside. Vixen raised her head, then thumped her tail against the coverlet.

Alicia sat up. "Has our lord and master returned, Vixen?"

The usually silent greyhound barked once. Her tail continued to wag. She stood up in the middle of the bed, gave herself a shake, then leapt to the floor. She stretched her forepaws out in front of her, while her hindquarters rose in the air.

The horn blew once more, nearer this time. The clatter of many hooves and the jingle of harnesses signaled the hunting party's immediate approach. Alicia swung her feet over the side of the bed. In the darkness of the early evening, she felt around with her toes for her discarded slippers.

"We must be down in the hall when Thomas arrives," she told the dog. "I cannot see if my gown is a mess or not. Sweet angels! How could I have slept so long? Why did no one awaken me?"

As if in answer to her question, someone rapped lightly on the door. "My lady?" Audrey called. "Are you up?"

"Aye!" Alicia replied. Her groping toe found her shoes. "Pray come quickly!"

The maid pushed the door open. She entered, carrying a lit taper and a pitcher of water. Vixen dashed out, leaving her new mistress to fend for herself.

Alicia smoothed out the wrinkles in her skirts. "What is the time, Audrey?"

The maid poured some water into the basin on a stand by the fireplace. "'Tis an hour past supper, my lady. Quick now, afore my lord comes from the stables. Have a wee wash."

Alicia patted the warmed, rose-scented water on her face. "Is my hair all in tangles? How could I have left our guests for so long? The noble ladies will think me very ill-mannered."

Audrey handed her a piece of rough toweling. "Nay, the day being so warm, they have drunk a great quantity of wine, and are now in mellow spirits. If you will pardon me for saying so, I do not believe that they noticed you were gone."

Alicia dried her face and hands. Then she tightened her braid and pinched some color into her cheeks. "How now, Audrey? Will I do?"

Smiling, she nodded. "Aye, my lady. You look glowing."

So will Thomas, once I have given him a large piece of my mind. Alicia whispered her thanks to the maid, then sped out of the chamber. She practically flew down the stairs to the great hall. Just as she reached the bottom step, the small army of boisterous men burst through the entranceway at the far end of the hall. Alicia paused, gathering her strength. Out of the corner of her eye, she saw that the trestle tables were lined along one wall. They groaned under the weight of platters of sliced roasts, cheese, fruits and sweetmeats. Ewers of wine and widemouthed wooden cups awaited the company. She closed her eyes for a moment of silent thanksgiving for Stokes's thoughtfulness.

"Good eventide, Lady Cavendish!" In the center of the hall, Lord Bolton bowed, followed by many of the other hunters.

Alicia cleared her throat. "Good evening to you, my lord. I trust that the hunt was successful?" She searched over their heads for Thomas.

A general round of laughter and much back-slapping greeted her inquiry. From the looks of the men's fine clothing, it appeared that Thomas had led his neighbors through a mire, a marsh and every one of last year's fallen leaves. It amazed Alicia that men never seemed so happy as when they were covered in mud.

Several deep barks brought the hall to silence. As if cued by a master of the revels, the company parted down the center. With a proud bearing, Georgie marched through the doorway. He looked five years younger. Beside him, Taverstock pranced as if he were a little boy harboring a big secret. Looming in the shadows behind his dogs stood Thomas.

He is afraid I am going to berate him for leaving me. I will do him the courtesy of waiting until we are alone. Alicia lifted her voice. "Welcome home, my lord. Did you shoot anything?"

More laughter erupted as the bridegroom proceeded down the makeshift aisle toward his wife.

He is dirtier than the rest combined. Alicia lifted her chin, and waited. If nothing else, her husband owed her some sort of explanation. As he drew closer, she stifled a cry. It looked as if he carried a large red bear in his arms. He appeared extremely pleased with himself. Andrew, his fine clothing reduced to a bedraggled state, followed behind his master.

Without uttering either an apology or a greeting, Thomas threw down the furry load at her feet. She gripped the stone banister, and willed herself not to flee. When she looked at the bundle, she nearly bit her tongue. A large pile of dead foxes! Their blood puddled on the flagstone floor. Vixen edged toward the carnage, then sniffed at a bloody neck. Alicia gripped the banister tighter. Dear Lord, do not let me faint now.

Thomas sank to one knee beside the foxes. "A gift for my bride!" he announced to the assembly in ringing tones.

A cheer answered him, though Alicia spied many of the nobles and their wives smirking behind their hands. One of the men tapped his forehead, and crossed his eyes. Others snickered.

She was glad her husband could not see what happened behind his back. His gaze was on her alone.

He continued in a whisper. "I had no time to get you a proper gift, Alicia. Until I can buy you something worthy at the Michaelmas Fair in York, these will have to do." His blue eyes brimmed with hope of acceptance.

She swallowed down her revulsion at the sight of the dead animals, then she lifted her head so that everyone in the great hall could see and hear her. She forced a warm smile on her face. "Foxes! I have often yearned for one, and you have given me an entire family, my husband. I am overwhelmed with joy and gratitude."

The snickering and sidelong glances ceased. Thomas beamed at her. Alicia stared at the pile, and wondered what on earth she was going to do with a dozen smelly foxes. She did not realize that Andrew stood behind her, until he whispered in her ear.

"My lord will have them skinned, tanned and made into a lap robe for you. The winter nights are cold here on the moor. Say something about the quality of the pelts, my lady. He drove us through every bog and nettle patch in the shire for them—and they *are* a good lot."

Her anger melted away like snow on a sunny hillside. Thomas's gift was certainly unconventional, but not without merit. In his own unique way, he had proved his affection for her.

She took his hand in hers. "I am very pleased, Thomas. Truly I am. I do not want for anything more at Michaelmas. Thank you for your gift."

He kissed her hand, then stood, and gave her a brilliant smile that sent her pulse racing. Her blood sang, as her senses leapt to life. He had never before looked so handsome as he did at that moment. Nor had he ever smiled at her with such genuine warmth. Alicia's breath caught in her throat, so that she could not speak, but only smile in return. He took her hand, and slipped it under his arm. Then he guided her around the red-and-white mound of fur and drying blood. Alicia gloried in feeling his strength under her fingers. Without exchanging words, but with many loving glances and more radiant smiles, he escorted her to the supper table.

The company fell to eating and drinking with gusto. Thomas heaped the choicest portions of food on their shared trencher. She nodded her thanks, but when she lifted a roasted chicken leg to her mouth, she found that her appetite had deserted her. Now that her husband had returned to his home, and evening had drawn its purple cloak around the castle, she realized that the time for bedding was near. She gripped her eating knife to keep her hand from trembling.

Just follow your husband's lead, her foster mother had advised her. *He will know what to do.*

Alicia sipped her wine. She wished that she could skip over this night, and tomorrow when she awoke, all that was necessary would have been accomplished. Not that Thomas didn't excite her. She tingled with pleasure when she recalled this morning's wedding breakfast, especially the sugar wolf.

After the supper, the hunters regaled their wives, and each other, with tales of the day's hunt. Alicia nodded, and clapped her hands at the appropriate times when Lord Palmerson told how Thomas nearly chased one fox up a tree. She laughed at the right moment when Sir Roger Ormond related how Andrew was unhorsed while leaping over a stile. The squire blushed to the roots of his brown hair, but he took the ribbing with rueful good nature. Lord Bolton set the hall in a roar when he recounted how half the party had gotten tripped up by the hounds, and found themselves surrounded by a hedgerow of thorns and briars.

Throughout the tale-telling, Thomas sat by the fire, his cup in his hand and a large ewer of wine at his elbow. Alicia noticed that he drank deeply and often. She shifted on her chair, and tried to display good humor and wondered when her husband would give her the signal to retire. Meanwhile their guests grew more uproarious as the expensive French wines flowed freely down their throats. Alicia gripped the folds of her crushed wedding gown, and prayed that Thomas would not insist upon the bawdy ritual of a ceremonial bedding.

The hours wore on. Thomas finished one pitcher of wine, and drank midway through his second. He rested his head against the back of the chair while the company around him joked and sang. Alicia saw that his eyelids fluttered. Just when she decided that she would steal up the stairs, Andrew whispered something in his master's ear.

Her husband blinked, then wet his lips, and nodded. He turned toward Alicia with a crooked grin. "Go up to my chamber, sweet wife. I will…ahem…attend on you presently," he said, slurring some of his words.

Scattered chuckles, nudging and sly winks applauded Thomas's command. Alicia felt her skin grow hot. Relieved that he had finally resolved the matter, she bade the guests good-night. Lifting her skirts, she ran up the broad stairway. Audrey trailed after her. Once inside the master bedchamber, the maid quickly helped Alicia out of her gown.

"You are shivering, my lady," she noted, as she untied her petticoats. "I will build up the fire."

Alicia licked her dry lips. "My thanks, Audrey." She would never reveal that she shook from nerves, and not a chill.

She allowed her finery to pool in fluffy billows at her feet. The maid drew Alicia's nightgown out of her chest that had been brought into the master chamber earlier that day.

She held up the delicate garment to the light. "Oh, my lady! 'Tis as light as a cobweb."

Alicia could see the firelight dance through the sheer lawn fabric. She swallowed with difficulty, then found her voice. "Aye, my mother made it for me. 'Twas her last gift." Stars in heaven! The gown would reveal more than it concealed.

Audrey dropped it over her mistress's head. The wispy material fluttered around Alicia's body. With shaking fingers, she tied the blue satin ribbons around the neck. Trying not to think of Thomas's reaction when he beheld her in such an indecent scrap of clothing, she busied herself by unbraiding her hair.

Audrey took the brush from her cold hand. "Pray, sit down, my lady. 'Tis my duty to attend you."

Alicia sank onto the stool before the fire. "'Tis an odd feeling for someone else to do what I have always done for myself," she remarked as Audrey drew the brush through her long, thick tresses.

The young woman grinned. "Nay, my lady. You are a countess now, and the mistress of Wolf Hall. 'Tis proper for you to give the orders, and for us to obey them. By my troth, I shall miss you in the kitchen. You made a merry place of that gloomy cave."

Alicia blinked. The reality of her new status struck her as if someone had slapped her face. With a pang of regret, she realized how much her life had changed since she had awakened this morning. She had given very little thought to her life after the wedding guests had gone.

"I shall still visit Master Konrad to make sure that he has not drifted back to his old ways. Never fear, Audrey."

The maid giggled. "I am glad to hear of that, my lady."

Would the inhabitants of Wolf Hall think less of her if Alicia did spend time in her own kitchen? And what of the folk in the village—would they respect their new countess, even if she was not a noblewoman? Alicia drew in a little sigh. *I am born of noble blood, but no one will ever know—except Thomas.*

Stepping back, Audrey regarded her handiwork. "You have a goodly head of hair. It covers you like a cape."

Alicia tried to return the maid's smile with one of her own, but her lips felt stiff. "Do you think I look pleasing?" she asked in a tiny voice. She had never before worried about such a thing.

Audrey's eyes sparkled in the firelight. "When my lord sees you like this, he will be speechless with desire." She pulled back the blanket, and smoothed the sheets.

Alicia slipped gratefully into the huge bed. She wiggled deep under the protective covering of the bed-clothes. "God give you a good night, Audrey."

The maid lit a large taper on the table beside the bed. "And may the good Lord grant you a merry one, my lady." With another giggle, she let herself out of the door, closing it softly behind her.

Alicia arranged herself amid the pillows, then folded her hands over her breast, and waited. She heard raucous male voices drifting up from the hall below. Their laughter grew louder, and the snatches of songs became more lascivious. She wiggled her toes, and wondered if Audrey had already told Thomas that his wife was ready for him. She prayed that the maid had been discreet. She had no desire to entertain the entire tipsy mob in her chamber.

Hot wax rolled down the fat taper, and plopped onto the tabletop. Alicia waited. The night watchman called the midnight hour. Alicia knit her brows together in a frown. Thomas had drunk a great deal of wine after supper. She wondered if he had consumed too much. How pickled would he be when he finally came to her bed? She had never known him to drink to the point of intoxication. *Then again,* she reminded herself, *I really do not know him very well.*

Katherine had warned her about the effects of too much wine on a man's amorous abilities. The spirit became more than willing, but the flesh hung limp and embarrassed. *Always be tactful,* her foster mother had counseled. *Never chide your husband while he is still under the sway of wine or ale. Wait until he has recovered from his splitting headache in the morning.*

Another hour dragged by. The candle sank lower in its holder. A pool of cool wax covered the top of the table. Alicia twiddled her thumbs. The sounds of the revelry downstairs subsided into a low hum. Where was he? Perhaps he would be too tired to breach her tonight. That thought gave her cold comfort.

The watchman called the first hour of the new day. Not a sound came from the great hall—not even Tavie's little yips. The candle burned a mere inch from the base of its holder. Alicia chewed her lower lip.

Thomas does not want to come to me. He finds the idea of bedding me too distasteful, despite all his assurances that he honors me. Ha! 'Tis the late King Edward whom he honors—not his bastard daughter.

She could not hold back a lone tear that trickled its way down her cheek. She did not bother to brush it away. *He has a mistress. No doubt he has gone to her, instead of me. By midmorning everyone in the castle will know of my shame. Thomas, how could you disgrace me this way?*

The candle sputtered in the last of its wax, then it winked out. Alicia lay in the cold darkness of the huge chamber, and grieved her plight. *In spite of all this, I cannot help loving him. I am fortune's biggest fool.*

Some time near dawn, she fell asleep.

* * *

A bell rang. Thomas awoke with a start. In his lap,
Tavie snorted, then yawned. Thomas discovered himself
slouched in his large chair in the hall. The fire had long
since died in the grate. Blinking the sleep from his eyes,
he gently shook his head from side to side. It felt like
it had swelled three sizes, and would burst at any moment. Moving gingerly, he sat upright. The village
church bell rang again, summoning early risers to the
day's first mass.

He attempted to moisten his cracked lips, but for
some reason his tongue had sprouted rabbit fur. A war
drum pounded against his temples. His stomach rolled
like a coracle in the stormy North Sea. He tried to remember what day of the week it was.

Tavie licked his master's face in a friendly greeting.
His tiny paws danced on top of Thomas's queasy stomach. At his feet, Vixen stood, then stretched her long
body. Georgie did not bother to open his eyes. Instead,
he merely thumped his tail against the flagstones.

The hall was nearly empty. Most of his guests had
slipped away to their beds during the night. Thomas
wondered why he had not gone to his own bed. The
answer hit him like a bolt of lightning. Alicia!

"God's teeth, Tavie. I should have been with
my...my wife, doing my manly duty, or whatever. I am
a double-dyed villain!"

He struggled to his feet. The room lurched alarm-
ingly. His supper threatened to make a nasty return appearance. Whispering to the dogs to keep quiet, he wove
his unsteady way out to the pump by the kitchen stoop.
Before he could douse his face with ice-cold water, he
had to empty his stomach into the compost heap. He
felt mildly better after that.

He pumped the handle. When the clear water gushed out, he stuck his head under the stream. The cold stung his burning skin. He grunted. He needed pain to fight the fumes of his wine-induced cowardice. He deserved severe punishment for the wrong he had done to his innocent wife. He tossed his soaking hair out of his eyes, then collapsed onto the stone steps.

"My poor, dearest lady," Thomas murmured to Taverstock, who had accompanied him to the gardens. "She must have lain in my bed all night, waiting for me—knave that I am." He shook his head, then winced as a bolt of pain bounced between his ears. "I do not deserve her forgiveness."

He must go to her immediately and apologize. He heard the first stirrings of the cooking staff inside the kitchens. Thomas swallowed hard. He could not let anyone in the castle know that he did not sleep with his wife on their wedding night. He did not care what anyone thought of his own unpredictable behavior. He was used to being the laughingstock of the shire, but he would never allow his stupidity to heap shame on sweet Alicia.

Looking up to heaven for guidance, he spied a thick-blossomed rose vine growing on a lattice overhead. With a grin, Thomas unsheathed his dagger, and cut down four of the biggest pale pink blooms. He shook the dew off their petals, then stole up the back stairs before anyone had noticed him. Tavie followed behind him. The dog's toenails scraped against the stone stairs. It sounded extraordinarily loud to Thomas.

Georgie and Vixen waited outside his chamber. They wagged their tails when Thomas and the little terrier appeared at the end of the gallery. He faced his own door with more trepidation than when he had faced a wounded boar last autumn. Alicia couldn't possibly be as angry as a tusked hog, could she? He wondered if she had inherited the infamous Plantagenet temper as well as the family's red-gold hair. Plantagenet! He cringed when he remembered who she really was. He had made his princess wait upon *him!* He was an ass of the first order.

Thomas gripped the roses. Their thorns dug painfully into his skin. He took a deep, lung-filling breath. Then he lifted the latch, and pushed open the door.

Before he realized what had happened, the dogs bounded inside his chamber as they had always done. Like salmon leaping up waterfalls, the three sailed through the air, and landed in the middle of the bed. The mattress shook with their added weight. To his mounting horror, Thomas saw Tavie stand on top of the fair sleeper.

"Taverstock, get down from there!" he whispered, snapping his fingers.

Alicia opened her beautiful eyes, and stared straight into Tavie's face, inches from her own. He cocked his head, and regarded her as if he had stumbled upon some unusual animal in his master's bed. He touched her nose with his wet black one. Meanwhile, Vixen pawed the top coverlet into a disordered mound. She circled several times, then settled herself against Alicia's pillow. Georgie flopped down on top of Alicia's feet. The surprised woman looked over Tavie's head at Thomas. Her clear blue eyes widened.

He wished that the floor would open up, and swallow him into the deepest pit of hell. All the words of apology that he had composed on the stairway fled his memory. Dumbstruck with acute embarrassment, he thrust out the roses at arm's length toward her. He tried to grin, but he felt his lips wobble.

Alicia lifted an eyebrow. ''Another bride's gift, Thomas?''

Chapter Sixteen

Thomas looked the picture of utter misery. Any words of upbraiding disappeared from Alicia's tongue. She could see that he was gripped by a most acute suffering. The odor of stale wine surrounded him.

She gently extracted her feet from under Georgie's heavy body, then she held out her hand to her husband. "The roses are beautiful, Thomas, but methinks they will be in desperate need of some water soon."

He nodded his head, and winced when he did so. "Aye—water."

He glanced around the chamber, saw the pitcher by the basin, and plopped the roses into it. Then he offered the pitcher to Alicia.

Biting back her urge to laugh, she accepted his gift. She couldn't help but wonder if these first twenty-four hours of her marriage were an indication of what life with Thomas was going to be like from now on. At least, things would never be boring.

Taverstock burrowed under the covers, and curled up next to Alicia's hip, pinning her against Vixen.

Thomas shifted his feet from side to side. "My fault," he mumbled.

A beginning, but I think I deserve a little more apology than two words and four roses. Aloud, she said, "I fear I am a little hard of hearing this morning, Thomas. What did you say?"

He pulled on the neck of his wrinkled surcoat, then cleared his throat. "Last night, you know."

Alicia buried her face among the roses to hide her smile. "Aye, 'twas a long one. The moon rose and set in a most becoming manner. Did you see it perchance?"

He reddened. "Blasts and fogs, sweet lady! I saw nothing, but the bottom of the wine jug, and the insides of my eyelids. The wine was a friend last night, but has turned into a mighty foe this morning. I confess my shame to you. In truth, I was as drunk as a drowned rat, and thereby hangs the tale."

She could not suppress her laughter any longer. "Oh, I see, yours is the tale of a drowned rat." She lay back against the pillows, and continued to laugh.

Thomas frowned, then he flashed another one of his heart-stopping smiles. "Methinks I hung on to the tail of that poor rodent, and so dragged myself here to you in this most disgraceful shape." He went down on his knees. "Pray, throw me a lifeline, sweet angel. Am I forgiven?"

Her traitorous heart swelling with love, Alicia nodded. She pulled back the covers, and patted a place beside her. "Aye, you are, Thomas. Will you come to bed now? The day has hardly begun."

He gasped when he saw her in her nearly transparent shift. Then he looked at the floor. He clasped and unclasped his hands. "We...we must not tarry, my lady. The cock has crowed." He covered the rising swelling between his legs with his huge hands. "We must be abroad."

His stammered words turned her newfound joy into ice. Stung by his refusal, she pulled the covers up to her chin. "I did not know that we had to go anywhere, my lord. I fear you did not inform me."

He staggered to his feet, and massaged his head as he spoke. "We must ride around the estate today." He cast her a beseeching glance out of his red-rimmed eyes. "The people expect me to introduce their new countess, and they would be disappointed not to see you." He approached her as if he anticipated an attack with a broadsword. "I will be proud to ride by your side, my lady, and to call you my wife." He sat down heavily on the edge of the bed.

Ha! Wife in name only! Giving him a sidelong glance, Alicia saw that he hung his head between his knees. Sheer agony etched his expression. She recalled Katherine's words about a splitting headache in the morning.

She touched his arm. "Does your head pain you much, Thomas?"

He shuddered. "Hell is empty, and all the devils are here inside my brain. They are giving me my just deserts for my shameful conduct toward you. I think I have died several times since daybreak. I may not survive this morning jostling around on the back of a spirited horse."

Once again, he thawed her with his words. She squeezed his arm. "Lie back, and I will try to drive away your tormentors."

With a sigh, he inched his way down onto the bed until his head settled in the hollow of her lap. "Am I too heavy for you?" he asked, looking up at her.

Alicia stroked him lightly across his forehead. "Nay,

Thomas. Methinks you will never be too heavy for me. Now close your eyes."

He did so without further comment. She massaged his temples with gentle circular motions, using only her fingertips. She felt him relax. While she worked, she admired his chiseled features. Thomas's long dark lashes fanned across his high cheekbones. A tremor ruffled his full, sensual lips. She had an overwhelming desire to kiss them.

"You have the touch of an angel," he murmured.

"Shhh," she replied.

Alicia snaked her fingers through his beautiful, though damp, sun-kissed hair. It was incredibly soft—almost like a baby's. Cradling Thomas's head in both her hands, she rubbed more vigorously. He moaned.

She paused. "Have I made the pain worse?"

"Nay, I am lost in pleasure."

His answer warmed her, melting the last of her icy reserves. A shameless idea sprang into her mind. *I will seduce him. The people can wait a while longer. Now...how did Katherine say I should start?*

She leaned over him, allowing her unfettered breasts to touch his hand. "Breathe deeply, dear heart," she suggested in a low voice. "'Twill banish all your pains and turmoil."

His eyes still shut, he turned his head toward her. His lips were less than an inch away from one of her nipples. She changed her massage into a caress, sweeping back his hair from his face. She trailed a fingertip around the contours of his ear. He shivered under her touch. Her nipples peaked and hardened. They tingled as if stroked by fire.

"Thomas," she murmured. "How do you feel now?"

He grinned. "I cannot remember if I am in heaven or on earth." He opened his eyes, and saw her breasts barely concealed inside the thin material. "Great Jove!"

She circled her arms around his head. "Is something amiss, Thomas?"

He gaped at her like a landed trout, but formed no words. Alicia felt scorched by the heat rising within her. Then his lips brushed her nipple through the filmy cloth. The desire within her surged at the intimacy of his touch. She pressed his head against her, much as a mother would hold a nursing babe. His tongue caressed her swollen rosy tip. She gasped with delight as the startling new experience propelled her into an undiscovered sparkling realm.

His eyes glowed with blue fire at her response. He cupped her breast with his palm. She arched under his touch.

"Is something amiss, Alicia?"

"Aye," she panted. "I think I have caught fire."

He untied the ribbon that held her shift in place. "You need cooling." He loosened the material, then took her bared breast once again in his mouth. He suckled her with growing abandon.

Alicia dug her fingers into the padding of his shoulders. "Kiss me, dear heart, or I shall die."

He released her with a final flick of his tongue on her nipple. Rolling over on his stomach, he bore her backward onto the pillows. His long body imprisoned hers with his passion. "Do not die." His lips touched hers as he spoke.

Then he claimed her mouth, crushing her to him. The hunger of his kiss thrilled her. She returned it with a reckless abandon. He growled his pleasure.

They rolled on top of a lump under the covers. With

a yelp, Taverstock clawed at them through the sheets. Then the little terrier pushed his way out of the bedclothes.

Paying no attention to the dogs, Alicia wrapped her legs around Thomas's waist. The hardness of his arousal pressed against her stomach. His heat drove her to greater heights of desire.

Without warning, Tavie took hold of her shift in his sharp little teeth, and ripped it almost in two. Vixen began to bark. Georgie added his bass tones. All three dogs joined in a chorus of yapping and baying, as they frisked around the couple. Thomas swore under his breath before he heaved himself upright.

"Taverstock!" He picked up the littlest one by the scruff of his neck, and shook him. The dog blinked with surprise. Thomas cast a look of supreme regret at his wife. "I had forgotten we were not alone."

Barking, Tavie wiggled in his grip.

Still a little dazed by the intensity of her first foray into lovemaking, Alicia gathered together the remains of her nightgown to cover her nakedness. She took a few deep breaths in an effort to control the rapid beating of her heart. Before she could say anything intelligent, someone knocked on the chamber door.

"Good morrow, my lord, my lady," Andrew chirped through the keyhole. "I have brought hot water for your bath. Master Konrad has already packed a fine picnic for you, and the horses will be saddled within this half an hour. The day promises to be a particularly fine one."

Thomas glared first at the squirming dog in his hands, then at the door. "Hang you, cur!" he growled at Taverstock. Then he raised his voice to Andrew. "And you, you insolent noisemaker, you can hang, too!"

Andrew merely laughed in reply. Tavie licked Thomas's nose.

Alicia sighed with regret at the sudden interruption of her seduction. "I see we are outnumbered."

"Aye," he agreed. "And outflanked as well. Cover yourself, Alicia. I do not want to give Andrew any more ideas than he already has running around that woolly head of his." Then he roared, "Come in!"

The squire entered the chamber, leading a procession of servants, who carried the bulky wooden tub and buckets of steaming water. All of them grinned at the bridal couple, and exchanged many a wink at each other. Alicia sank deeper among the pillows as she watched chaos bubble around her. The squire and Audrey, now promoted to lady's maid, bustled around the chamber with self-important airs as they laid out fresh clothing for their master and mistress.

The line of bucket-bearers seemed never-ending. Alicia suspected that everyone in Wolf Hall used this excuse to catch a glimpse of the newly wedded couple after their first night together. She gripped the sheet tighter under her chin. The dogs added their own accompaniment to the general din by barking and skittering around the servants' legs. Stokes watched the scene from the doorway with a broad smile on his face.

How disappointed everyone would be if they knew the truth! Alicia cast a quick glance at Thomas. He struggled to appear perfectly calm in spite of his flushed face and his obvious headache. He drew the curtains around the bed, enclosing Alicia within their velvet confines.

When the last of the servants had finished gawking, Andrew pushed everyone, including Audrey and the dogs, out the door, then shut it behind them. With a great deal of merry chatter, he helped Thomas out of his stained wedding finery. Alicia covered her mouth lest they heard her gasp of shock. She had not realized that Andrew meant to strip Thomas to the skin, and bathe him practically under her nose.

'Tis natural, now that we are man and wife. Everyone thinks we have already seen quite a lot of each other. She pulled the sheet up to her eyes. She could see them through a tiny crack in the curtains at the foot of the bed.

The boy lifted Thomas's silken shirt over his head. "Did you pass a good night, my lord?" he asked with a wide grin.

Thomas inspected his fingernails. "Tolerable, tolerable," he muttered. Then he whistled woefully out of tune.

The squire chuckled, then called to Alicia over his shoulder. "Your good husband could never sing, my lady. Pray, never allow him to serenade you."

She tried to answer him, but all that came out was a strangled "awk." She had no breath left to speak. She had never seen Thomas bared to the waist. His body was magnificent. His broad chest and powerful shoulders looked as if they were molded in bronze. Thick muscles rippled across his flat stomach. She felt very light-headed.

Andrew knelt to take off his master's boots. Then he untied the laces that held up Thomas's golden tights.

"Oh!" Alicia squeaked, then threw the covers over her head.

"Be quick, stumble-fingers! I grow cold," Thomas growled.

Huddled under the bedclothes, she strained to hear what happened next. Thomas said nothing, nor did Andrew. She drew up her courage to take another peek. Perhaps they had left the room. Then she heard a great sloshing of water, and realized that Thomas had gotten into the tub that stood on the other side of the drawn bed curtains. He grumbled under his breath.

Curiosity got the better of Alicia's maidenly virtue. She parted the hangings, so that she could see a little more through the crack. Thomas sat with his back to her, while Andrew scrubbed his master with silent industry. Alicia admired her husband's back almost as much as she had enjoyed his front. She wished it were her hands that roamed over his glistening skin. She shivered at the thought.

The squire poured a bucket of clean water over Thomas's head. His master reacted with a deep bellow, then shook his long hair. Water droplets flew in all directions. Before she realized what would happen next, he stood up. Water rolled down the hollow of his spine, past his slim hips, and between his tight, flat buttocks.

She stuffed a corner of the sheet into her mouth. Sweet Saint Anne! Her husband was no mere mortal, but some demigod come to earth—and to her.

Andrew handed a large piece of toweling to his master. Thomas threw back his head, as he rubbed the material across his back. Then he turned around, and faced the draped bed.

Alicia nearly choked on the linen wadded in her mouth. She couldn't help staring at the most private and intriguing part of her husband's anatomy. "Oh!" she moaned, chewing on the sheet.

Thomas looked up, saw that he had an audience, and turned scarlet—all over. Quickly wrapping the toweling around his middle, he stepped out of the tub. "Take my clothes to the antechamber,'' he snapped at Andrew. ''My lady needs some privacy.''

He stomped out the door. Andrew followed, but paused long enough to toss a wink at Alicia. She ducked behind the curtains until she heard the door close behind them. Then she lay very still, and listened to her blood pound in her ears.

An hour later, the bridal couple rode out of Wolf Hall. A small retinue accompanied them. Andrew wore his most outrageous cap decorated with many feathers and colorful baubles. Mary, freed for the day from the onus of Mistress Genevieve's dull lessons, challenged everyone to race with her. The master huntsman carried a prized peregrine falcon on his arm—''just in case we see something,'' Thomas explained to Alicia. Audrey perched nervously on a gentle gray mare.

Kip, one of the cook's boys who was placed in charge of Master Konrad's lavish picnic, sat astride a sleepy mule behind a half-dozen men-at-arms. He led a second pack animal that was loaded down with provisions, rugs, pillows and other assorted comforts. One of the assistant huntsmen rode ahead of the party, and blew his horn whenever they approached a hamlet, farm or village. With their heads up and tongues hanging out, Taverstock and Georgie ran alongside the horses. Heavy with her litter, Vixen chose to remain at home.

Alicia lifted her face to the sun. The day proved a glorious one with the earth in its fullest summer ripening. In the fields, families harvested hay and wheat. Plump green apples hung heavily from the trees. Hidden birds caroled the party as they trotted along the byways of the vast Cavendish holdings. The sweet-scented breeze banished the last vestiges of Alicia's marital concerns. She reveled in the cheerful company, especially that of her handsome young husband who rode by her side.

Once past the stone battlements of Wolf Hall, Thomas underwent a transformation—almost as if he had shed a dark, heavy cloak. His serious expression changed into one of boyish enthusiasm when he pointed out his favorite haunts to his wife. He laughed at the slightest provocation, and teased his sister, who gave back as good as she got. He smiled often at Alicia, and constantly asked if she was comfortable, if she was enjoying the ride, if she was thirsty, hungry or tired. Though she was not used to riding a horse, she returned her husband's smiles, and assured him time and again that she was very comfortable. To herself, she vowed to soak for hours in a hot bath at the day's end.

At every cottage and humble croft, the tenants waited to do courtesies to their lord and his new lady. Alicia was overwhelmed by the people's genuine love for their overlord, and the warmth of their welcome to her. At every stop, they were offered something to eat as a token of hospitality: bread and butter at the poorer homes; sharp cheese and blackberry pastries from the more affluent. Their health was toasted with foaming mugs of ale. Alicia suspected that they would never be able to do full justice to Master Konrad's picnic.

Village children capered beside her horse, and offered her ragged bunches of flowers gathered from the fields. Alicia's cape soon overflowed with daisies, buttercups, blue cornflowers and red poppies. She was deeply touched by the many little kindnesses showered upon her, as the company progressed over hill and dale.

Women of advanced years used the handsome earl's visit as an opportunity to kiss his hand, and to be rewarded with a peck on the cheek and a silver penny in return by the red-faced bridegroom. Alicia didn't blame the old dames one whit. Thomas's good looks appealed to females of all ages, from six to sixty. She was very lucky to be his wife, she told herself.

At one farmhouse, the children offered Thomas a reed-thin puppy. He dismounted, tossed the horse's reins to Andrew, then hunkered down in the mud of the stable yard to inspect their furry gift. Georgie helped himself to the water in the horse trough. Tavie stared at the pup with a jealous expression on his face.

Mary nudged her sister-in-law, then pointed to the terrier. "Tom will have a great deal of trouble on his hands, if he takes another dog under his wing."

Alicia nodded. "For once I agree with Tavie. I am just getting used to three dogs—a fourth might make me lose my wits."

Holding up the pup, Thomas scrutinized its paws, teeth, legs and joints. "Aye, you have a right fine hound here," he complimented the three little barefoot girls in front of him.

The eldest bobbed a curtsy. "He is yours—and the lady's—so please you, my lord."

Thomas leaned closer to her. "Pray, does this most excellent dog have a name yet?"

The girls looked from one to the other. Then the youngest volunteered, "Da calls him that deuced dog."

Their father, who stood behind the trio, coughed behind his hand. The men-at-arms chuckled. Thomas managed to keep a straight face though Alicia saw that it was a struggle for him.

"Deuce is a brave name," he agreed. "Methinks he will make a good hunter when he is grown."

Alicia glanced at Mary, and whispered, "By my troth, he means to keep it."

Thomas looked up at his wife, then at Tavie, then he returned his attention to the girls. "Your Deuce is a bit young to follow the pack now. Pray, will you keep him for me until he is half-grown? Then my master of hounds will train him for the chase."

The little girls nodded with great seriousness. Their father looked taken aback. Alicia suspected the man wanted to be rid of the gaunt animal. Thomas rose, then dug into his pouch, and gave the farmer a gold sovereign. "Methinks this will pay for Deuce's board with a bit left over to buy these pretty posies of yours a few fripperies. Do not forget your good wife, my man. I have recently discovered that wives cherish a loving gift or two." He grinned at Alicia.

With a laugh on her lips and a fluttering in her heart, she acknowledged his salute.

The farmer smiled broadly as he fingered the gold coin in his hand. "'Twill be as ye say, my lord," he promised.

Thomas remounted Silver Charm. With many a wave, they continued on their progress.

Once out of sight of the farm, Alicia leaned over her pommel, and said, "I am right glad you did not add Deuce to our family circle."

He nodded. "Aye, our bed is crowded enough as it is," he replied in a low voice.

She blushed to remember the early morning's debacle. Thomas reached over, took her hand, and kissed it.

Her skin sizzled where his lips touched. She struggled to maintain her composure. "You treated the children well."

He grew serious. "'Twas little enough for them, poor

poppets. The children look healthy in the summertime, but when the winter winds howl down from the north, they suffer with coughs and fevers. Their parents almost lost the youngest last year. When the girls are a little older, I plan to take them into service at the Hall—with your permission, of course.''

His concern for this poor family touched Alicia more deeply than she had expected. ''Aye, the girls will enliven our hearth with their sweetness.''

He wiggled his brows at her. ''More likely they will enliven the pot boys to lusty thoughts. Have to watch that.'' After kissing her hand again, he accepted Mary's challenge to race to the far side of the nearby meadow.

Alicia reined in her horse, and watched her husband and his gray charger dash across the waving grasses dotted with colorful wildflowers.

What a wonderful father Thomas will make—if I can ever get him into bed without those deuced dogs!

Flash and Demon stood by their horses under the cover of the forest that edged the meadow. They watched the Earl of Thornbury gallop after a flaxen-hair chit on a white palfrey.

''He is a monstrous brute,'' Demon observed.

Flash shrugged. ''Aye, but 'tis his wench we want.'' Shading his eyes, he peered across the grassy expanse at the tall woman who watched her husband's progress. ''She is a match to him. Methinks she is a head taller than you, Demon.'' He cuffed his associate on the shoulder.

The other man spat on the ground. ''Not so, neither. There is not a woman alive I cannot tame.''

Flash merely smiled to himself. Then he considered the problem at hand. It had been sheer good luck that they had spied the earl and countess leaving Wolf Hall this morning. Easier to waylay them somewhere on the road, than to attempt an abduction from within the stout walls of the castle. He narrowed his eyes with speculation. The attending men-at-arms outnumbered them three to one. Only a simpleton would attack with such odds.

Demon tugged at Flash's sleeve. "They have turned at the stile, and are coming back this way."

Flash shook his arm free from the other's grasp. "Make no move, and they will pass us by as they did before. Should the earl spy us, bow your head like a humble peasant, and smile. A cheerful face hides the devil's own, my da often told me."

Demon grinned, displaying gaped teeth. "Yer da was a right proper cutpurse in his day."

Flash didn't answer. Instead he went very still as the earl's warhorse thundered past their hiding place. A little brown-and-white dog panted after the riders. He stopped, lifted his nose in the air, then turned toward the spot where the brigands hid.

"Do not move an eyelash," Flash whispered out of the corner of his mouth.

The dog crept closer, his beady little eyes fixed on Flash. The man drew in his breath. One of their horses stamped the soft ground. The movement distracted the little cur. Just then the notes of a hunting horn sounded over the meadow. The dog froze with one forepaw lifted off the ground. He pricked his ears. The horn called again. With an answering bark, the dog turned, and raced back to the earl and his party. Demon sagged against a tree. Flash released his pent-up breath.

He threw himself into his saddle. "Mount up, Demon. Our hunt continues."

"How long?" his companion whined, as he pulled himself up onto his rented nag.

Stroking his rough chin, Flash watched their quarry ride down the road. "Until we get her." He gave his friend a wink. "She will have to take time to relieve herself sooner or later."

Demon's chuckle answered him.

Chapter Seventeen

The late-afternoon sun dropped down behind the tips of the tall pines when Thomas and Alicia drew near to the forest that marked the boundary of the Cavendish lands. The pace of the bridal progress had slowed considerably since the stop to consume the picnic lunch. The fresh, clear air, and the steady riding had preserved the company's appetites, despite all the hospitality they had enjoyed. Full of food and more ale than she usually drank, Alicia found she had a difficult time staying awake.

Thomas caught her when she pitched forward in her saddle for the second time. "Are you ill?" he asked, concern clouding his brilliant eyes.

Smiling, she shook her head. "I must confess that I have grown numb. 'Tis a weakness I must remedy— but not today." She covered a yawn with the back of her hand. She hated to show her lack of riding experience in front of all of the men.

Thomas drew their horses to a halt. "The devil take me for a pudding!" He dismounted with an easy grace, then lifted his wife out of her saddle. "The day has been so merry, my mind forgot that you are city-bred,

and not used to long hours on horseback. Forgive me.''
He gave her a look of genuine sorrow.

Alicia made light of the matter, though she ached in
every joint. '''Tis nothing. I have enjoyed myself—and
the company.'' She squeezed his hand.

He grinned like a schoolboy. '''Tis cool and pleasant
among these old trees. We will take our ease here
awhile.'' He made a rueful face. ''My own backside
has been well used, and could do with a rest.''

Alicia doubted that he felt any discomfort at all, but
he was kind to pretend that he did to cover her frailty.
Gratefully, she sank down on a springy bed of moss
that grew beside the wide trunk of a sweet-smelling
spruce. Andrew offered his lord and lady a skin of cool
watered wine. The drink tasted like nectar after so many
dusty hours in the saddle, and so many mugs of rough
ale down their throats. Contentment seeped through her
every fiber. With another yawn, she laid her head
against the fragrant bark of the sheltering tree. Her eyelids fluttered closed.

Thomas chuckled in her ear. ''Do you mean to pass
the night here, my lady?''

With her eyes still closed, Alicia rolled her head from
side to side. ''Not the night, but a century,'' she murmured.

He draped his riding cape over her. ''A half hour is
all I can spare you. We must be home before the moon
rises.''

''Home,'' she echoed with a contented sigh. She
drifted on a gentle current of sleep.

Georgie startled her out of her half dream when he
suddenly gave a sharp yelp. ''What...?'' She squinted
through her lashes.

"A hare, my lord!" Andrew called. "A fat one, who begs to be the guest of honor at your supper this night."

Thomas leapt to his feet. "Then let us accept his kind invitation with pleasure. Mary, you stay with Alicia while she rests."

His sister groaned. "And miss all the fun? I am not tired."

Alicia gave her new sister a sleepy smile. "Be off with you, poppet, and show your brother who is the better hunter."

Mary mounted her palfrey without waiting for a hand up. "'Tis a challenge I accept. To it, Tom! I wager three gold angels that I shoot it before you do."

He dropped to one knee beside Alicia. "I did not know that my sister possessed such a fortune," he said with a grin. "Will you give me leave to uphold my honor?" He cast an anxious glance over his shoulder to make sure that Mary did not get a head start.

Alicia reached up to sweep a stray golden lock out of his eyes. "Ride on, Thomas. I am content to stay here, and dream of rabbits, not chase them."

He caught her hand, and kissed it. "We will return in a short time, I promise. Taverstock will guard you. Stay," he ordered the little terrier.

Tavie whined, licked his nose, then crawled under the cape and curled his body next to Alicia's.

She patted the lump beside her. "Methinks I will be the one guarding Taverstock."

Thomas kissed her hand again. "Methinks you are right, but do not tell him. Sleep well, sweet lady."

Her heart swelled with love to hear him whisper such tender words to her, and to feel the print of his lips caress her hand. Before she could tell him of her own warm feelings, he left her, and ran for his horse. He jumped into his saddle without his feet touching the stirrups. With a shout that surely frightened any hare within twenty miles, he kicked Silver Charm into a canter. They dashed away through the trees, followed by Mary, Andrew and the men-at-arms. Audrey and Kip, having discovered a mutual interest in each other, wandered out of Alicia's sight.

She settled herself back against the tree, and pulled up the cape to her chin. "Heaven help the poor hare," she murmured to Taverstock. Then she drifted into a cozy sleep.

She dreamed of a black cloud that descended upon her, hiding her from sight. The more she fought against it, the heavier the cloud became. It smothered her, blocking out light and air. She called for Thomas, but the cloud filled her mouth and silenced her. She couldn't breathe. It smelled of onions, sweat and dirty wool. When she tried to thrust it away, something clamped around her throat.

Taverstock barked.

She opened her eyes, and gasped. She wasn't dreaming but awake, and bound in the folds of a thick, filthy cloak.

A man held her, and swore. "Zounds, the wench is stronger than I thought. The rope, you laggard! Step lively!" he growled, his voice low and raw with anger.

Alicia kicked at him, but her assailant proved to be too agile. She clawed at the foul material that covered her. She felt a face through the cloth. Getting a good grip on him, she squeezed his cheeks and nose together.

He shook her. "Hold, bitch, or I will give you a few bloody teeth," he snarled. He bent her hand back at the wrist, until the pain forced her to release him.

Alicia tried to roll away from the ruffian. God in

heaven! Where was Thomas? She managed to pull a corner of the cape away from her face.

"Taverstock! Go to Thomas!" she shouted to the little terrier, who danced out of the man's range. "Bring Thomas here!"

The dog laid back his ears, and snarled, baring his little sharp teeth.

A short, black-haired man drew his dagger. "My tooth is greater than all of yers, cur!"

Alicia kicked and clawed at the taller man, who tried to straddle her. "Run, Tavie! Find Thomas!"

The terrier perked his ears, then turned and raced through the thick underbrush. The short man started to follow the dog.

"Nay!" Alicia's captor called to him. "Leave off, and bring me the deuced rope, Demon! We will be long gone ere his wee legs can carry him beyond the briars." He slapped Alicia across the face. "By the devil and his dame, she fights like a Fury crowned with snakes."

His blow made Alicia's ears ring. Blue sparks danced before her eyes. Warm salty blood rolled into her mouth from a cut on her lower lip. She glared at the man above her.

"Toad!" She spat out the word. "Ugly and venomous swamp creature!"

He grasped her by her braid, and yanked it hard. "I swear I will cudgel you if you dare to speak to me again."

She curled her lip. "Aye, I would rather throw my words to the dog. He is better company." She tried to free her hair from his grasp.

The man drew his free hand back, and dealt her a second blow harder than the first. Tears welled up, though she bit her lips to keep from crying out. She refused to give her tormentor any satisfaction. Instead, she shut her eyes, and went limp in his grasp.

"God's death! Did ye kill her?" the darker one asked.

In answer, the first man gripped her face in his large paw, and wobbled it to and fro. "She breathes still. Fainted, by the look of it."

Alicia prayed that he would relax his hold. A minute of inattention was all that she needed to make her escape. Instead, he maintained a tight grip around her middle with his thighs. At least, he let go of her hair. Her head fell against a root of the spruce tree with a teeth-rattling crash. She clamped her jaws together, and managed to maintain her subterfuge. The man then threw the stinking cloak back over her face, and tied it down with a thick coil of rope around her neck.

With a grunt, her assailant got off of her. "There is a pretty package for the king," he said as he bound her hands behind her back.

Demon chuckled. "And a pretty penny for us!"

A well of panic bubbled up inside Alicia's throat. *Sweet Jesu, protect me!* Her worse nightmare had come to life. She had been captured by hirelings of her sworn enemy, the Tudor who called himself England's rightful king. She bit her tongue to keep from crying. *Oh, Thomas, will I ever see you again this side of heaven?* She took a deep breath through her swollen lips. The seed of her Plantagenet courage grew stronger within her breast. *We still have a long way to go before I lodge in the Tower of London, you churls. Do not count on your reward so soon. Besides, I have not yet enjoyed my wedding night.*

The taller man scooped her up, and carried her as if she were a sack of wheat. He tossed her over a horse's back. "She is a tall one!" he remarked as he swung himself into the saddle behind her. "I like my women tiny, like the one who sent us here. Now *there* is a toothsome piece."

Alicia remained very still, though her mind grew keener. She could not image why any woman would employ these knaves to do the king's dirty work. Her captor spurred his mount. Her head hanging down, she bounced and slipped across the pommel as the man's horse broke into a gallop. Her abductor held her by the rope around her waist. She prayed he had tied the knots tight enough. She preferred to arrive at her destination in one reasonable piece, rather than to be dashed headlong into a ditch.

Thomas reined in his horse. Georgie pawed at a small hole under a rotting stump.

Andrew took off his cap, and mopped the perspiration from his brow. "Our rabbit has gone to ground, my lord. Do you want us to dig her out?"

Mary drew up between them. She wrinkled her nose. "What is the sport in that? 'Twould be like digging up a turnip. I say spare the poor thing, and let us return home. She has given us good exercise, and deserves the boon of her life."

Thomas reached out, and chucked his sister under the chin. "Methinks you are too tenderhearted to be a true huntress."

She pulled herself up in her saddle. "Give me a mighty stag or a stout boar, and I shall show you how ruthless I can be!"

Her brother opened his mouth to make a jesting retort, but instead cocked his ear. Taverstock's barking resounded through the woods. Georgie ceased to dig at the rabbit hole. He lifted his muzzle, and answered Tavie with a deep bay. The mastiff's neck hairs bristled.

Andrew jammed his cap back on his head. "How now? What is amiss?"

Thomas wheeled his horse around. "'Tis Tavie's cry of alarm."

The terrier burst through the underbrush, dashed up to Silver Charm's hooves, and circled himself several times. Standing in his stirrups, Thomas peered into the wood behind the dog. More crashing sounds followed the terrier. Thomas drew his sword.

"Prepare yourselves. Mary, behind me!"

Audrey, accompanied by Kip, staggered into the clearing. Their clothing hung half-off their bodies, and many scratches from thorns and twigs scarred their arms and faces. The distraught maid sank to the ground, threw her apron over her head, and wept with loud wails. Kip clutched Silver Charm's harness.

"Two men," the boy gasped. "They have taken Lady Alicia, and—"

A blind rage filled Thomas. "What?" The forest echoed his roar. He leaned down, and collared the white-faced lad. "Why did you not protect her?" He shook the frightened youth like a doll made of rags.

Kip's teeth chattered. "We did not hear them until 'twas too late, my lord. They were evil-looking brutes, and well armed."

Thomas tightened his grip. "And you let them take her? Did they...harm her?" He glared at the cowering lickspit.

Tears shone in the boy's frightened eyes. "No harm, my lord. I swear upon my soul. She fainted, and they tied her up, and rode away."

Thomas released the lad, who dropped to the ground

as if his legs could no longer support him. "They were on horseback?" he muttered under his breath. "Then they were no ordinary thieves." He shuddered to think of his precious wife in their company.

Taverstock barked with an impatient air. He skittered back and forth at the edge of the clearing. His dark eyes glowed.

Thomas sheathed his sword. "Cullum," he shouted to one of the men-at-arms. "Take my sister and these two servants back to the castle, then call out the guard." He turned again to the kitchen boy. "Did you happen to see the direction they were headed?"

Kip nodded. "Away from the sun, my lord."

"Perchance to York?" Andrew suggested.

Kip nodded again.

Thomas ground his teeth together. The blood lust boiled in his veins. "To hell itself! Taverstock! Find Alicia! Go!"

Without a backward glance, the little dog streaked into the underbrush. His feet did not appear to touch the ground. Georgie flashed after him, howling as if all the furies of damnation pursued him. Spurring Silver Charm into a gallop, Thomas leaned low over his charger's neck. Rider and horse melded into one. They flew through the forest after the dogs. Thomas heard Andrew and the men-at-arms thudding behind him.

Brambles tore at his cape, and slapped against his horse's flanks. Thomas urged his courageous steed to an even faster pace. His mount responded. They galloped into the gathering twilight, following Tavie's blur of white, and the deep howling that Georgie hurled to the purpling sky.

One thought burned in Thomas's brain. *I never told her that I loved her.*

* * *

Alicia had no idea how long they had been riding, except she knew they were not on a well-traveled road. Her hands had grown cold and numb from the ropes that bound them. Her stomach ached where the ridge of the saddle pressed into it.

"Flash, hold!" the darker man shouted above the sounds of their horses. "A word, I crave ye!"

Flash pulled on the reins. His horse skipped sideways before coming to a halt. Alicia held her breath as she started to slip downward. Flash gripped the rope, and tugged her back into place.

"A pox on you, Demon! Has your nag thrown a shoe?"

Demon rode his horse so close to the other that the animal bumped against Alicia's head. Under the concealing cloak, she strained to hear their conference.

"Nay, 'tis the woman I speak of," Demon replied.

Flash tightened his grip on the rope that held her. "Which one?"

Demon chuckled. "Aye, there is the rub. Two fine ladies in one night, if we be lucky."

"There will be nothing for us if we do not deliver her as we were ordered," Flash replied.

"We nipped her in the bag so quick, I could not tell if this wench had any jewelry about her," his partner complained.

Alicia thought of her too-large wedding ring, her necklace of gold chains and freshwater pearls, and most of all, her father's ruby and pearl brooch. That jewel alone would incite these knaves to cold-blooded murder. She swallowed back the sour bile taste on her tongue.

Flash did not speak for a long moment, then he asked, "What do you have in mind?"

Demon chortled again. The sound grated against Alicia's nerves.

"We have traveled a goodly distance, and 'tis growing too dark for anyone to track us. Let us unwrap our pretty prize, and see what she's wearing. The lady said we could," he added with a whine in his voice.

Alicia licked her bruised lips. *What lady?*

Demon continued his plea. "If we wait until we get to the inn, 'twill be no time to search her at our leisure, if ye catch my meaning, eh, Flash?" His laughter rang with an ominous tone.

Alicia truly did feel faint. They meant to use her body before delivering her up to her unknown enemy. She squeezed her eyes shut at the horrible prospect. *Come soon, Thomas, before 'tis too late for me.*

Flash patted her backside. She willed herself not to flinch. They must think she was still unconscious. Perhaps they will drop their guard. She knew she would have only one chance to escape, if she even got that slim opportunity.

"You speak the truth," her captor conceded. "Methinks we have put enough miles between us and the earl's men. We are safe for a while. There is a thick copse yonder. A fair trysting spot if ever I saw one." He chuckled as he urged his horse into a walk. "This piece of work will not take long."

Alicia prayed that she would not tremble when they uncovered her. Branches lashed her head and feet as Flash guided his horse through a grove of trees. All too soon, they stopped.

Flash dismounted. "'Tis a fine place for fine work."

"'Tis a bit of honey that I crave," Demon replied.

Rough hands grasped Alicia by her feet, and pulled her off the horse. She willed herself not to stiffen at their touch. She must not give herself away too soon.

Flash grunted as he hefted her over his shoulder. "She is more than a bit, my friend. 'Tis a lass to entertain an army. And soft." His hand fondled her buttock again. Alicia pressed her lips together. She could feel an angry flush steal into her cheeks. *Guardian angel, hide my color, or they will know I am conscious.*

"This spot is as good as any." Flash laid her down on the pebble-strewn ground.

One of the stones bore into the small of her back. She remained still. He pulled the cloak off of her. The cool air of the evening kissed her face. She welcomed the scant relief, though she did not move, nor open her eyes. Her stomach churned with fearful anticipation.

Demon sucked in his breath through his teeth. "Pretty piece that."

"The woman or her jewels?" Flash asked with a trace of sarcasm.

"Both. First we take one, then the other."

Alicia's skin crawled at the varlet's insinuation.

"Cut her loose, Flash. She's no a-danger. I cannot mount her if her legs be tied together."

Alicia bit the inside of her cheek.

Flash said nothing, but stroked her hair. Then he drew out his knife. The blade rasped against the scabbard. He began to saw at the thick ropes around her legs.

"Did you ever lay eyes on old King Edward?" he suddenly asked his partner.

Alicia held her breath. Why did the man say something like that?

Demon snorted. "Nay, only ministers of the king's justice." He spat, narrowly missing her face.

Flash proceeded to cut the bindings from her wrists. The men were so close she could smell their filth. Her gorge rose in her throat. Flash removed her rings from one hand, while Demon helped himself to the other with many a harsh chortle. Her outsize wedding ring slid easily off her middle finger. Alicia experienced a pang to be parted from it. It felt as if the knaves stripped her husband away from her. *Thomas, my heart, where are you?*

Flash dropped his booty into his poke, then turned back to her. "I saw King Edward once when I was a lad. Giant of a man, and all golden. Made me almost believe in angels again." He again took a lock of her hair, and rolled it between his fingers. "She has his look," he continued, with an odd catch in his voice.

Demon thumped him on the shoulder. "Be ye a Yorkist?" He spat again. "York or Tudor, makes not a whit of difference. The devil take me! Look at the bauble she wears on her breast."

He started to reach for it. Alicia wondered if she should make her move now. Her muscles strained with the agony of waiting. Flash grabbed his henchman by the wrist.

"Aye, 'tis a gladsome sight, but soft, my friend. I want to be sure the glittering stone does not slip away, never to be seen again."

Demon cursed as he tried to pull himself away from the other's grip. "Calling me a thief, are ye?"

"Aye, you have a most unsavory smile, and are swift of fingers in other men's pockets. Yet I also know you to be as true a coward as ever turned a back, so do not threaten me with your empty oaths," Flash replied in a low icy tone. "I will take the jewel myself, and will broker it with one I know whose shop lies near Micklegate. By and by, you will get your share of the coin. Be content with that."

Demon leaned over her, and shoved Flash. "Content, my foot! You are the veriest varlet that ever chewed with a tooth!"

Alicia trembled as the men fell to cursing each other above her. She realized that her eating knife had been overlooked. It still hung from her belt. A small weapon against two villains, but enough, if she could use it at the right moment. Her hand lay only a foot away from its sheath, yet it seemed like a mile.

She stiffened. She thought she heard the distant sound of a dog's deep bark. While the men continued to argue in more heated terms, she inched her hand closer to her belt. Again, she heard the sound of a dog in full pursuit of his prey. This time she could not mistake its tone. Only Georgie howled like rolling thunder. Her heart leapt to her throat. She prayed her ears had not deceived her. Her fingers closed around the handle of the knife.

Alicia froze as one of the men struck the other. She heard the sickening sound of flesh smacking against bone. Demon fell half on top of her, but struggled to his feet almost at once. Peeking out of one eye, she slid the little knife from its case. Neither man noticed her. They continued to flail at each other. Moving as quickly as she dared, she hid her hand with its poor weapon under a fold of her skirts.

Hurry, Thomas! Pray God, 'tis you!

Flash grabbed Demon by his jerkin. "We waste the last of the light with this fool's farce." Giving him a shake, he let go of his partner, then knelt by Alicia. Demon dropped down on her other side.

Her eyes closed, Alicia gripped the knife harder. The hilt bit into her palm.

Flash unpinned her father's brooch. With a grunt of satisfaction, he added it to his booty in his poke. Demon unclasped her necklace. Then his hand closed over her breast. He squeezed it hard.

She gritted her teeth. *Nay! I will not yield up my*

precious maidenhead to this churl. I belong to Thomas Cavendish!

Without warning she sat bolt upright. Before either man could react, she swiped at Demon with her weapon and felt her blade slice through the flesh of his cheek. The impact so unnerved her, she almost dropped the knife in horror. With a roar, he drew back his hand to hit her, but she curled into a ball. The blow landed on her shoulder.

Flash grabbed her around the waist, though she fought and clawed at him. She searched for another target with her knife. Demon drew his own weapon, twice the size of hers.

Flash clamped a large hand around both her wrists. Still holding her in a death grip, he kicked the dagger out of Demon's hand. "Are you moonstruck? The lady wants her alive."

"The bitch cut me! I'll have my own back at her."

Flash pulled Alicia behind him. "She is worth nothing to us if she is dead! Use what is left of your sodden brains."

Demon stalked toward them, his eyes gleaming like a maddened animal's. Blood gushed down his neck. "She has marked me for life, and I will have my revenge. Get ye gone, Flash, or I will kill ye, too. 'Tis all one to me!"

Just then a tremendous howling filled the forest. The underbrush crashed with an unseen fiend. All three stood stock-still, and listened as the unearthly sound reverberated amid the dark trees around them.

Demon's eyes widened. He crossed himself. "'Tis a pooka hound! He has come to drag us down to hell! God shield me!"

Chapter Eighteen

Georgie burst into the clearing. Even Alicia gasped at the fearsome sight he presented. His wide black muzzle opened, and exposed two rows of large white teeth. Silver strands of saliva dripped from his jaws, as the mastiff rose on his powerful hindquarters, and hurled himself onto Flash.

The man let go of Alicia, and fought to ward off the maddened animal's attack. They crashed to the ground. Demon stared at the struggle between man and beast with terror-stricken eyes. Meanwhile, Alicia scrambled away from their twisting bodies.

"Cavendish! To me!" Thomas's battle cry filled the air. Silver Charm plunged through the hawthorn bracken into the melee. His rider brandished his sword, looking like Saint Michael the archangel himself.

Demon raised his dagger to plunge it into Georgie. Without waiting for his horse to stop, Thomas leapt from the saddle, and hurled the dark man to the ground. Alicia screamed as her enraged husband lopped off the villain's hand with a single slash of his sword. The bloody thing fell to the earth, still gripping the knife.

Demon shrieked in pain, and clutched his mangled arm to his chest.

His sword dripping with blood, Thomas wheeled round. Flash gripped Georgie by his leather collar, and twisted it tighter. The huge dog thrashed against the choke hold. Without blinking, Thomas thrust his sword between the two. Flash gasped as if all the wind had been knocked out of him. Then he went limp when the sword pierced his heart. Gasping for air, Georgie backed off the body.

Alicia clutched the nearest tree for support. Never had she witnessed such a heated rage. She felt shaken to the core by the display of her husband's raw power.

Thomas stepped over the dead man, and strode to her side. "How fare you, Alicia?" he asked with infinite tenderness. He took her cold hand in his warm one, and kissed her nerveless fingers.

She tumbled into his arms. Her blood roared in her ears. "W...well, my lord," she answered when she could find her voice.

Dropping his weapon, he crushed her against his chest, and buried his face in her unbound hair. "Did...did they...? Are you...harmed?"

She slipped her arms around his waist. "Nay, but 'twas a near thing." She could feel his heart thudding against her own. She could not stop shivering.

His lips trembled. "I have never killed a man before." The two of them clung to each other in silence for several long minutes. Thomas's warmth seeped into Alicia. Laying her head on his shoulder, she drank in the comfort of his nearness, and wept with relief. His great body shook with emotion.

Andrew and the guards milled around the small clearing within the thicket of hawthorn. The exhausted Taverstock rode in the squire's saddlebag. When he saw his master and mistress, he uttered several hoarse barks. Meanwhile, Demon's screams of pain had subsided to moans.

Lifting his head, Thomas stared into Alicia's eyes. "Later, I will make amends to God for my killing, but, by my troth, I would have skinned the villain while he still lived until he begged for death, if he had touched—"

She placed her hand over his lips before he could say anything else. The force of his anger frightened her. "I am whole, Thomas. All they took was my jewelry—and your wedding ring." She showed him her bare finger.

He brushed his lips over her ravished hand. "You shall have it back anon—with interest." His eyes gleamed in the dusk.

Her skin burned where he had caressed her. She started to reply, but Thomas turned to Andrew, and lifted Taverstock out of the leather pouch.

"Here is your true champion." He held out the little dog to her. "I have never seen Tavie run so fast, nor so far before. He guided us from the clearing where you had been attacked to the old wagon track before his legs gave out. There Georgie picked up your scent, and led us onward."

Alicia took the terrier, and cradled him against her. Tavie closed his eyes, and sighed through his nose.

"He and Georgie shall have a special feast when we return home."

Thomas traced his knuckle down her cheek. "Aye, they deserve it, but first, I must finish what was started."

He strode over to Demon, and nudged the prostrate

churl with his boot. "Cease your caterwauling, fool. Tell me your master's name and his intent."

Demon acted as if he had not heard Thomas. He continued to rock on the ground, and cry.

The tall knight knelt beside him. "Speak, butcher's cur, or you will lose your other one in a trice."

The varlet only whimpered, "My hand, my hand! How can I make my living now?"

Thomas grabbed the man's good hand, and raised his sword. Alicia stifled a scream. Her husband's beautiful blue eyes glowed like ice chips. He looked like the angel of death.

Demon squealed like a stuck pig. "'Twas no master, but a lady," he babbled.

Thomas flourished his sword an inch above the man's arm. "Come again, I did not hear you well enough. The name of your master, churl!"

Alicia took a step forward. "He speaks the truth. I heard them say 'twas a lady who had hired them to abduct me."

The man nodded. "By my mother's soul, 'tis a rich lady named Isabel Cavendish, who waits for us at the Black Dog Inn on the Ainsty road."

Alicia gasped. She had not realized how deep Isabel's hatred had flowed. What would Lady Cavendish have done with her?

"Why?" Thomas's voice crackled like ice in February.

Demon sucked in his breath. "She claimed to be an agent for King Henry. She said your lady was an enemy of the king, and that he would pay a rich ransom for her."

Alicia closed her eyes, and breathed a prayer of

thanksgiving. Isabel would have delivered her up to certain death—and all for a few coins in return.

Thomas swore a blood-chilling oath. His fingers tightened around the hilt of his sword. For one terrifying moment, Alicia thought that he meant to run his blade through the brigand. Instead, he slid his weapon back into his scabbard.

He spoke to one of the men-at-arms. "Crocker, take this piece of vermin into your care. Bind up his wound so that he will be healthy when he hangs in York." He glanced at Flash's inert body. "Throw this offal over his beast, and bear both knaves to the master gaoler of York with my compliments. Andrew, escort my lady and the dogs back to Wolf Hall, and see to their comfort. I have some business to attend to in Ainsty at the sign of the Black Dog."

Alicia touched his arm. "Nay, my lord," she told him in a quiet voice. "I will go with you."

His eyebrows knit together into a dark frown. "'Tis not a matter for a woman."

She lifted her chin. "Isabel is *my* enemy, not yours. She wanted to betray me unto death. 'Tis my right to face her."

Husband and wife stared at each other for a moment, then Thomas relented. "Your beauty hides the heart of a lion, my sweet. You do your noble father proud." He gathered her into his arms once again. "Breed me only warriors," he whispered in her ear. "Methinks I could not handle more than one woman made of your fiery mettle."

He took Tavie from her, and handed the sleeping dog back to Andrew. "Care for my heroes until we return, Master Ford."

Bending in his saddle, Andrew swept his master a

courtly bow. "'Tis my honor and pleasure, my lord."
He tucked Taverstock back inside his saddlebag, then
whistled to Georgie. The rising moon caught a sparkle
in the boy's eyes. "We will prepare Wolf Hall for a
grand celebration. Godspeed, my lord and lady."

Thomas patted Andrew's gelding on the rump. "And
with you, lad."

The squire turned his horse about, then disappeared
through the hawthorns. Georgie followed behind him
with his long tongue hanging nearly to the ground.
Some of the men-at-arms trussed Flash's body across
his horse while others tied Demon into his saddle.
Thomas slipped his arm around Alicia's waist.

"Are you certain sure you want to see this affair to
its end?" he murmured in her ear.

She leaned against him. "On my life, Thomas. My
very life."

He pressed his lips to hers. At first, he only caressed
her mouth. His touch sent a thousand tingling shocks
through her body. She rose on tiptoe, and returned his
kiss with fervor. He twined his tongue with hers as if
he would devour her, then he pulled away. She clung
to his shoulders. Her mouth burned with his fire.

"We ride," he whispered, his hot breath fanned her
cheek. "We will meet the devil's handmaiden in her
lair. Later, by God, I will do you full justice."

His promise made her heart leap for joy.

He lifted her onto Silver Charm's saddle, then swung
himself up behind her. "Kirby, Ozwald, attend on me,
and follow!"

Thomas spurred his charger into a canter. Alicia held
tight to the pommel as the horse swept through the hawthorn branches. The cool night air blew into her face.
Thomas pulled her back against his solid chest.

"'Tis good that you accompany me, my sweet," he said. "Your pure heart will keep me from doing an injury to that shrew."

She squeezed his arm that held her around her waist. She gulped great draughts of air, and thanked all the saints in heaven for the gift of her husband and protector.

You chose wisely for me, Sir Edward Brampton.

Isabel had waited until nearly midnight for her minions to return with their prize. When the candle on her sideboard began to sputter in its wax, she decided that they had been unsuccessful that day. No use to lose her own sleep over their ineptitude. She climbed into the inn's sorry excuse for a bed, pulled the covers up to her chin, and had no difficulty falling into a deep sleep.

The chamber's door burst open with the force of a whirlwind. Wood splintered against the plaster wall. Isabel bolted upright. In the dim light of the moon through the tiny dormer window, she saw her room fill up with men brandishing swords and daggers. One of them grabbed Meg before the imbecile maid could utter a scream. Isabel shielded herself with a pillow.

"Who dares to disturb my sleep in this unholy fashion?" she demanded in the bravest voice she could muster.

Someone struck a flint to the candle. In the flickering light she beheld Thomas standing over her. Wildfire danced in his eyes.

"Good evening, Isabel," he growled.

She snorted in reply. "What jest is this, Thomas? I am in no mood for any mad prank of yours. Begone!"

He bared his teeth like one of his dogs. "No jest,

sister-in-law, unless you consider abduction, theft and rape to be entertaining.''

Her words of rebuke died on her lips when Thomas stepped aside, and she saw Alicia standing next to him. The woman's long hair hung unbound and tangled; her rich gown was torn and muddy. Despite her fear, Isabel felt a certain satisfaction with her usurper's bedraggled appearance.

She glanced again at Thomas. He looked like one of the dreaded horsemen of the apocalypse. All he lacked was a fiery sword. She realized belatedly that she had pushed the Earl of Thornbury too far. The blade of his dagger glowed red in the candlelight.

Alicia placed her hand over his that held the knife. At her touch, he visibly softened a little, though he still looked like a sinner's worst nightmare. Isabel's intuition told her that her only hope of salvation lay with Alicia. She pasted a weak grin on her face. She must brazen out this debacle. Her lips trembled.

''I am relieved to see you here, sister-in-law,'' she said. ''I beg you to take your poor husband home, and nurse him well. 'Tis obvious that he is in the throes of one of his fits, and—''

The dagger sang through the air. Thomas sliced open the pillow that Isabel clutched to her breast. Goose feathers fluttered around them like snowflakes in winter. Isabel bit down hard on her lower lip to contain her scream of fear. *He has truly gone mad!*

''Why did you seek the life of my own?'' he asked in a deceptively soft voice.

She tried to swallow, but her throat had gone dry. ''I…I have no idea what you are talking about. As you can see, I am a-bed. How could I possibly—''

Thomas leaned over the bed. His face was mere

inches from Isabel's. The smell of her fear tainted his nostrils. "One of your men languishes within York's dank gaol. After due process of the law, he will suffer a cruel death for his crimes against my wife. I regret that his companion has already paid the full price, and will miss the excitement of a public execution."

Isabel turned paler, but said nothing.

He continued. "We had a long ride to York this evening. Your henchman talked a great deal. Indeed, he did nothing but babble his misdeeds over and over. With every other word, he pronounced you as the employer of their criminal talents. 'Twas a tiresome thing to hear him repeat, and repeat your name. Have you anything to add to his confession?"

Like a cornered cat, she narrowed her eyes. She glanced at Alicia, then back to Thomas. "How dare you accuse me of wrongdoing when you yourself have committed a worse crime?"

Thomas stiffened. What game did the little witch play now? he wondered. "How so?"

A thin, cruel smile touched her white lips. "Treason, my lord. You harbor a sworn enemy of the king of England."

A dart of fear burst inside his chest, though Thomas made sure he exhibited nothing but mild surprise. "Who?" he asked as he put his arm around Alicia's waist. He could feel her trembling under his fingers, though her expression did not betray her anxiety.

Isabel pointed her finger at his wife, as if it was an arrow to Alicia's heart. "Her!" She directed her attention past Thomas's shoulder. "I beg you all here to be my witnesses."

He looked behind him. Beside Ozwald, who held the fainting maid in his arms, the doorway had filled with a number of the inn's customers. Alicia gasped under her breath. Thomas gave her a reassuring squeeze. Now that an audience was present, he knew exactly what course to take. He had had years of practice.

He chuckled. "I fear that the lady is moonstruck," he tossed over his shoulder to the gawking crowd. "My wife is the virtuous daughter of Master Edward Broom, a well-known and respected gold merchant in the city of York."

Several of the onlookers murmured their agreement. Thomas thanked the stars for their witness.

Isabel tossed her black hair out of her face. "Ha! She is a Plantagenet. I heard her say so with her own mouth. She is one of King Edward's misspent seeds grown to maturity."

Thomas shook his head with a show of sadness. "Alas, grieving creature," he murmured. Then to the people behind him, he added, "My sister-in-law's mind is unhinged by my poor brother's untimely death."

A few muttered sympathetic sounds.

"Look at her!" Isabel shrieked. Her face changed color from white to mottled red in a matter of seconds. "She is the very image of the late king."

Thomas pretended even more surprise. "In truth? Were you a close friend of King Edward?" He remarked to the onlookers, "Methinks she is older than I first suspected."

The people chuckled at his witty observation. Thomas gave Alicia another squeeze. *Do not swoon, my love. I have not yet finished this piece of mummery.*

Isabel rose to her knees in the middle of the bed, so that the crowd could see her better. Thomas obligingly stepped to one side, pulling his beloved into deeper shadow.

"I have seen the late king's portrait," Isabel announced. "And I have heard tales of that man. They said he was a golden giant." She pointed again at Alicia. "That one is tall and has golden hair, the same as the king. Indeed, there are few women in all of England who are as tall as she, except for our queen, Elizabeth Plantagenet—her royal half sister."

Alicia clutched Thomas's hand. Her skin was ice cold. He folded his fingers over hers, and warmed them as best he could.

"I saw the queen once," Isabel continued as her audience grew silent. "When she was crowned in London. My father took us there to take part in the festivities just before I was wed to William Cavendish. The queen and that woman are as alike as two peas from the same pod. Mark you!"

Thomas noticed that Isabel's finger shook. He exulted silently, then he pulled up a deep roll of laughter from the pit of his stomach.

"The lady's brain sickness grows worse and worse," he told the growing crowd who now poured through the chamber's door. "I do fear for my poor sister-in-law, my friends. Aye, I fear that she may do an injury to herself if she is allowed to continue with this mad delusion."

Many of the men nodded their agreement with him.

Thomas released his wife, strode over to the bed, and sat down next to Isabel. He put his arm around her shoulder. She started to resist, but he held her more firmly, and pulled her against him so that he could speak to her alone.

"Listen to me well. If you are not suffering from lunacy, then you will stand trial for the same crime as your maimed hireling who attacked Alicia,'' he whispered.

Isabel ceased to struggle, and became very still in his grip.

''On the other hand,'' he continued, ''if you have lost your wits and cannot tell a hawk from a hand, then you must be cared for.''

She gulped. ''What do you mean?''

He smoothed her hair over her brow. ''You must be put in a dark, safe place, given cold baths every day, and fed only plain foods that will purge your madness.''

She shook her head, and renewed her efforts to pull away from him. Thomas dug his fingers into her bare shoulder.

To the people, he said, ''Methinks we have found her just in time.''

The crowd responded in the affirmative.

Thomas lifted his voice so that even the people out in the hallway could hear him. ''As her loving brother-in-law and the Earl of Thornbury, I have power over her care. 'Tis my merciful will that she will be conducted this very day to the Abbey of Saint Luke on Holy Isle in the North Sea, and there—''

''Nay!'' Isabel twisted, then flung herself at him, her fingers curled into claws to scratch his face.

He grabbed her wrists, and flattened her backward onto the mattress. He pinned her down with the weight of his body. Her eyes grew wide when he spoke again in her ear.

''There, the holy sisters, who have dedicated their lives to healing the brainsick, will lay their gentle hands on you,'' he whispered to her, ''for the rest of your natural life.''

Isabel went very still. He released her, and again addressed the company. "Good friends, I thank you for your concern, but I beg that you withdraw in order to give my poor sister-in-law time to dress." He stood up, his great size filling the small room. "Good night, and pleasant dreams to you all," he said as he ushered the rabble out of the door.

Isabel dragged herself to her knees again. Tears streamed down her face. "Forgive me, Thomas," she sobbed. "Alicia, please! Have mercy on me!"

Thomas ignored the soft look that crept into his wife's blue eyes. He crossed his arms over his chest. "Forgiveness comes from God alone, Isabel. While you are healing your mind, perchance you can heal your soul, as well."

He glanced at Meg, who had revived from her swoon. "Get your mistress dressed," he ordered. "She rides from here in an hour, and I care not how she is clothed. The quicker you are, the happier you will be anon."

Once again, Isabel hurled herself at him. "Thomas! You cannot do this!"

He caught her as if she weighed nothing. "Aye, I can, and I will." He tossed her back on the bed amid the hundreds of goose feathers. "Have done with me, woman, and count your blessings that you will not face the burning stake for your sins. For my part, I wash my hands of you forever."

He slipped his arm around Alicia. "Come, my sweet. You must be exhausted." He led her out the door, and closed it softly behind him. "Stand guard," he told Oz-wald.

As they descended to the first floor, they could hear Isabel's bloodcurdling screams behind them. Alicia shivered. Thomas held her tighter against himself.

"Stark, staring mad," he explained to the gaping landlord, as the couple passed by him.

Chapter Nineteen

Once he had recovered himself, the landlord of the Black Dog showed Thomas and Alicia to his best room. For a brief moment, Alicia wondered if she was going to have her long-awaited bedding in a roadside inn, but her husband quickly scotched that idea.

"A warm posset for my lady," he instructed the man. "She has had a long day and a night on a horse, and is tired beyond caring."

The little florid-faced innkeeper glanced at Alicia, then nodded his head like a jay bird. "At once, my lord."

When he had gone, Thomas pulled back the covers of the simple bed. At least the sheets smelled clean with a hint of lavender. As if she was a child, he unbuckled her shoes for her, then massaged her aching feet. Alicia lay back on the mattress, and purred with pleasure.

The sweet-smelling posset of milk, honey and sack wine arrived just as he tucked her into bed. He stirred the hot mixture for her before he allowed her to sip from the steaming mug.

"'Twill do you a world of good," he murmured.

"You are very kind to me, Thomas." She stroked his cheek.

In the distance, they heard a muffled scream.

His jaw clenched. "I wager 'tis Isabel." He glanced out the window at the setting moon. "She has a scant half an hour to get ready. She would do well to dress warmly, and scream less. I understand Holy Isle is a very cold place."

Alicia looked up at her husband. "Do you not think you were too hard on her?" she asked in between sips of the posset.

His eyes turned bluer. "After what that witch nearly did to you? She would have handed you over to the Tudor king to be killed at his pleasure. She is fortunate to still possess her own life."

"But, Thomas—"

He placed his finger over her protesting lips. "'Tis the only way I could think to silence her accusations against you. No one will believe a mad woman's ravings." He cradled her face between his large hands. "I will not have you live in fear for the rest of your life."

She kissed his fingers. "Will you come to bed, Thomas?"

To her surprise, he flushed, and looked down at his boots. "Sleep well," he mumbled. "I must attend to Isabel's departure. Once I know she is safely away in the keeping of my guards, I will take you home."

He kissed her forehead, then left the chamber. Home, she thought. That simple word held a wealth of joy. She curled on her side. Sleep engulfed her faster than she expected it.

The sun stood almost overhead when Alicia and Thomas finally rode away from the Black Dog Inn. All the way back to Wolf Hall, he entertained her with snatches of funny songs, clever riddles and word puns, and with more tales of his youth. Neither of them spoke of Isabel whom they knew traveled in the opposite direction. Though Thomas did his best to banish all sad thoughts from her mind, Alicia could not help feeling sorry for her sister-in-law. Silently she said a little prayer that Isabel might find some contentment within the convent walls.

Evening shadows lengthened across the courtyard when they rode through the open gates of Wolf Hall. Alicia saw at once that Andrew had been true to his word. Colorful banners hung from every tower and battlement. Lights blazed from every window.

"That boy will beggar me yet," Thomas grumbled under his breath.

Alicia cast him a quick glance, and was relieved to see that he smiled.

He waved at the windows' cheerful glow. "Mark how my squire has used every candle from the storeroom." He grinned at her. "'Tis only fitting to greet the lady of my house."

She inclined her head at his compliment. "And her lord," she added.

Mary burst through the main doors, and dashed down the steps. "Thomas! Alicia! Oh, Tom! I am so glad you are back! You will never guess in a month of Sundays what has happened!"

He rolled his eyes at his wife. "Welcome home, my lady. As you can see, you do not even get a chance to shake off the dust from the road before a crisis ensnares you."

As he helped her down from her rented horse, she whispered to him, "Do you think Mistress Genevieve has abandoned her charge?"

He chuckled under his breath. "One can only hope and pray."

Mary flew into his arms. "Thomas! You will never guess! Put me down! I am not a little girl anymore!" she added with the merest trace of indignity.

He placed his sister on her feet. "How now, mistress? What is all the fuss about?"

Mary opened her mouth to speak, but Andrew's sudden appearance interrupted her.

"My lord and lady! You must come at once. 'Tis such a sight as you will never imagine."

Mary stamped her foot. "Do not say one more word, Andrew. 'Tis for *me* to tell, not you."

Thomas puffed out his cheeks. "By all that is holy, what are you two babbling about?"

His sister drew herself up until Alicia wondered if the child would burst out of her gown.

"Vixen has had her puppies!" she announced. The news echoed around the stone walls of the courtyard.

"Six!" added Andrew.

A warm, wonderful smile enveloped Thomas's face. "Healthy?"

The girl giggled. "Aye, every last one of them is nursing like a little piglet. Vixen looks very pleased with herself, though why, I cannot understand. By my troth, the puppies look as if every dog in the village had sired them."

Thomas hugged Alicia. "Then all is well. Where did she have them this time? In the loft? Under the stairs? In the buttery?"

Mary and Andrew exchanged looks. The squire cleared his throat. "In your absence, Vixen picked her most favorite spot in all the world, my lord. She had them in the middle of your bed."

Alicia covered her mouth to hide her laughter. Thomas looked thunderstruck. She hoped he was thinking about where he would sleep with his new wife tonight.

Vixen greeted her visitors with a regal demeanor. She had created a soft nest amid the tumbled sheets and blankets of Thomas's great bed. Stokes had kept the room warm with a great fire blazing in the grate, and he had cleaned up the birthing before his master's return. The half-dozen puppies slept in a heap next to their mother.

Alicia's heart melted at the maternal sight. She had often seen newborn kittens when she was growing up, but never puppies, since Katherine had not been partial to dogs.

"Oh, Thomas, they are so sweet—and so tiny!"

He chuckled. "You have outdone yourself this time, Vixen. Good girl!"

The greyhound laid her ears back, and wagged her tail at his words of praise. He stroked her smooth head. She closed her eyes with contentment.

Leaning over the bed, he regarded the mix of black, white and tawny balls of fluff. "Methinks I will have to dower this lot with silver pennies to find them good homes."

Alicia touched his shoulder. "Oh, Thomas! Do not think of giving them away so soon when they have only just arrived. Poor Vixen! How can you talk of taking her children away in her presence?"

He cocked an eyebrow at her. "How now? You wish to keep this motley pack? You shall see anon. In six weeks' time, Vixen will be *anxious* to flee them all."

He sat down on the bed near the headboard, taking care not to jostle the new mother and her brood. Watching him, Alicia prayed that next year at this time, *she* would be the one lying in this great bed, beaming with pride as she presented her lord with his first child—that is, *if* she could ever get Thomas to make love to her.

"'Tis a good omen," she said aloud, then laughed when he gave her a perplexed look.

Something rustled when he shifted his weight on the bed. His expression changed to one of surprise when he looked down where he sat. "What is this?" He reached between the headboard and mattress, and drew out a crumpled piece of paper.

Alicia nibbled her lower lip. She heard his quick intake of breath as he smoothed out the love letter she had hidden there. Sweet Saint Anne! How could she possibly explain this damning piece of evidence?

He held out the note to her. "The words did not please you?" His astonishment was obviously genuine.

She licked her lips, trying to think of a placating answer. "The words are fair and fine, my lord. 'Tis the hand that wrote them."

His eyes darkened. "What is wrong with my penmanship?"

His question caught her off-balance. "Your handwriting is a good one, and easy to read."

He looked down at the paper. "Then 'tis the author who does not please you." His face paled, and his good humor disappeared.

Alicia swallowed. She did not want to get Andrew into trouble. "I did not think 'twas proper for someone to be sending me such…personal letters when I was betrothed to you."

Their gazes locked. For one eternal moment, she thought her heart had stopped beating. Then he threw back his head, and released a deep, rolling laughter.

"You truly do not know who sent you this, and the ones before it?" he asked when he finally could speak.

Something clicked in her mind. "Methought 'twas Andrew," she answered slowly. "Audrey told me that he can counterfeit your writing quite well."

Again his rich laughter filled the chamber. "That popinjay? He flees from books and pens as if they would infect him with the plague, instead of learning."

Alicia drew closer to her husband. "'Tis *your* letter?" The shock of the truth hit her with the force of a pitcher of cold water dashed into her face. "*You* wrote all those beautiful things to me?"

Thomas jutted out his chin with a hint of injured pride. "Of course. If anyone else had dared to write to you in this intimate manner, I would have boiled him in oil, and poured him down one of the murder holes."

Alicia traced her finger across his cheekbone. "That is what I thought. And why I...I destroyed them." Now she mourned their loss.

He drew her to him. "But you *did* read them first, I hope." Despite his cheerful expression, she sensed his vulnerability.

Sitting on his knee, she put her arm around his neck. She massaged his tense knot of muscles. "Aye, I could not resist their poetry." She planted a light kiss on his nose. "Truly, Thomas, you are most amazing. Why could you not just *tell* me that you loved me?"

His cheeks flamed. "I am a man of action, not speech," he muttered.

She cocked her brow at him. "A man of action, you say? Then, if you love me, *do* something about it."

His lips wobbled. "Now?"

"Aye," she whispered, staring into his beautiful eyes. "This very minute."

Without saying another word, Thomas swept her into his arms, and carried her out to the hall. He strode down the corridor with Georgie and Taverstock trotting at his heels. Her heart swelling with a mix of joy, anticipation and apprehension, Alicia twined her arms tighter around him. She buried her face in the warm place between his neck and broad shoulders. He smelled of horse, leather, wool and some indefinable musk that was all his own.

When they reached the royal suite, he pushed open the door with his foot. The dogs raced ahead of them, and jumped onto the richly appointed bed. Georgie settled himself in his accustomed spot at the foot, while Taverstock pawed at the pillows, seeking a way to get under the covers. With a quick kiss on her forehead, Thomas set Alicia on her feet. Then he hunkered down by the fireplace, and began to pile logs onto the grate.

She eyed the bed. Finally, it was going to happen—except for two little problems. "Thomas." She spoke his name quietly so she would not alarm him.

Not looking at her, he grunted a reply.

She cleared her throat. "Thomas," she said a little louder.

He turned from his work. "Aye, sweetheart?" He wore a silly grin on his face.

"Methinks there are a few too many of us in this chamber for a proper wedding night." She smiled at him playfully, then gave a meaningful nod toward the bed.

Thomas followed her gaze. Georgie lifted his great head, and banged his whipcord tail against the coverlet. Tavie paused in his burrowing, and barked, as if inviting his master and new mistress to join him.

Thomas rubbed the side of his nose. "Aye, you have a point." He rose, then snapped his fingers.

Puzzled but eager to do their master's bidding, both dogs scrambled off the bed, and stood before him. Clasping his hands behind his back, he regarded the mastiff and the terrier. "Gentlemen," he began, "there will be a new order in this household. Henceforth, that is to say, tonight…" He coughed. His neck reddened. He pointed to the door. "Go find Mary. See Andrew! Look for Stokes!"

Tavie held up one paw, sneezed, then dashed into the corridor. Georgie looked up at his master, then to Alicia. He crossed the floor with all of his ancient dignity. Thomas closed the door softly behind them. Almost as an afterthought, he bolted it. Then he looked at his wife.

She saw the heartrending tenderness in his eyes. "Thank you, Thomas," she whispered.

His face flushed crimson. He stared at his boots, then back to his half-laid fire. "Got to finish that," he mumbled.

He is nervous. Good! So am I. Aloud she asked, "Shall I prepare for bed, Thomas?"

He opened his mouth, but no words came out. Instead, he nodded, then turned his back to her. He made a great deal of bustling noise while he built up a bonfire in the fireplace.

Hiding her smile, Alicia pulled back the covers, and smoothed the bottom sheet. She kicked off her shoes, and peeled down her torn stockings. Thomas did not move from his position. She untied her laces, and allowed the mud-stained gown and petticoats to billow to her feet, leaving her only in her light shift. She kicked her tattered garments aside. She glanced at her handsome husband over her shoulder. He still hunched in front of his now-roaring fire. His head hung low between his shoulders.

Alicia hummed a lullaby under her breath as she brushed out the tangles of the past twenty-four hours from her hair. In her mirror, she spied him casting swift glances at her. She tried to assess his expression. While she studied him anew in her looking glass, her body ached for his touch. She replaced her brush on the dressing table.

She crossed behind him, and sat down on the edge of the wide, yawning bed. The ropes that held the mattress in place groaned under her weight. Thomas's shoulders stiffened at the sound. Folding her hands in her lap, Alicia waited for him to turn around. He did not move.

We will never get anywhere at this rate.

"Thomas," she called in a gentle voice. When he looked over his shoulder at her, she patted the mattress beside her. "I am ready for you." She held her breath. This prolonged anticipation was almost unbearable.

With a deep, soul-stirring sigh, he stood, then turned to face her. His short hunting jerkin could not conceal the outward manifestation of his growing interest. Alicia saw the full measure of his aroused desire. Her heart danced with excitement. She moistened her lips with her tongue. Thomas's eyes widened. He swallowed with a gulp.

He cleared his throat. "This is the first...that is... Mayhap you think...I mean...I...I..."

"Is something wrong, Thomas?" Alicia asked with growing misgivings.

"I have never lain with a woman before now," he blurted out. His voice echoed around the chamber.

Alicia bit her lower lip to hide her surprise. She saw how embarrassed he was. "Then we are alike," she answered with a shy smile. "For I have never lain with a man—until now."

Looking a little more relieved, he came closer to her. "I assure you, I know what I am supposed to do, and I swear upon my soul that I am more than willing to do it." Perspiration glistened on his forehead.

She found his proximity almost overwhelming, but she resisted the urge to reach out and grab him. "And I am more than willing to learn, sweet Thomas."

He clasped his hands as if she was a holy statue in a cathedral, and he was a pilgrim supplicating her intercession to heaven. "Your patience, I pray you, my love. I know that I cannot just leap at you like Georgie does with one of the yard dogs."

She gave him an encouraging smile. "I am glad to hear that you know the difference. I understand that some husbands do not."

He bit his lip, then said, "I am mortally afraid that I will hurt you."

The pent-up tension eased out of Alicia's body. So *that* was the problem. "I have never been afraid of you, Thomas. I am not afraid now." *Not very much, anyway.*

He came closer still. "Furthermore, I have not the slightest idea how to pleasure you!" he confessed in a rush. He flashed her a tender smile.

Alicia blessed Katherine for all her lessons in lovemaking. She stood up beside her husband, and took his hand in hers. His mere touch sent a shiver of longing through her. She kissed his cold fingers. "Methinks that things will progress more quickly if you get undressed, my darling."

He nodded, but did not move. After another kiss, this time on his chin, Alicia slid under the bedcovers. Thomas turned around, and fumbled with his laces, swearing under his breath at the stubborn knots. Meanwhile, she wriggled out of her shift, and stuffed it under one of the pillows. The cool sheets soothed her flushed skin.

Thomas hurled his jerkin across the chamber. It landed on top of the chest under the window, then it slipped to the floor. His shirt followed in quick order. He stretched his arms, causing the muscles in his back to ripple under his skin. Hopping about first on one foot then the other, he pulled off his riding boots, leaving him attired in only his black hose.

The glow of the firelight accentuated his quiet strength, and his golden body. Alicia's pulse skittered. She barely breathed when he began to roll down his tights over his firm buttocks. At long last, he stood naked with his back to her.

Slowly Thomas turned around. She could not suppress an exclamation of admiration when she saw how *very much* he wanted her. Thrusting aside her apprehensions, she hungered for the fulfillment of his love. She allowed the bedcover to slip down to her waist, baring her breasts for him. His gaze burned her with his desire. In two swift strides, he crossed the distance between them. She pulled back the coverlet, and smoothed the place beside her.

"You will catch a chill if you stand in the night air like that for much longer, my love. Come to bed."

She swallowed tightly as he eased himself down next to her on the sheet. His hard-muscled thigh brushed against her, sending a quiver of excitement through her.

She stroked his arm. "'Twill help if you relax, my darling." Her lips trembled against his as she spoke.

Thomas groaned. "You ask too much of me, my princess. I am a man of honor, but I fear I am no monk."

With a low growl, he took her in his arms, and

molded her soft curves against the hard contours of his body. Clasping her against his heart, he gently rocked her back and forth. She reveled in the feel of his strong arms around her.

She moistened her lips and waited for the gift of his kiss. Lowering his head over her, he traced the soft fullness of her mouth with his tongue. As if she had been touched by lightning, her heart skipped a beat. She welcomed the message of his growing passion. Alicia's mouth burned with his fire. The headiness of his musky scent overwhelmed her. She wove her fingers through his thick hair. His lips seared a burning path down to her shoulders. Shivers of delight followed in his wake.

He cupped one of her breasts, and fondled it. His touch was gently tentative. Her nipples firmed shamelessly under his fingers. His tender massage sent currents of fire and ice whirling through her. She gripped handfuls of his hair, and moaned.

He paused his sweet torture. "Have I hurt you?" he whispered.

"Nay," she gasped, "but if you stop now, you will kill me." Her heartbeat hammered in her ears.

His lips recaptured hers, and became more demanding. His cool fingers brushed across her skin, and danced down her spine. As he drank deeply from her spring, his hands explored the hollows of her back. When he reached her rounded bottom, he pulled her hard against him. Arching her back, she silently pleaded to be consumed.

He slid his hands over her hips. With a featherlight caress, he explored her thighs—then moved up to her moist center.

Writhing under him, she forgot all her carefully memorized lessons in love, especially when he brushed his fingertip over her throbbing core. Shivers of delight coursed through her. Her passionate moans only encouraged him to seek newer delights.

He moved over her, then slowly lowered himself. Her hips rose to meet him as their legs intertwined. Flooding with desire for him, she welcomed him into her body.

They moved in exquisite harmony with one another. Together they found the tempo that bound them closer. Alicia's heart beat with the pulse of Thomas's rhythm. She buried her face against the corded muscles of his broad chest. He sang her name over and over in her ear. The flames of their newfound passion burned bright within them.

Thomas's lovemaking swept over Alicia like a summer storm. His power thundered within her, while his hands sent lightning bolts darting through her. Her body vibrated with his liquid fire. She cried out for sweet release.

His ardor mounted to a fever pitch as he sent her to the highest peak. She gasped with sweet agony, then shattered into a million glowing stars. He roared in triumph, as his love flowed into her like warm honey. For one indescribable moment, she felt transported on a cloud of silver and gold, where she experienced the torrent of uncontrollable joy.

In the quiet aftermath, Thomas rolled to his side, then gathered her close against him. He sighed with pleasant exhaustion. Filled with an amazing feeling of completeness, she curled into the curve of his body, and laid her head on his shoulder.

He kissed her forehead with infinite tenderness. "I am sorry," he murmured.

She trailed her finger down the center of his chest. "For what?"

"For hurting you."

With a giddy sense of joy, she released her happiness

with a ripple of laughter. "If that is your idea of hurting me, I cannot wait to discover your ideas of pleasure."

He twined a tendril of her red-gold hair around his finger. "Give me some time, my love. I am not a stallion." He stared at her for a long moment, as if he beheld a wondrous new creature in his bed. Then he said, "Roll over, Alicia."

She blinked. "Why? Is something amiss?"

"I want to see the marks of your virtue."

Hot embarrassment filled her. "Do you doubt that I was a virgin?" Insult stabbed her soul.

Chuckling, he erased the furrows in her brow with his thumb. "I never doubted you for an instant, my sweet, but I want to survey the damage I did to you."

"'Twas nothing, I assure you."

In reply, he made a twirling motion with his finger. Seeing that he would not be denied, she did as he requested. Thomas hitched himself up on his elbow, and flipped back the coverlet. The crimson proof of Alicia's virginity proclaimed itself boldly on the white linen sheet. She chewed on her lower lip.

He inspected the area closely. "Six…seven…ah, and a tiny one. Eight altogether." He grinned his satisfaction.

She blew a lock of hair out of her face, and stared at the velvet bed curtains. "Eight what?" she finally asked.

He took her hand in his, and pressed a kiss upon her palm. "Eight spots of your blood."

She snorted. "And I suppose you will order the trumpeters to blow eight blasts from the battlements, so that all the world will know how well you bedded me!" She pulled the covers up to her chin.

Leaning over her, he kissed her on each eyelid. "On the contrary, my love. I do not care to proclaim my virility, nor your former innocent state to anyone. 'Tis no one's business but ours.''

Alicia stared at him, trying to fathom the workings of his mind. ''Then why—?''

He silenced her with a gentle kiss on her lips. She relaxed, and opened her mouth to receive him. It was a kiss for her perplexed soul to melt into.

''We shall ride to York in a week or so—when you have recovered from your last outing on a horse—and...er...other activities.'' He gave her his appealing schoolboy grin. ''And I shall order for you a necklace of gold chain links with eight rubies—one for each virtuous tear you shed for your love of me.''

Her eyes widened. ''You do not have to do that. The fox pelts—''

Another one of his kisses stopped her protests. ''But I want to.''

Alicia was too emotion-filled to speak. Tears shimmered in her eyes.

He drew her to him again. ''I am glad to see that you approve of my plan. Sleep now, my darling, for methinks we shall romp in these pleasure fields again before morning.''

She hugged him. ''Thomas Cavendish, I have completely underestimated you!''

He closed his eyes with a chuckle. ''Most people do.''

Then he blew out the candle.

Epilogue

Wolf Hall
December 1499

The fire in the master bedroom crackled with a particularly cheerful note this fine December night, Thomas thought, as he stretched out his legs before its welcome warmth. How could a man possibly be happier?

From the kitchens below wafted the appetizing scent of roasting venison. Today had been the best day's hunting he could ever remember. Perfect weather. Up at dawn. A promise of winter in the crisp air. And most excellent sport.

The noble buck had given Thomas and his men a good chase for most of the day. It didn't matter. The way he had felt, he would have chased that animal all the way to Scotland if necessary. He had promised Alicia a stag, and, by God, he would get her one. Thankfully, the good Lord and the buck cooperated.

Closing his eyes, he pictured the eighteen-point rack of antlers hanging in the great hall, just below the beautiful new wolf's head banner that Alicia had embroidered while she waited out her pregnancy.

He heard a small sound in the great bed behind him. He stood, and tiptoed over to the side where Alicia lay. Her beautiful hair, freshly brushed, fanned over the pillow in a cascade of gold. The firelight enhanced all her red Plantagenet highlights. She smiled up at him.

He kissed her forehead. "Methought you were sleeping. You have had a hard day's work."

Her smile widened. "I have been watching you for these past ten minutes, Thomas. I like to see my men at my fireside."

She touched the little flannel-wrapped bundle that he held carefully in the crook of his arm. "Is he still asleep?"

The new father's chest swelled with pride as he looked down at his newborn son. "Aye, his day's labor has tired him out as well."

With a sense of wonder at the tiny being he had helped to create, Thomas smoothed the little tuft of reddish gold hair on the babe's head. Then he stroked his son's downy cheek. The child sighed in his sleep, then opened one exquisitely formed hand. Thomas touched it with his thumb, and chuckled when the baby clamped his tiny fingers around it.

"He has a good grip," he told the baby's mother. "He will make a fine swordsman one day."

Still smiling, Alicia shook her head at her husband. "Let the child get all his milk teeth before you start teaching him how to lose them."

He considered her request. "How long will that take?"

"About six years—at least."

He grinned. "Plenty of time for swords. In the meantime, he can start riding a pony at four. Chase a rabbit.'' He dropped a kiss on the top of his son's head. "You will like chasing rabbits, my boy. Easy to catch." He grew more serious. "You did not mind that I was not here when he was born?" he asked Alicia. He felt a little guilty about racing off with horns and hounds the minute she had announced that she was in labor.

She took his free hand in hers, and gave it a squeeze. "Nay, my love. You would have done me no good at all if you had been cooped up downstairs while I did a lot of screaming. You would have driven the midwife and all the maids to distraction. In fact, Stokes sent me a message of thanks for getting you out from underfoot. I believe he called you a roaring bull."

Thomas raised his eyebrows. "Did he now?" He chuckled. "'Tis a fine stag I got you, Alicia. Will make you a good stew to give you strength. And when this one is old enough to understand, I will show him those antlers, and tell him how I brought that buck down with only one arrow on the day he was born."

Alicia patted his hand. "I am sure you will begin to tell our son even *before* he is old enough to understand. Thank you, my love, for the beautiful stag. I look forward to tasting the fruits of your labors."

"Aye, well…" Thomas tried to think of something very complimentary to say, but nothing came to mind, except how proud he was of her. "In a fortnight, or so, when you have recovered enough, we will ride into York."

A glow lit up Alicia's eyes. "Whyfore, now?"

Thomas kissed her hand. "I will order you a necklace of gold chain links and blue sapphires to honor your eyes, and those of our first-born son."

She laughed with pleasure. "Thomas, you will drown me in gold necklaces."

He nibbled at her fingers. "Aye, 'tis my life's goal. I love you so much, Alicia."

She stroked his cheek. "And I love you, Thomas."

The baby stirred in his arms, and began to whimper. Alicia reached for her son. "Methinks he is a true Cavendish. He is hungry *again*."

Thomas watched as she suckled his son. He wanted to throw open the casement windows, and bellow his joy across the countryside, but he knew his wife would tell him to hush up. Later tonight, when everyone else was asleep, he, Andrew and Stokes would have a little celebration of their own with the cask of good malmsey wine that Thomas had laid by especially for this happy occasion.

"Do you have any choices for the babe's name?" he asked her.

Alicia smiled down at her son. "I had thought of naming him Edward, after my father and my guardian."

Thomas nodded. "'Tis a noble name."

She furrowed her brows. "But, methinks this child may look too much like his grandsire for safety's sake. Have you noticed his large feet? They are Plantagenet through and through."

Her expression took on a faraway look. "And the same is true for the name of Richard." Her lips trembled.

Thomas squeezed her hand. "I have paid for a hundred masses to be said for the soul of your dear brother. He is not forgotten in this household."

And cursed be Henry Tudor's craven heart for executing the boy!

Alicia looked up at her husband, her eyes glazed with tears. "I am ever grateful to you, Thomas."

He knelt by her bedside. "Nay, 'tis I who thanks God every day for sending you into my life, my princess."

Her smile returned. "So, then, we are agreed. We will not burden this child with the name of a king. But he must be named before his christening. Is there any family name that you particularly like?"

Thomas recalled the harsh years of his childhood under the stern discipline of his father, Giles, and the taunts and blows of his brothers, John and William. "None come to mind," he replied.

"Was there a friend of your childhood? Someone very special whom you would wish to honor?" she persisted.

Immediately the perfect name leapt onto Thomas's tongue. A slow smile spread across his face. "Brandon," he said.

Alicia nodded. "'Tis a fine name. A good strong one, too. I like it well. You will be Brandon Cavendish, my little one." She kissed the babe who, sated with his mother's milk, had fallen asleep. "Was Brandon a good friend of yours, Thomas?"

His smile grew broader. "As true a friend as any man could have."

Later, after Alicia had fallen asleep again, Thomas left the chamber, and sought out Georgie, Vixen and Taverstock by the fire in the empty hall. He hunkered down among them with a sigh.

"'Tis a red-letter day for Wolf Hall, eh, my friends? The tenth Earl of Thornbury sleeps in his cradle above us."

He massaged old Georgie's ears. The years had been

kind to the greathearted mastiff. Thomas bent low, and whispered into his ancient friend's ear.

"You will be proud to hear that we will call my son Brandon after the truest friend a lonely boy could ever have, But please, upon your word as an honorable gentleman, never tell my lady wife that Brandon was your noble sire. Methinks she might not like the idea of naming our son after a dog."

* * * * *

Author Note

Even after five hundred years, Perkin Warbeck remains one of the more enigmatic figures to play upon the stage of English history. Historians still debate exactly who was this handsome young man who appeared in 1491, at age eighteen or thereabouts, claiming to be Richard of York, the second son of King Edward IV. The world presumed that Richard and his older brother, Edward V—known as the Little Princes in the Tower—perished sometime during the reign of Edward IV's younger brother Richard III.

Legend has it that the elder of the princes, Edward V, died in the Tower of a fever, but the younger one had been spirited out of the country, and sent to Flanders—by Sir Edward and Lady Katherine Brampton. Brampton was a godson of Edward IV, and a strong Yorkist sympathizer. Perkin Warbeck bore a striking physical resemblance to Edward IV, and was well-versed in life at the English court.

Many historians believe that Warbeck was one of Edward's many illegitimate children. Others suggest that he was a complete impostor, schooled by the Yorkists at the Court of Margaret of Burgundy to assume the role of Richard, and depose Henry VII. A few believe that Warbeck was indeed the real Richard, who had returned to claim his rightful inheritance.

After giving Henry VII eight uneasy years of insurrection and warfare, Warbeck was captured and sent to the Tower in 1497. Henry then began his systematic reprisals against all members of the royal Plantagenet family. Warbeck, along with Edward, Earl of Warwick, a true claimant to the throne, were executed in November 1499. Both men were in their midtwenties.

I love to hear from my readers. Please write to me at: P.O. Box 10703, Burke, VA 22009-0703.

 HARLEQUIN®

Not The Same Old Story!

HARLEQUIN PRESENTS® — Exciting, glamorous romance stories that take readers around the world.

 — Sparkling, fresh and tender love stories that bring you pure romance.

HARLEQUIN® 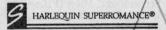 — Bold and adventurous—Temptation is strong women, bad boys, great sex!

HARLEQUIN SUPERROMANCE® — Provocative and realistic stories that celebrate life and love.

 HARLEQUIN® AMERICAN ROMANCE® — Contemporary fairy tales—where anything is possible and where dreams come true.

HARLEQUIN® INTRIGUE® — Heart-stopping, suspenseful adventures that combine the best of romance and mystery.

 LOVE & LAUGHTER™ — Humorous and romantic stories that capture the lighter side of love.

Look us up on-line at: http://www.romance.net   HGENERIC

COMING NEXT MONTH FROM

HARLEQUIN HISTORICALS